Dixbury Does Talent

Cover illustration http://www.andrewdelf.co.uk

Visit the author's blog at https://maxinesinclair.com

To the wonderful (real life) ballet teacher, Nicky Gibbs, who has inspired me more than words can say.

TABLE OF CONTENTS

Dixbury Does Talent

The Before

'Thank God I don't have to live this day again.' I think, turning the door sign to 'closed'.

Plonking myself down on a chair near Hip Snips' plastic hood dryers and with streetlights filtering through the dark brown tinted windows, I burst into tears. At least I made it through the day, but if I had to force another smile to the back of one more head I think I would have screamed. Images of last night, finding Steve sitting in the lounge and immediately knowing something was wrong, flash before me.

"What is it, Steve? Is it Basil?"

Steve smiled wryly. "Typical you think it's the dog - no, Amy, it's not Basil." His face was taut and his body looked stiff from anxiety.

"Steve, you're scaring me – what is it?"

"Amy – things haven't been right between us for a while…"

I stopped dead in my tracks - was this a break-up speech? I hadn't seen this coming. His words blurred as I stood there in sheer disbelief.

"...unhappy...didn't mean for it to happen...met someone else...sorry..."

The room swayed as I found myself rooted to the floor. I had lost all feeling in my body and couldn't comprehend what he was saying.

"What?" I asked eventually, my eyes wide and frightened.

Steve looked at his shoes, with his hands plunged deep into his jeans pockets. He slowly lifted his gaze, but was barely able to look me in the eye.

"I'm sorry, Ames, it just wasn't working for me."

His words hung in the air as he left the room. The next sound I heard was the front door closing.

Chapter 1

I have no idea how long I stay sobbing in the salon but eventually I get up and check that everything is switched off. I set the burglar alarm and leave for home.

Sitting on the bus, the numbness persists. Ten years of living together and two years of marriage, and this was it! He hadn't even stayed long enough to discuss it. Had things not been working out between us? I knew that we weren't blissfully in-the-first-throws-of-a-relationship happy, but I didn't think things were that bad. Thinking about it, he had been going out on his own more than usual, and he had been distant, but I had just assumed it was maybe a work problem that was troubling him. We had often talked about having children and recently, when I'd raised the topic, he had uncharacteristically flown off the handle. Maybe I had been pushing too hard. Just at that moment, a text pops up on my phone. It's Steve.

Will you be home late Saturday afternoon? We need to sort out some stuff and talk? Say 5.00pm?

I dryly note there is no usual kiss at the end of his message. He needs to sort out 'stuff' – was that possessions or emotional stuff? I take a deep breath.

Yes that's fine. I'll be there.

The following morning, I awake and look across at the empty space in the bed. My eyes are sore from too many tears the previous evening, and the taste in my mouth reminds me of the white wine I'd consumed to block the pain. I can still smell him on the bedcovers, and this provokes another barrage of tears. I switch on the radio, and they are playing a song that reminds me of him. I abruptly switch it off and set about my morning routine. Putting make-up on to look 'normal' and void of misery is a genuine challenge. I settle for styling my dark layered bob so that the sides kiss my face and hide a proportion of it too. Two tons of hair lacquer and a splash of distracting bright red lipstick later and I am good to go.

In the salon, I check the day ahead. Great – Gloria has an appointment. Gloria has been coming to the salon for many years, and I consider her more of a friend than a customer these days. Since both my parents died, I look to Gloria as a mother figure, although, in truth, she is nothing like my mother. Gloria is pure sophistication, whereas my own devoted mother had been squat and plump, smelling of rose perfume and freshly baked bread.

Sitting down heavily in the staff room with a sigh, I look up and see the sign on the wall.

"YOU DON'T HAVE TO BE MAD TO WORK HERE – BUT IT HELPS"

I have never liked that sign, but Steve had given it to me just after I'd bought the shop. He thought it was hilarious, and I'd faked laughter, as you do for the person you love. Tears bubble up as I had been so genuinely happy at that time. I had my own business and a loving, gorgeous, supportive man at my side. We were enjoying romantic dinners, long Sunday lie-ins, nights cuddled up in front of the fire and long dog walks. Life was good. Rising from the chair I angrily rip the sign from the wall.

"Oi, what d'you fink you're doin'?" Gina's familiar Essex twang sounds out.

"Oh G – didn't hear you come in," I say, quickly looking down, wiping my eyes and nose.

"Blimey, Boss, you look rough! You OK? You coming down with summink? My Barry 'as 'ad a cold type thing for about three weeks and it still ain't shiftin'. I told 'im to go to the docs, but will

8

he 'eck as like! He's a fella ain't he, no bloody good at looking after 'imself."

I promptly burst into tears.

"Oh whoa whoa – whassup, Babe?" Gina asks, putting her arms around me. The familiar scent of Vera Wang 'Princess' engulfs me, and I feel genuinely pleased that I work with this roughest of diamonds with the softest of hearts. There is a reason in life why we have stereotypes, and Gina is one of them. She wears the required foundation, hairstyle, fingernails and fashion of the 'Essex girl' with unabashed pride.

"He's left me, G. He's met someone else. Didn't even talk about it really," is what I try to say, but the sobs are so heavy that some words get lost.

"Nah...I don't believe wot I fink you just said." Gina has a look of shock.

"What's going on?" Karen, the young apprentice asks, walking into the room.

Over my shoulder, Gina mouths to Karen to put some coffee on.

"Urgh, the customers will be here soon," I say, pulling away and wiping my eyes. "We'll talk later, eh G?"

She has genuine concern in her eyes.

"Yeah, course. But really, if it's too much, you should go 'ome, Love"

"And sit there and think of him all day?" I smile drolly. "No, honestly, G, I'm best occupied. It'll take my mind off it."

Gina gives me a sympathetic smile and rubs my arm.

I dart to the toilet to fix the teary damage, and, right on cue, the bell on the door rings, signalling the arrival of the first customer.

Mid morning, Gloria turns up for her usual blow dry and the sight of her heartens me. She's in her sixties, and exudes youth and beauty. She has the most glorious steely grey hair that she wears in a stylish sharp shoulder length cut. In fact it would be true to say that Gloria is the epitome of classiness. Fixing my best smile, and, with as much breeziness as I can muster, I greet her.

"Hi there, Gloria, come and take a seat."

Gloria sweeps through the salon and, fanning her designer skirt, sits facing the mirror. Looking at me, her brow wrinkles.

"Amy, my dear girl, what on earth is the matter?"

Nothing much gets past Gloria.

I lean forward over her shoulder, and making eye contact in the mirror, I lower my voice.

"Steve has left me, Gloria. I got home two nights ago to find him packed and leaving. We haven't talked properly, but he told me he's met someone else," I say, barely managing to choke back the tears.

"Oh, My Dear, I'm so sorry. This must be a dreadful shock for you! For once, I am speechless," she pauses. "Am I allowed to say something mean or call him a name, or are you not at that juncture yet?" Gloria's eyes ooze sympathy and a small sad smile forms at the corners of her mouth.

Despite myself I smile. It's always a comfort to talk to Gloria – she's a good listener and today she adds soothing noises of support.

"You know, My Dear, after the dust settles and you have finished putting the voodoo pins in the doll that I shall give you, you need to find something to occupy yourself." She pauses to think. "I know!" She clasps her hands together. "You should come with me to my ballet class – it's exquisite! You'll enjoy the exercise, feel like a lady and, My Dear, you will look beautiful."

Me? Graceful? That's funny – I mean I'm not exactly fat, but neither do I possess the physique of a ballerina! Steve used to describe me as his 'pleasantly plump' wife. I can't quite imagine being in a ballet class again after all these years. In fact, I haven't done any exercise since those very classes as a fourteen year old, and in the intervening years, I have become good friends with Miss Chardonnay and Mr. Cadbury.

"I'll get back to you on that, Gloria, thanks," I smile.

We continue to chat easily whilst I wash and dry her hair.

As she is paying at the desk, she can't resist having another quick word.

"Promise me you'll think about that ballet class. Might be what you need for now – just get you out for an evening." She smiles kindly.

"I promise I'll give it some thought, Gloria., thank you."

As she is leaving, she takes my hand and looks at me in earnest.

"And it will work out, my darling girl, these things always do, you know."

She pecks me on the cheek and glides out of the shop – I do   hope   with   all   my   heart   that   she's   right.

Chapter 2

The questions that whirl in my mind never end. How long has he been having an affair? Why has he left me now? Do I know her? Is he sure about this? Is this somehow my fault? And underlying all those thoughts is my lamented wail; 'but we were so happy!'

I don't announce our split to the world in the hope that he regrets what he's done and returns, begging for forgiveness. In fact, it's my favourite fantasy – Steve appears at my door, his dark hair lank and lifeless, clothes crumpled and stained, and with hunched shoulders and sorrowful eyes he begs me to take him back. Wishful thinking? I would think so.

The more I scrutinize our relationship, the more it occurs to me that maybe we weren't so happy. Back in the day, we used to play Scrabble on Sunday nights. It was a simple routine, we would cook a big roast, have a bottle of wine and, after we'd cleared up, we would sit down and play Scrabble. We'd be jovially competitive and the winner would jog a lap of honour around our small lounge, cheering and punching the air in celebration. We would laugh at our ridiculousness. When did we stop doing that? When did Sunday nights become a time when we silently watched television? When did we stop holding hands whilst walking Basil, our beloved Cocker Spaniel? And when did we start going to bed at different times?

Saturday eventually comes around and I am finishing the last customer of the day. It is dear old Mrs. Henson with her biweekly shampoo and set. I am so nervous about the impending meeting with Steve that I neglect to brush out her hair thoroughly. It really isn't my finest work.

"Boss, she looked like she 'ad a bunch of grapes on 'er 'ead," Gina laughs as Mrs Henson leaves.

"I know." I cringe. "But I'm afraid my need to get home outweighs my remorse." Gina pulls a sympathetic face.

After spending a long time thinking about what I should wear; of the image I want to project, I need to get home and preen. I don't want to look like the sad, forlorn, frumpy, dumped wife.

I race home and charge around plumping cushions, (like that's going to make him return to me – 'oh darling, just seeing that puffed up cushion makes me realise how much I love you, need you and want to be with you!') - putting things away and spraying air freshener. A quick shower, clean clothes, some light make up and I'm ready to face him.

Just before four thirty, I'm pacing, unable to sit still. Basil knows that something is happening and is vying for attention by following me around.

"It's OK, Basil," I say soothingly, stroking his long floppy ears. "Daddy's coming round and Mummy just wants it to go well. Can't have you choosing between us in a bitter divorce, can we?"

Basil looks at me with sad eyes.

I continue to straighten pictures that don't need straightening and moving ornaments that were fine where they were. Eventually the doorbell rings. He's not even using his key. Is our home no longer his? Has he literally moved on?

"Hi," I say, with a hopeful smile, opening the door. He is standing there in his work clothes (he clearly hasn't bothered!), still looking awkwardly guilty.

"Come in," I let him pass me in the hall. He walks into the lounge and takes a seat.

"Do you want a coffee?"

"No, no thanks, I won't," he shakes his head.

My heart sinks again as I presume he isn't planning to stay long. Guess he's not going to announce that this has all been a big mistake then.

"Right, I just wanted to come over to pick up some stuff and maybe sort out a few things," he says, eyes lowered, looking visibly detached.

"OK – what exactly would you like to pick up?" I try to control the quiver in my voice.

"Just some music, clothes, other stuff that I didn't take with me."

"Oh, OK then." There is a long pause. I stare at him, willing him to make eye contact, but he averts his gaze to anywhere but my face. I can't stand it any longer.

"OK Steve, enough! I need to know what the hell happened!" I surprise myself with the ferocity of my outburst.

"Amy, I told you, I've met someone else."

"Who Steve? Who have you met?"

"It doesn't matter who she is," he snaps.

"Of course it does! Don't insult me, who have you met? Do I know her?" I feel my blood pressure rising with every exchange.

Fidgeting nervously with his head lowered, he says, "It's Justine."

"Justine? From the pub? The barmaid? Oh my! Steve – really? THE BARMAID? Did you pour out your troubles to her over the bar? Aw, was she a sympathetic ear? Or maybe a comforting bosom for you to cry into? Any more clichés up your sleeve?" I am beyond consolable.

"It just happened, we didn't plan it..." he starts.

"Oh spare me, can you hear yourself? What about us! What about our marriage! Two years, Steve! And ten years before that! Thrown away over a tart in the pub! Did you ever think about talking to me?! We could've worked it out!"

Against all my wishes, I begin to cry.

"I don't expect you to understand, Ames, and I am sorry," he says gently.

His soft tone only serves to increase my tears. I sit with my head in my hands as I hear him leave the room. The floorboards above creak as I hear him in our bedroom, and then in the spare room. He appears a few minutes later with a case in one hand and a sports bag in the other.

"We still need to sort out money," his voice trails off.

"Why, Steve? Was it me?" I ask pathetically, looking up at him with mascara streaking down my cheeks.

"Amy, no - it was just the way things worked out." His shoulders fall as he sighs. "I suppose my feelings just changed. I'll always love you, just not in the way that a husband is supposed to love his wife."

That strikes a chord. We *had* become more like brother and sister but however much I sense this to be true, I am in too much pain to accept it right now.

"I'm going to go, let's talk about money another time. Here's the mortgage money for this month though, OK?"

I nod silently as he places the pile of notes on the coffee table in front of me. I sit there, feeling pathetic and weak, staring at the money as he walks out of the house and out of my everyday life.

Chapter 3

I sit with my head in my hands, crying with Basil snuggled at my feet desperate to comfort me, when I look out of the window to see that dusk is forming. I really should walk him before it gets too dark. In robotic fashion, I put on extra warm clothes, grab my wellies, place collar and harness on Basil, and leave the house.

I take the usual walk through the back lanes to the neighbouring village. It's a beautiful route with wide-open farmland and pheasants wandering around the roadsides, but today I feel too desolate to appreciate the beauty. Basil trots along obediently off the lead, frequently looking up to check on me. My mind is in knots but the fresh air feels good on my face and I walk briskly, enjoying the sensation of blood pumping around my emotionally pained body.

Reaching the village hall, Basil disappears around the side to sniff out other recent canine visitors, leaving me with little else to do other than to peruse the large notice board. There are the usual adverts of karate classes, slimming clubs and flower arranging sessions and then one notice catches my eye: -

<u>ADULT BALLET CLASS</u>

WOMEN – Are you tired of the usual aerobics/step/yoga/boxercise classes? Want to get fit and toned AND look beautiful at the

same time? Come and try ballet! No experience necessary.

MEN - ever wanted to be the adoration of beautiful ballerinas? Always looking for men to partner. No experience necessary.

Call Helena on 07989 333047 or just drop in.

All welcome*!*

This must be Gloria's class! I wonder whether this *could* serve as a welcome distraction – it'd be a fun challenge, and spending time with Gloria would be lovely. I'm single so I am going to need something to fill my evenings. Who knows, I might even lose some of my plumpness! I type the number into my phone, and then, shouting for Basil, we head for home.

The rest of the weekend is spent in a haze of dog walking, eating the contents of the cupboards and shedding tears. Wrapped in my favourite pastel fluffy blanket, I lie on the sofa and watch back-to-back DVDs, and cry at the sad and happy parts. I try to push the memories of good times with Steve to the back of my mind. When we had first met back in 2003, in a local pub, we were instantly drawn to one another. His floppy dark hair and thick eyelashes over dark blue eyes had me mesmerized. We spent the evening like magnets, unable and unwilling to be separated. We talked, laughed and generally spent the evening gazing at each other. When it was time to say goodnight - we didn't. Instead, with racing heartbeats, we enjoyed the first of many passionate nights. We were like happy drunks, staggering around in the joy of a new love.

And now my heart physically hurts at the thought of him. It feels as if he has died, and with the painful feelings of betrayal, I wonder if it might be better if he had.

***

Monday morning's alarm brings music flooding into the room and I awake to find Basil jumping up eagerly to greet me. I know that his ulterior motives are food and a walk, but I appreciate his enthusiasm anyway.

"Morning Bas, how you doing?" I stroke his soft head. His doleful eyes study and then lick my face. Dog breath first thing in the morning isn't great, but in lieu of having anyone else to kiss, I grimace and go along with it.

Padding to the shower I discard my checked pyjamas and hit the 'on' switch. The pipes start banging but no water comes out of the showerhead. Grrrrr! 'Well Steve, you weren't the most DIY-savvy man in the world,' I think, 'but you could do general repairs and you'd been promising to do this one for at least a couple of months! Guess you had more important matter to attend to...'

I follow the usual routine of switching it on and off again a few times, and as I'm peering up into the showerhead looking for signs of life, the water splutters and blasts me in the face with great force. Recoiling from the cold gush of water, I rub my eyes - how can water hurt so much? After a minute, the water warms and I immerse myself, lathering lavender body wash all over in an attempt to scrub away some of my pain. With the exception of my parents' deaths, I honestly cannot remember a time when I felt this lonely or this bereft.

***

"Morning, Boss!" Gina bounces into the salon.

"Morning, G. How are you?"

"Good good – how 'bout you though? How woz Sat'day?" Gina asks, concerned.

"Eugh – don't ask!" I feel the pain of knowing that I am going to be telling this story many times in the coming weeks. "You know who he's with? Justine from The Feathers!"

Gina opens her mouth and closes it again with no noise coming out.

"G? You OK?"

19

"Yeah, yeah, just surprised that's all." Gina's eyes avert to the ground.

"Kind of a cliché isn't it? Husband runs off with local barmaid."

"It ain't original," Gina concedes.

"You know, if he wasn't happy, why didn't he talk to me? I feel such an idiot. Guessing I'm the last person to know." Gina opens her mouth again but the door opens, and the first customer of the day appears, diverting her attention.

Taking a coffee break between clients, I hear Gloria at the reception desk. I lean out of the staffroom and wave for her to join me. Posture perfect and with ballet dancer duck feet, Gloria sashays her way to the staffroom.

"Hello, Dear. I've been so worried about you, I've thought about you all weekend. How are you?"

"I've been better, Gloria. You got time for a coffee?"

"That would be marvellous, Dear."

I fill Gloria in on all the details of my meeting with Steve, while she sips her coffee, nodding sympathetically. "So," I conclude, "I was walking Basil and passed the village hall where you dance, and I saw the flyer for it. I'm going to take it as a sign, and join you in your twinkle toes class," I announce, knowing she'll approve.

"Oh, darling – that's marvellous!"

"Do I need to phone and book?"

"No, no, just come along with me. We need to boost numbers and you'll adore it!" Gloria enthused. "It's tonight – I can pick you up if you like?"

"OK, sounds good to me. So tell me, what do I wear? I don't have any ballet shoes."

"Don't worry my little ballerina-in-the-making, you can just wear leggings and a t-shirt. You can dance in bare feet or I have a spare pair, size five. What size are you?"

"Oooh, I'm a five! Fabulous, thanks. Let me give you my address." I jot it down and pass it to her.

"That's settled then, Dear. See you around six o' clock at..." She looks at the piece of paper. "...'Rose Cottage' - what a delightful name!"

Gloria pecks me on both cheeks, flings her overlarge scarf over her shoulder and sweeps out of the salon, bidding farewell to the staff as she goes.

I have to smile to myself. Did I really just agree to go to a ballet class tonight? It really isn't how I envisaged filling my time. But what's the alternative? I could certainly do with a night off from tears and wine. So ballet it is.

Chapter 4

Pulling up outside my cottage, Gloria waits in the car, studying her near perfect make-up in the mirror. Locking the front door and offering goodbyes to Basil, I run up the path to Gloria's small BMW for the ride to the village hall.

It's a typical red brick village hall, slightly run down but functional, and once inside, Gloria leads me to the small changing room. Struggling to squeeze into a purple Lycra leotard is a large woman in her thirties with olive skin and dark wild curly hair.

"Amy, this is Lucia," Gloria introduces us.

Lucia has got one arm in the leotard and is trying desperately to get the other one in. Her breasts are barely contained by a push-up lacy bra, and it seems highly possible that the leotard is a couple of sizes too small. Despite the tangle she's in, she smiles a big toothy grin.

"Hi there! Nice to meet you! New recruit eh? Well done, Glo!" she says, heaving her arm into an opening and stretching the front of the leotard to cover her bosom. It barely covers her and I have serious concerns that it may not preserve her modesty whilst dancing.

"Have you done ballet before?" Lucia asks, now pulling on animal print purple leggings.

"Not for a long time - it was Gloria who talked me into it, " I smile.

"Ah, you'll love it! Helena, the teacher, is great and it's a giggle." Leaning over conspiratorially, she stage-whispers to me.

"And Glo is fantastic! A proper ballerina, you'll see." Lucia smiles, revealing a smudge of bright red lipstick on one of her front teeth.

"Darling," Gloria says, gesturing her finger to her teeth.

"Oh, OK, thanks," Lucia says, heading off to the mirror.

Gloria and I change our clothes. Gloria certainly looks the part in black leotard and pink tights with a small black wraparound cardigan. I have chosen to hide in black leggings and a plain black t-shirt.

Entering the hall, there is a long wooden pole, a barre, along one side of the room and full-length mirrors on the other. Two women are already there warming up. One is a small wiry looking woman who looks in her sixties. She is wearing all pink and has badly dyed blonde short curly hair. The other is a tall slender woman, wearing an off-the-shoulder top with tights and a traditional georgette ballet wrap skirt. She has a ruddy complexion with a bun high on her head and she eyes me with a snooty air. In the corner of the room there's a woman sorting out CDs, who I assume is Helena, our teacher. A young woman with a perfect willowy ballerina figure also arrives, smiles at me, and takes her place at the barre.

"OK, ladies, gather round, let's do 'Prayers and Pains'," Helena calls from the front of the class.

I was already nervous and this only exacerbates my anxiety. What on earth are 'Prayers and Pains'? Just then, Helena's eyes land on me.

"Ah! A new face! Hello, err...?" she smiles.

"Amy."

"Welcome, Amy! My name is Helena and I'm your teacher. Don't look so worried; we can incorporate introductions into 'Prayers'.

'Prayers', it transpires, is the ritual at the beginning of class when each member of the group speaks of what they want to achieve in that particular class.

Gloria is first.

"May I develop increased flexibility in my poor old feet," she smiles.

24

The snooty looking woman is next.

"May I continue to dance with grace," she sniffs.

"Could you introduce yourself, please," Helena interjects.

"I'm Julay," she says, theatrically placing her hand on her chest.

Lucia coughs. "Julie," to correct her. Julay stares at her with daggers.

Lucia pulls an innocent expression.

"Hello, my name is Marion," says the small curly haired woman, smiling at me. "And may my balance improve!"

"I'm Samantha," says the young woman with the willowy frame. "May I achieve the elusive double pirouette...and then I'd like to land it!" We all kindly laugh.

At that moment, an older man appears at the door.

"Hello?" Helena calls to him. "Are you here for the ballet class?" The women all stare at him.

"Er, yes I am," he nervously replies. He is clearly in his sixties, tall with grey hair and a distinguished look about him. Even though he is older than most of us, he certainly looks in good shape – better than me anyway.

"Welcome, welcome!" Helena smiles, waving him into the room. "We're just going around the room introducing ourselves and saying what we want to achieve from class tonight, and you're not alone, we do have another new starter this evening," she says, nodding to me.

"Hi, I'm Amy," I say to the group. "I suppose I just hope that I don't get too lost or make a complete idiot of myself," I feel my face flush a little. All the participants, with the exception of Julay, smile encouragingly at me.

"And you, Sir?" Helena asks.

"My name is Brian," he says, in a Home Counties' accent. "May my arms be strong enough to lift any of you," he smiles, looking at everyone and bowing slightly. The class ripples with laughter. Finally it's Lucia's turn.

"May I lose an ounce or two."

"Or three or four," Julay mutters under her breath, barely audible. Helena shoots her a reproachful look and then turns her attention back to the group. She clasps her hands together and smiles.

"Right, hoping there aren't any, but can I hear your 'Pains', please."

Lucia jokingly cries out as if in pain and we laugh.

Gloria starts off.

"Nothing to report."

"Nothing," Julay says with her nose in the air.

"My ankle is still slightly sore," Samantha adds.

"OK, well take it easy then – don't push it," Helena answers kindly.

"Feeling a little dizzy today," Marion says with a small blush in her cheeks. Julay raises her eyebrows.

"Don't do the turns then," advises Helena, as she finally turns to Brian.

"Any injuries, Brian?"

"Not at the moment, but I haven't danced for years, so goodness knows what kind of injury I'll have by the end of the class," he chortles.

"We'll be gentle with you, I promise," Helena reassures.

My turn next. "I haven't moved off the sofa for years, except to walk my dog, so I guess I'm with Brian."

"No pressure, People," Helena continues. "You don't have to be super fit to take this class, but you will be super fit if you stick at it," she says enticingly.

"The only pains I have are from this leotard," Lucia says, showing the group where it is cutting her across the bosom. Brian coughs almost choking with surprise and collectively we are staring at her plentiful breasts. Lucia, however, is completely unperturbed – I smile, imagining that not many things flummox her. Leaving Lucia to find comfort by yanking and rearranging her overly tight clothing, we turn our attention back to Helena.

"Right, Ladies...and Gentleman...places at the barre, please," she instructs.

Helena faces us from the front of the hall with the mirrors behind her. She's in her thirties and can only be five feet tall but with perfect posture she appears much taller. She's pretty with dark cropped hair that accentuates her striking brown eyes.

"As we have two new starters tonight," she smiles at Brian and myself. "We're going to return to basics. Later, I'll give those 'who can' more advanced exercises, and for our beginners I'll keep it nice and gentle."

I feel myself starting to ease.

We are led through gentle exercises that warm up every part of the body. I am grateful to be behind Gloria at the barre so, when I'm lost, I can follow her.

Helena demonstrates each exercise and before we begin, to ensure we are all facing the same way, she instructs,

"Left hand on the barre."

I spot that Marion is facing the wrong way.

"Left hand on the barre," Helena repeats over her shoulder, walking away to start the music.

Marion is still standing face to face with Samantha. Samantha signals with her eyes to Marion that she's facing the wrong way, but to no avail. Out of nowhere, Lucia yells in a banshee fashion.

"OI MARION! Left hand on the barre, Love!"

"Oops!" Marion admonishes herself with a headshake. "Sorry folks!"

Chuckling, she turns, and we begin.

All thoughts of Steve have to take a back seat as I can't think of anything else – the class requires my full attention. I am completely in the moment and enjoy the escape from the questions that continually buzz around my mind. My body is alarmed at being required to move and the increasingly difficult combinations test my memory.

In the second half of the class, I realise how much I like the barre when we have to leave it to dance independently in the centre of the room. Helena demonstrates the combination of steps and I aim to place myself at the back. I soon realise that, in a class of only seven, there's not really anywhere to hide. At the front is ultra-confident Julay, and excluding Samantha and

Gloria, the rest of us are a shabby bunch. Helena gives necessary corrections and some praise.

"Brian, don't forget to point your toes."

"Lucia, relax your shoulders."

"Marion – that's a wonderfully exuberant jump!"

Marion doesn't appear so sure as she quite comically staggers to the wall to steady herself. She bends double, trying to draw in some much needed oxygen.

I wonder if any one here is a first aider.

With the exception of Lucia enthusiastically leaning over in a forward bend and ripping her tights, the rest of the class passes by without incident.

At the finish, we stand, drenched in sweat, applauding our teacher who applauds us, and I decide that I definitely like this class.

"Oh, Gloria, thanks for talking me into this - I really enjoyed it," I say, putting my arm around her as we walk to the changing room. "I tell you though, I'm going to ache tomorrow!" I smile and wipe a sweaty half curl away from my forehead.

"That's wonderful, Dear. I thought you might enjoy it!"

We're on a collective gabbling high as we change. 'Wasn't that exercise at the barre tricky?' 'Isn't Helena the most divine dancer.' 'Will I ever be able to turn my feet out more?'

Getting into Gloria's car, I suddenly realise that I've left my scarf in the changing room.

"Won't be a mo, 'Glo'!" I laugh at my unintentional rhyme and run back in to retrieve my scarf.

Entering the changing room, I see a man mopping the floor.

"Oh, sorry," I say, not wishing to tread on his newly cleaned floor. "I think I've left my scarf here."

"Is this it?" he asks, walking towards me, holding up my much-loved baby-blue spotted scarf.

"Yes, thank you," I say, taking it from him. He smiles.

"Were you in the ballet class?"

"Yep – it was my first time and I loved it!" I enthuse, not having realised until this moment just how much the raging endorphins have lifted my mood. I am buzzing. The man chuckles. He has a beautiful smile and gorgeous light brown, slightly ruffled curls.

"Might give it a go sometime myself," his eyes twinkle.

"Yes, you should! You know, we do have another fella in the class. And it's great fun!"

He is still smiling and I feel slightly stupid – he's clearly making fun of me.

"Anyway, better get going, nice to meet you, err…" I say, raising my eyebrows.

"Joshua the Handyman."

"Joshua the Handyman," I smile. "I'm Amy."

"Bye, Amy, the new ballerina!" We hold each other's gaze for a second too long before I skip out of the building back to Gloria waiting.

"I just met Joshua, the handyman," I say, climbing back into the car.

"Ah yes – nice young man." Gloria looks across at me. "Amy, Dear, you're blushing!"

"No, I'm not! I'm just flushed from the over-exertion of dancing," I say, trying to nip that line of thinking in the bud. Gloria pulls away and smirks.

"If you say so, Amy, if you say so."

Chapter 5

By the time the weekend comes around, I have recovered from the energetic ballet class. Thursday morning had been tricky getting up and down the stairs, but gradually the feeling returned to my muscles, and I stopped walking like The Wizard of Oz' 'Tin Man'.

I spend the rest of the week working by day and returning to my empty house by night, eating slimming meals and curling up on the sofa with Basil. I am starting to get used to Steve not being here, but the emptiness in my house and my heart is hard to bear.

The thought of the next ballet class keeps me going. In fact I'm developing quite a passion for it - it certainly beats brooding over Steve. My body has extra lumps and bumps that ballerinas don't possess, and the baggy top and leggings certainly didn't flatter me. (Do they flatter anyone?) What I need is some figure flattering ballet-wear and with that thought in mind, after the Saturday close, I head to 'Chappelle Dancewear.' Remembering that Helena told us that 'dressing the part makes a dancer feel the part,' I peruse the rails of leotards, tops and skirts. I select a handful of different styles and head to the small curtained cubicle.

I find a long ballet skirt; leotard, footless tights and a wraparound cardigan all in black that are slimming and make me look quite the ballerina. I pay for my new apparel and, feeling quite pleased with myself, I skip out of the shop. A celebratory skinny latte is needed and with that thought in mind I head to the best coffee house in the city – Expresso High. Walking along the cobbles past the exclusive boutiques and trendy 'white hearts and birdcage' shops, I spot Samantha. As I have only ever seen her in balletic clothing, she looks quite different in her civvies, although she is instantly recognisable by her upright-posture and turned out feet.

"Hey! Samantha!" I call, waving. As I get nearer, I can see that she's been crying. Mascara marks her cheeks and her face looks red and blotchy.

"Oh, what's the matter?"

She looks slightly taken aback from seeing me.

"Oh, hi, Amy. Sorry," she sniffs. "It's my mum, she's in hospital. I've just left her…" she crumples into tears, long hard sobs.

"Oh dear," I wrap an arm around her. "Look, I'm just going to Expresso High, why don't you join me? Let me buy you a coffee."

"Thank you. That would be lovely," her voice shakes through the tears. I link her arm as we walk to the café.

We enter the up-market coffee house of choice for literary types, trendsetters and vegetarians. Most of the patrons are effortlessly cool. The dark wooden distressed floorboards squeak and groan and the place is adorned with abstract artwork.

"Really," I joke, looking around. "A blank canvas put in a frame – even I could do that!"

Samantha smiles weakly, appreciative that I'm befriending her. I find us a small table situated in a quiet corner and a waitress soon appears to take our order.

We sit facing one another and I wait for her to speak.

"My mum's been ill for quite a while," Samantha sighs. "The doctor said today that the second round of chemo hasn't worked as well as they'd hoped." Her voice is constricted. "And now it's a matter of weeks rather than months."

"Oh, I'm so sorry," I say, leaning across and placing my hand on hers.

"My dad left years ago and it's always been just me and mum. We've been on our own together for what seems like forever. I can't imagine my life without her." Samantha hunches over, her tiny frame shaking with long heart-wrenching sobs. The waitress brings our coffees. I search in my bag for a tissue.

"I'm so sorry, Samantha, it must be a dreadful time for you."

"Things like this put everything into perspective, don't they," she says, taking the tissue. "I work at Dalton's Garage on reception, and I hate it but I'd work there for the rest of my life if it meant I could have more time with my mum."

"Yeah, I know what you mean."

My own sorry situation comes to mind, but I instinctively know that now is not the time to discuss my sorrows. I cannot compare a cheating husband to a dying mother. Nothing comes close to the pain of losing a parent.

"I lost both my parents within months of each other," I offer.

Samantha looks up at me with surprise. "Oh, I'm sorry."

"That's OK – it was a while ago. It was a tough time though," I sigh.

"Can I ask what happened?" she timidly asks.

"Yes of course. It was an ordinary Saturday afternoon and Dad was sitting in his armchair watching the football after spending the day decorating their spare room, and that was it, he had a massive heart attack. No one could have saved him. It was such a shock."

I am surprised at how calmly I can talk about this now. For a long time my throat would tighten when I tried to relay the details of his death.

"My mother didn't really carry on living without him. I mean, she functioned but she took no joy in life. Before my eyes, she became stooped and old. Her mood was invariably low and the light left her eyes. It really didn't come as any surprise when she died a couple of months later. She literally gave up the will to live. If it wasn't my parents and I hadn't been affected so deeply

32

by their deaths, I would say it was utterly romantic." I wryly smile and sigh. "But in truth, it left me orphaned and bereft."

"I'm so sorry," says Sam.

"Anyway, I bought my own hairdressers, Hip Snips, with the money they left me." I continue. "I'm determined to work hard and make a success of it, just so that something good can come of something so utterly sad. And also, somehow, to make them proud of me," I tail off, shrugging my shoulders.

"My mum always encouraged my dancing," she says, "She worked extra hours to afford me the 'ballet life.' I think she was disappointed that I didn't pursue it as a career. I just wasn't confident enough to take that route. I love dancing, but, to be truthful, I don't really like the performing side, which is a bit odd, isn't it?"

"No, I don't think so," I assure. "You just enjoy the dancing. And you *are* a beautiful dancer!"

Samantha blushes. "Oh, thank-you." Her watery eyes smile. "I love it so much, but I do feel that I let my mum down by not becoming a professional dancer. And then to make it worse, I end up in Dalton's Garage!" she rolls her eyes.

"You talk like your life is over! How old are you?"

"Twenty-three."

"See! That's so young! You still have your whole life ahead of you. You can do whatever you want! You certainly don't have to stay in a job you don't like. What would you like to do?"

"That's the problem, I'm not quite sure." Samantha looks downward.

"Ah well, you have time on your side. Plenty of time to ponder life's big choices!" I say lightly. With her mother so ill, it's probably not the time to be making life-changing decisions. One step at a time.

"Hey look, in the meantime, let's just drink to blossoming ballerinas – and let's face it," I say, pointing to myself. "Some of us need to blossom more than others!"

Laughing, she says, "We just need to enjoy the dancing and the rest will sort itself."

"I'll drink to that."

And with that, we smile and raise our coffee cups.

Chapter 6

I am slowly readjusting to days and nights of not hearing from Steve. Although I still have many questions that I want answered, I can't bring myself to contact him. It is sad to witness Basil behaving like the abandoned child, regressing to chewing the furniture, something he hasn't done since he was a pup.

"Bit of a readjustment for you eh, Bas?"

I take his mottled brown and cream face in my hands. "You know that mummy and daddy still love you. It's just that daddy stopped loving mummy. It's not fair that the kid gets caught in the middle, is it?"

Planting a kiss on his nose, I leave him lounging in his favourite spot, by the French windows that overlook the garden. It's a vantage point for watching the wildlife. Basil doesn't mind being left alone for a few hours, so I don't feel guilty about going out to ballet. I'm so grateful for my new-found interest and I skip to the bedroom to collect my stuff in anticipation of the class.

At seven o'clock on the dot, Gloria pulls up outside. Grabbing my bag and bottle of water, I fly out of the house. Gloria has Tchaikovsky's Swan Lake blasting out of her car stereo and is grinning from ear to ear.

"C'mon my little cygnet, your audience awaits you," she teases.

"There is no audience alive that wants to see my dancing!"

"...yet!" she adds.

We drive along to the village hall, chatting and laughing and 'singing' along to the better known parts of Swan Lake.

As we pull into the car park, Brian is getting out of his silver Volvo.

"Good evening, Ladies," he pretends to doth his cap.

"Hi, Brian," I smile.

"Good evening, my dear man," Gloria fakes a curtsy to him. He takes her hand and they giggle. Do they rather like each other? When she turns back to me, she has blushed a deep shade of red. I'd say that answers my question and I register a feeling of warm satisfaction.

Five years earlier, Gloria and her husband, Stanley, had been out for the evening at an upmarket cinema in town, when a drunk driver careered into their car. The collision was on the driver's side, and Gloria, the passenger, came out of it totally unscathed. However, Stanley had not fared so well. He was initially in intensive care and was battling for his life. The hopes were that after a few days he would be out of the woods, but sadly, the days turned into weeks and eventually the doctors explained to Gloria how they saw Stanley's future panning out. He was irrevocably brain damaged and would not be regaining his faculties. Gloria's tears sprung sharply to her eyes and with those words, all hopes and plans for the rest of her life with Stanley died. She hated the term 'vegetable', but this would best describe him now. He didn't know where he was, who she was, or indeed who he was. Her husband was no longer her husband. The teasing, twinkle eyed, big-hearted man she had adored for thirty-eight years had, for all intents and purposes, died in that car. Her heart broke, knowing that her life axis had shifted, and that it would never return to its former position. The doctors advised Gloria to look for a home that could cater for Stanley's needs. Gloria found a delightful one and uses the compensation from the accident to fund it. She visits him often to sit and hold his hand and stroke his hair. He never knows that she's there.

Life has plodded on for Gloria but, looking at her now, she is radiantly alive. We enter the changing room to find Lucia already there, again trying to squeeze into a three sizes too small pink Lycra leotard. Having squished her ample flesh into equally tight leggings, she exhales happily with the accomplishment,

"Come on ballerinas – let's get our bums in there and start pointing our toes!"

We take our places at the barre.

"Prayers please People," Helena announces.

Julay starts, "I wish to perfect my rond de jambe en l'air"

I wouldn't know one of those if you hit me round the head with it.

"I merely want to lose myself in class and be in the moment," Samantha adds.

"Make that grand plié my own," Brian smiles.

"Nothing special, just to enjoy the class," Gloria twinkles.

"Not split my tights," adds Lucia.

"I want to have as much fun as last week," I smile at my classmates.

A quick scan of the room shows Julay to be resplendent in purple, Brian is sporting black tights and a white t-shirt and Samantha looks beautifully pristine with high bun and regulation style black leotard and pink tights.

"How are you doing?" I whisper across to her.

"OK, thanks – and thanks for the coffee, I really appreciated it."

"No problem," I smile.

"Pains?" Helena enquires.

Mumbles of nothing to report reverberate around the room

"Right, if that's the case, is everyone ready to start?"

We begin with gentle bends and warm-ups, and are just getting into the exercises when Marion comes running in. She takes the place next to me at the barre, and we exchange smiles. This evening, poor Marion seems to be struggling with her coordination, and at one point, she topples and lurches toward me. The strong smell of alcohol hits me and I see her eyes are watery and glazed. I don't think alcohol and ballet would mix well for me. I have enough trouble doing it sober, but then, I'm not about to start judging.

Watching Julay, I notice how she punctuates her dancing with snootily held poses; performing as if she were on stage. She projects dramatically to the third balcony and appears to want to curtsy at regular intervals to lap up her applause. Her dancing is really quite lovely, but her manner is questionable.

Helena stops the class, calling for our attention.

"Julay, your grand jetés are the perfect combination of height and shape. You're using your feet into the ground and your legs are beautifully stretched to the maximum. I wonder if you could show the others please?"

Julay could not look prouder. Puffed up like a peacock, she walks to the corner. All eyes are on her as she makes the most of her moment in the spotlight.

She prepares and lurches herself forward into the gallop followed by a split leap grand jeté. In mid flight, there is an unmistakable sound of breaking wind. Upon landing, her ruddy complexion is even redder as she struggles to maintain her haughty demeanour. Apart from the sound of small stifled giggles, the room is plunged into silence.

"See, you'd expect that from me, wouldn't you?" says Lucia under her breath.

"What did you say?" Julay asks indignantly.

"I said that you wouldn't expect a jump like that from me," Lucia replies, her eyes wide with innocence. The room vibrates with suppressed laughter.

"That was a beautiful grand jeté, Julay," Gloria says, kindly deflecting the situation. "Wish I could leap that high."

With earnest expressions we all enthusiastically echo the sentiment, and then, with a call for warming down and stretching, we, thankfully, move on.

***

Driving home, Gloria and I are in hysterics from the sheer joy of class and Julay's lapse in etiquette.

"Oh Amy, I do feel sorry for her. She was embarrassed, wasn't she!"

"Well maybe she needs to get that stick out of her backside!"

"Second thoughts, might be better to keep it in!" Gloria says, between the guffaws of laughter.

I cannot remember the last time I belly-laughed like this and, even though it's not kind to be laughing at the expense of another, it feels wonderful!

Until this moment, I hadn't even realised that, of late, Steve and I had stopped laughing. In fact, thinking about it, we weren't embroiled in massive arguments either. That surely shows our lack of passion. We didn't even care enough to fight. We were indifferent. I shelve thoughts of Steve as I'm keen to discuss our classmates further.

"You know Marion? Well, I don't mean to be nosey but…"

"You mean the…" Gloria mimes drinking and raises one eyebrow.

"Oh, is she known for having a drink?"

"Or two," Gloria exhales. "I really don't know the full story, but once we went out for a drink after class. We weren't there long – maybe an hour or so. Well, we were huddled around a table having a giggle about our lack of ballet expertise or some such silliness, when we suddenly became aware that someone was standing at the bar watching us. It transpired to be Jack, Marion's husband. He was just standing there, staring at us, with his hands on his hips looking mightily cross. Marion, as quick as anything, jumped up from the table and said her goodbyes. We watched as he stalked out of the pub with her frantically scurrying behind him. When we saw her again at class she made an excuse that he was only annoyed because she'd forgotten that she was supposed to be meeting him somewhere that evening. But between you and me, Dear, I think it was a weak excuse. I think he's not a very nice man."

"Poor Marion. Do you think that's why she drinks?"

"Quite possibly." Gloria frowns. "She's lovely, but I fear that her marriage isn't exactly rosy. Talking of which, have you heard from that errant husband of yours?"

"Nope, not a dickie bird. I keep waiting for him to walk in the door and tell me it was all a huge mistake and that we can work at our marriage and get back on track."

Even I can hear that I am trying to convince myself.

I look at Gloria's face and I can see that she wants to say that he's not coming back and that I need to get on with my life, but Gloria being Gloria is far too kind to hurt me, so instead she squeezes my knee.

"Give things time, My Dear. No one knows the future and what's in store. Just, in the meantime, concentrate on you, and above all, be kind to yourself. And don't forget that there are people around like me who are more than happy to offer a helping hand when it's needed."

Her kindness brings the tears flowing once more.

"Now now, Dear, come on, think of that wondrous explosion of wind tonight," she teases naughtily. "That was comedy gold!"

As my rollercoaster of emotions changes direction once again, the soggy wet tears dissolve into raucous laughter.

Chapter 7

I had left school and gone straight into a hairdressing apprenticeship. It was all I had ever wanted to do. As a young child, my mother's hairdresser had multi-coloured hair and funky clothes, and I would sit transfixed watching her work. The shop itself smelt of potions and perfumes, and I believed it to be the most glamorous place on earth. Right there and then, I decided that hairdressing was the career for me.

Progressing through my apprenticeship was hard work, but the endless sweeping up, shampooing and taking towels to the launderette was done with enthusiasm. I worked a six-day week for little pay but I was happy. If there was one thing that slightly irked me was that apart from actual holidays, I never had a Saturday off. All my friends would be shopping for new outfits to wear out at night, and I could never join them. So when I came to run my own shop, I set about compiling a rota that gave every member of staff one Saturday off every few weeks. Waking up on this rare delightful Saturday morning, I reflect that my rota is a stroke of genius and I am sure that my employees would agree.

I'm going to take the day at my own pace. Apart from Basil, I have no one else to consider. I sit in my dressing gown at the dining room table with a pot of tea and two slices of toast, looking out at the garden. In it I see the first signs of autumn, and I'm once again reminded that life never stays the same. The garden's shades of brown tell me that before I can feel the hope of spring's new beginnings I must trudge through winter. I know well enough that, in time, all things pass. I think of Samantha's dying mother, of how her life has been lived, how her time is passing. With that in mind, after showering and dressing, I decide to walk Basil to Dalton's Garage to see how Samantha is faring. I become distracted by a squirrel darting up the oak tree at the far end of the garden, and decide to plump for one more cup of tea before doing battle with the shower...

Dalton's Garage is about a forty-minute walk, starting off on country lanes that eventually lead into a residential area. It is a small petrol station and garage that is popular with local residents. I tie Basil up to a drainpipe around the side, and then open the shop door, triggering the bell to ring loudly. It is fair to say that it is an old-fashioned garage shop, selling only car parts and accessories. A man wearing a blue grey boiler suit, with dirty hands and a black smudged face, is helping a customer choose some oil. I find Samantha behind the desk on the phone.

"Yes, Mr. Chan, it's all booked in for Tuesday. Yes...if you can bring the car in first thing, we'll call you when it is ready." She looks up and smiles brightly at me. Her tiny frame is swamped in a deeply unattractive mid-grey overall with 'Dalton's Garage' on the breast, and yet somehow she still manages to look supremely feminine.

"Amy, how lovely to see you! How are you?" she says, putting down the phone receiver.

"I'm fine, thanks. Just thought I'd pop in to see how you're doing. How's your mum?"

"She's doing well, actually. I think it's a relief that she doesn't have to go through any more chemo. She gets to enjoy whatever time she has left to do things that she wants to do. It feels a little like the calm before the storm, but I'm just trying to support her and enjoy the time I have with her."

"That sounds good," I smile.

"I am exhausted though...oh hold on." She reaches across to reset the petrol pump. "I try to help out as much as I can, and I'm really not complaining, but working full-time and then popping round there to do chores, you know, it's a lot to do."

"I can imagine," I empathise. "Actually, why don't you..." My words hang in the air as I notice, through the glass-paned door, Steve, my Steve, walking towards us. He hasn't seen me yet, as his head is down, looking in his wallet.

Samantha follows my gaze towards him.

"Amy, you OK?"

"Oh Christ," is all I can say before he enters the shop and we come face to face.

"Amy," he says, with a look of shock mixed with guilt.

"Hi," is all that will come out.

"How are you?"

"Fine," I automatically reply a little too quickly.

He looks different. He's wearing a different style of clothes. If I had suggested he wore a Jack Wills hoodie, he would have laughed and told me that no way would he 'pay more for a poncey name.' But there he is, if I'm not mistaken, top to toe in Jack Wills.

"Sorry I haven't been in touch, I know we need to sort out things, finances and stuff," he bumbles.

"Yes, we do. In fact, the council tax will be due soon," I say, trying to keep my voice level and devoid of emotion.

"Oh, ok, I can give it to you now if you want? I've got cash in the van...hold on a sec..." He eagerly runs to his work's van. This is him salving his guilty conscience.

"Amy? *Who is he?*" Samantha asks, furrowing her brow.

"That, my dear Sam, is my estranged husband."

Steve re-enters the shop, and hands me a wodge of banknotes. As I take them, it is then that I notice he is no longer wearing his wedding band. We both stare at his naked finger. I suppose I shouldn't be surprised, but I am. It feels so absolute that he's taken it off. I haven't even thought of removing mine. His reflex is to cover his ring finger with his other hand and, by his awkward stance, I can sense that he doesn't want a scene.

"See you soon, Ames," he says, and with that, he turns to the counter to pay for his petrol.

Sam is processing his card, and he reminds me of a horse with blinkers on, as he steadfastly keeps his eyes forward. Having paid, he leaves the shop without looking back.

Rushing round to my side of the counter, Sam puts her arms around me.

"Oh my God, Amy, are you OK?"

"I will be," I sigh.

At that moment, more pumps need to be reset, and Sam is clearly needed to attend to her duties.

"Why don't we go for a drink after ballet on Wednesday?" she calls over her shoulder as she races back behind the desk.

"That'd be lovely," I reply. "See you in class."

She blows me a kiss as I leave the shop feeling quite dazed.

Chapter 8

"OK, Ladies and Gent, tonight we're going to try something a bit different," Helena says, switching off the music.

By the looks on all our faces we are all clearly wondering what she has in store. Helena is a great planner – each lesson is constructed in detail. She has a system of following the same exercises for a three-week period, and then amends and introduces new ones to keep them fresh. She constantly strives to find new ways of teaching us the same things. Her instructions are repeated constantly and she introduces imagery to help us. For example, the torso must be kept straight and square, so she asks us to imagine that we have headlights shining out from our hips. These lights must never dip – they must always be facing straight ahead. It's helpful. We love Helena - she has the patience of a saint.

"I would like you to pair up as we're going to work on turning."

A collective "ooooh" goes around the room.

"I was with my niece recently," she continues. "She's five. I watched her twirl madly across the room. They weren't perfect pirouettes, but she was lost in the joy of turning. Now, being adults we've mostly lost that ability. We need to get it back. We consider too much the nuts and bolts of turning, and we need to forget that for a while and just turn. I want to inspire you to twirl!" Helena should be a motivational speaker.

"Now – in pairs, let's have Samantha and Amy, Gloria and Brian, Julay and Marion and, Lucia, you can work with me."

We all stand with our respective partners.

"What I want is for you to face each other. One of you will be the turner and the other will hold her, or his, arms out to guide the person turning and to make sure they are safe. Apart from the actual turn, the only other thing I want you to do is to keep eye contact with your partner. Don't worry about turned out legs or pointed toes – we need to focus on just getting round!"

There's an excited buzz as everyone starts chatting.

"OK – do you want to go first?" I say to Sam.

I hold my arms out and she begins to turn and her head whips around as she tries, and mostly succeeds, to maintain eye contact.

"Wow, Sam, you're good at this!" I say, as she completes her umpteenth turn.

"It's called spotting. When you keep your eyes on something stationary. Without it, believe me, you feel like a drunken sailor!"

I giggle and then it's my turn. To say that I fail miserably would be an understatement. The turns are off balance, despite Sam trying to harness me in place and my spotting is non-existent. Feeling exactly like a drunken sailor, I stop turning and bend over double, putting my hands on my knees.

"Shall we observe the others for a while to learn from them?" Sam kindly offers, nudging me with a smile.

The height difference between Julay and Marion is comical. Julay must be at least five foot eight, and Marion is a dot of a woman at around four foot nine. Julay is turning, but poor Marion is struggling to get her arms to stretch around her bigger partner.

Helena is perfectly guiding Lucia, who has taken to spotting very well. But by far the most interesting couple to observe is Gloria and Brian. They seem to be in a different place altogether. They have no trouble holding eye contact and they are laughing, collapsing into each other as Brian struggles to turn. I don't think they would notice if we all upped and left the room. Gloria's skin is shining with a mix of perspiration and old-fashioned romantic glow. Brian looks down at her and his eyes are full of fondness. Gloria takes her turn at twirling and he holds his arms out, gently guiding her round. She isn't spotting in the slightest as her head is thrown back in laughter. As she stops, they both realise that the whole class is watching them. They look like a couple of teenagers caught in a compromising position. With flushed cheeks, Gloria smooths her clothing and coughs delicately. Brian looks like a cat with the cream, but quickly adjusts his expression to feign solemnity.

"OK," Helena coughs, diverting attention away from them. "Now we'll try it with the nuts and bolts back in place."

Helena continues to instruct us in the ways of the pirouette. "Feet in a strong fourth position, arms in third, a sharp snatch up onto one leg, turned out legs, pull up, spot and turn!"

There are so many parts to it that my mind is sent into a dizzy spin – and that might accurately describe my pirouettes too.

As we all face the mirror to practise, we must look like out of control spinning tops. Occasionally, there's a triumphant cheer as someone either lands one or at least makes it round, but mostly we are like blind newly born kittens veering off in different directions and falling off balance.

"Well done, everyone," Helena finally says. "We'll do more of that next week. For now, we need to cool down and stretch out."

***

"Lucia, are you coming to the pub?" I ask, as we head out of the hall.

"Yep, count me in," she replies, wiping her forehead with a small towel.

"Julay? Marion? Brian? Gloria. You guys coming?"

"I can't, Dear," Marion says. "I have to get home."

"OK, no worries," I say, feeling the injustice of Marion's

situation.

Is she not coming because of her husband? Is he the bully that Gloria described, or had it been a simple husband and wife misunderstanding? I like Marion, so I truly hope it's the latter.

We head to the changing room, chatting affably. There is a leaky underwhelming shower in the corner of the women's changing room and we take it in turns to have a quick spin in it. I am the first to finish and, as the changing room is quite pokey, I decide to wait in the corridor.

As I step out, I find Joshua loading bottles of cleaning fluid into a large wall cupboard.

"Hi!" I smile, hoping that I don't still look lobster-red and flustered from class.

"Oh hi, Amy, how are you?" he flashes a wide smile.

All the better for seeing you.

"I'm fine, thanks. Just had a great class," I say, fingering my hair in an attempt to flatten it.

"Yes, I saw that through the window."

I am mortified that he has been watching.

"Isn't there some kind of caretaker code that doesn't allow that?"

"There might well be," he grins. "But I'm a handyman."

"And a comedian."

"Ah now that's not officially in my job description," he counters.

As our laughter curtails, we keep eye contact. Is he looking at me in a certain way? Or has my imagination gone into overdrive and I'm willing him to? Goodness knows my ego is in need of a boost.

He is utterly gorgeous. He must be around six feet tall, slim with broad shoulders. His brown curls are again looking slightly unruly and he has a smile that could win over the hardest of hearts. I might be drooling slightly.

Pull yourself together, Amy, you're a married woman and you certainly aren't looking for any kind of romantic involvement.

The rest of the group emerges chatting and laughing from the changing room.

"Ah, Josh, my man – how you doing?" Lucia slaps him hard on the back.

He laughs. "I'm fine thanks, Lucia."

"We're going for a little drinkie over at The Swan – you wanna join us?"

Oh crikey – supposing he says yes…

"Sorry I'll have to pass," he says, not looking me in the eye. The others try to cajole him into coming but when they see that he is resolute, it turns to cries of 'kill joy' and 'party pooper.'

It really shouldn't bother me that he doesn't want to come with us, and yet it does. My 'ego brain' says that if he liked me, he'd want to join us. I cannot help the deflated sensation I feel. This is ridiculous. I hardly know the man. But then again, maybe not spending time with him is for the best.

Heading out from the village hall, I steal a glance back at him. He is shaking his head and smiling. Gosh – should I really be having these thoughts about him? I am only just separated for goodness sake! And I absolutely do not need any more affairs of the heart to deal with. Talk about out of the frying pan and into the fire. Why on earth would I be looking at someone else at this point in my life? Craziness!

And no, I don't think I am protesting too much.

Chapter 9

Joshua watches the gaggle of women and the one token gent leave the building. He shakes his head, smiling sadly to himself, and continues loading the cleaning fluids into the cupboard. Actually, as he has declined to join them in the pub, he could quickly do the hall floor before shutting up for the night.

Dragging the broom across the floor, he can't stop thinking about that woman, Amy. He had glanced through the hall window, and had become charmed by watching her chewing her lip while trying to master a turn. She was completely committed but when she couldn't do it, she was laughing wholeheartedly. Her eyes were alive and shining, and he had stood there for far too long, enthralled by her. Then she had appeared in the corridor, and he'd felt a natural ease of warmth towards her, and he suspects that she'd felt the same. If that is true then, to him, she is already an almighty disappointment as she is clearly wearing a wedding band. Women! It would just be like Sophia all over again, and he's still nursing the wounds that she inflicted on him.

No, this woman is not going to feature in his future plans. He is working all the hours he can to save enough money to get on a plane back to where he was born, New Zealand. His parents had been working there twenty-eight years ago and he was born in Wellington on the north island. At the tender age of three months, they had brought him back to England, but his dual nationality allows him to live there should he choose to. And that is his choice.

He finishes sweeping the floor and then fills the bucket with water and detergent, and starts mopping it thoroughly. He finds it therapeutic. He is a plumber by trade, but a few years ago, the local college approached him and told him that they were desperate for tutors for their City and Guilds Plumbing course. They paid for his Teacher Training and employed him at the college. This covered two thirds of his week and so he took other jobs to boost his income. Hence, he came to be the handyman at the village hall. Strictly, he should only be fixing and maintaining, but he's quite happy to pitch in with some cleaning. He finds that working alone gives him plenty of opportunities to let his mind wander and then resettle and focus on his goals.

She crosses his mind again. She does have a beautiful smile...but it's the smile of a married woman. And even if she were single, she's not going to distract him from his plans of moving abroad. Avoidance is the key here. Don't get sucked in. Don't let another woman turn his life upside down again. Abstinence is what is called for – and he can do that!

So why was he wishing so very dearly that he was in that pub...

Chapter 10

"Oi, Fancy Knickers! Get another round in!" Lucia has clearly had one too many and Julay tuts, clearly not appreciating her new moniker.

"Last one, then," Julay says disapprovingly, as she gets up to go to the bar.

I am in the middle of the horseshoe leather seating booth with Sam on one side and Gloria on the other. Gloria is once again locked in conversation with Brian so I chat mostly to Sam.

"Are you OK after the other day? I take it you've only just split from your husband? " she asks gently.

I falter to answer. I don't want everyone overhearing, and the evening becoming a mass discussion about my broken marriage.

"Sorry, look you don't have to tell me. I'm too nosey by half, forget I said anything," she backtracks.

"No, no, Sam, it's fine, I really don't mind," I half smile. "Yes, it is recent. Just a few weeks ago, I got home from work to find him packed and ready to leave. It seems that he has 'a thing' with the local barmaid. I had no idea – which, believe me, makes you feel rather foolish. But it's interesting, you know, since he left, I've really thought about our relationship. I suppose we take things for granted after being together for so many years – but I can't help thinking back to when we used to have such fun together, really laugh, you know? We were inseparable and in love…" I trail off feeling the familiar lump in my throat.

"Sorry, didn't mean to upset you." She eyes me kindly.

"It is what it is," I sigh resolutely. "I guess it just wasn't built to last. It feels odd though, being apart, and it's strange being on my own in the house. To be truthful though, I'm just not sure if it's having someone around that I miss or actually him. We'd definitely drifted apart. And you know what I hate? I used to poo-poo the idea of people 'drifting apart.' I refused to believe that it was something that happened outside of our control – as if we're powerless to stop it happening." I find myself getting fired up. "I thought it was a lazy excuse for a break-up. I kind of blamed people for letting their relationship drift apart. How can you let a solid, lasting love just go? How can you not work at the relationship to stop from drifting apart?"

Sam's wide-eyed expression tells me that I have definitely got carried away.

"Sorry," I say contritely, raising my hand to touch my burning face. "Guess I'm still coming to terms with it and I suppose I never thought I'd stop caring enough to let us 'drift apart.' We took our eyes off the ball."

"And he put his on the barmaid," Sam looks at me with a small smile, not sure if her witty observation will be appreciated.

"Ha ha – you're right!"

"Don't be so hard on yourself, Amy. It takes two, and from what you've said, you weren't the one looking for something outside of the marriage."

I blush a little as I think of Joshua and my wayward emotions towards him earlier in the evening.

"Yeah, I suppose you're right."

Julay returns with the drinks and I notice Lucia staring towards the bar.

"Lucia – didn't your mother ever tell you it's rude to stare?" I tease.

"But look at them – it's amazing!" she says, barely dragging her attention away.

I follow her stare to see five men in a circle near the bar laughing. What has captivated her is the fact that they are all using sign language. Their hands move deftly as they communicate. There is not one word spoken and I must admit, it is rather fascinating to watch.

"Can't exactly go and join in, can you?!" says Julay.

"I don't know," Lucia slurs a little. "I do know the alphabet you know. Learnt it in Guides."

"Ah well, in that case, go forth and communicate!" Julay says sarcastically.

"You know what, Fancy Pants, I must just do that!"

Lucia uses her arms to hoist herself up from her chair. She's not completely drunk but neither is she sober. She walks a wavy line to the group and stands there beaming at them. They stop signing and turn to her, and we watch as she spells out something on her fingers. They all stare at her hands. One of them, the ginger haired, freckly one, smiles kindly and spells something back to her. It's too fast and she waves her arm in a 'slow down' motion. The others resume their conversation, but he continues to engage with her. We have no idea what she is trying to say (if indeed she does!) but it is highly entertaining. We screw up our faces and with tilted heads, we try to decipher her message; it's a bit like watching your grandmother play charades. We feel an alliance with the chap, and we can see that he wants to laugh but, to his credit, he keeps a straight face and encourages her to continue.

"Should we go and rescue him?" Sam asks.

"I don't know – he doesn't seem to be too bothered," I answer.

"Goodness knows what they've agreed!" Julay chips in. "She's three sheets to the wind and they can't speak the same language – sounds like the start of a match made in heaven!"

We all laugh.

"Anyway," Julay continues, turning to me. "I understand from Gloria that you're quite a good hairdresser. And I'd like you to do my hair."

"Yes, of course!" I realise that this is the closest to a compliment I will get from Julay, and feel quite flattered. "When do you want to come in?"

"When are you free?" she says, opening her bag to retrieve her small diary.

"Well I know that I'm fairly booked up this week, but actually, thinking about it, Gloria is in for a deep conditioning treatment on Friday, so while it's working its magic, I could squeeze you in then."

"That'll do fine. Thank you," she curtly replies. "What time?"

"Say 11.30am?"

"Yes, I'll be there." She jots it down.

We look up to see Lucia writing on a piece of paper and handing it to the grinning ginger guy.

"Do you think she just gave him her number?" I ask.

"Do you think she can even remember her number?" Sam replies.

Lucia stumbles away from the smiling man, blowing a kiss over her shoulder.

She falls back into her seat and bangs her empty glass down on the table. We all look at her in disbelief. A big smile covers her face.

"Misshion accomplissshed!"

Chapter 11

It's Tuesday morning and Basil leaps on the bed to alert me that it's time to wake up. I much prefer Basil waking me than the alarm, so I make a fuss of him for a few minutes before rising and padding to the bathroom.

I hit the shower switch. From the emitting groaning noise, I know that it's not good news. I try the usual on/off trick but this time to no avail. I feel like drawing the sign of the cross over the shower unit and I inwardly cry at the thought of how much this is going to cost me. If only Steve had fixed it before he swanned off to his bit on the side.

More pressingly, I wonder how I'm going to become clean and refreshed for the day. I consider my childhood and how my parents would only bathe me once a week. Did I smell? When did showering on a daily basis become the norm? Regardless of my normal hygiene routine, without a morning shower, I know I am going to feel grubby.

Cursing that I had dispensed with the only flannel I owned when Steve once inadvertently used it to wipe his boots, I go to the cupboard and fish out some facial cleansing wipes. I wipe all over my body. This doesn't make me feel particularly clean – just incredibly cold. And then using much more deodorant than normal, I dress and head out to catch the bus.

Steve, the shower has gone on the blink and as this was something you promised to do before you left maybe you could put some extra money in the joint account so I can pay someone to come in and have a look at it. A.

I fire off the text feeling irate that I have to ask him to do this. I gaze out of the bus window thinking that, even though I make a reasonable living from Hip Snips, recently the bookings have been down. I think it's the same everywhere – everyone is feeling the pinch. Folk can't afford the nice things in life, and so they stretch out the weeks between haircuts. It's totally understandable. I pay the staff before I pay myself, so consequently, I have been taking a lesser wage for the past few months. Steve really did pick his time to leave.

The morning goes by in a whirl of blow dries and shampoo and sets, until Gloria turns up for her treatment.

"Hello, My Dear." She enters the shop looking as immaculate as ever in a pink polo-neck and smart wide legged trousers.

"Morning, Gloria, good to see you. How are you?" I smile.

"I'm marvellous," she twinkles.

Sitting in the chair at the basin, I apply the deep conditioning treatment to her hair.

"So, how are things with you, Amy?" she asks.

"Well, not bad, except that my shower has finally given up the ghost. Steve had been promising to fix it for ages and, of course, he never got around to it. This morning it was making this horrid noise and absolutely no water came out of the darn thing. I had to resort to wet wipes!"

"Oh dear, nasty business. Don't you know anyone *else* who could repair it?" Her words are innocent but it's clear that she's teasing me. Her words hang in the air.

"No, Gloria, I don't," I say, deadpan.

"Well what about that nice handyman at the village hall…now, what's his name…?"

I smile at Gloria's clunking lack of subtlety.

"Gloria, you know his name. It's Joshua!"

"Ah yes, Dear, that's the one. Nice young fellow. I'm sure he'd help you, if you asked."

58

I'm thankful to be positioned behind Gloria so she doesn't witness my brightly flushed face.

"I might do that, Gloria, thanks."

I choose a quick change of conversation.

"So, enough about my hygiene deficiencies, how about you? How are you doing?"

"Me, Darling? Oh you know, plodding along."

"Nothing new in *your* life?" It's my turn to dig.

"Ha ha – you've noticed, have you?" she giggles.

"I would have to be blind not to have noticed! You and a certain gentleman do seem to get along terribly well," I prod.

"Don't think badly of me, Dear," she lowers her voice slightly. "I will always love Stanley, but he doesn't even know who I am anymore. It is heart-breaking and I never purposely went looking for someone, but when Brian turned up at the bridge club... " she stops abruptly.

"Gloria! You knew him before the ballet class? You sly dog!" I exclaim.

"Shh... shh...now, Dear. OK, I might have met him already, but it was quite a surprise when he turned up at the class. I really didn't think he would join!"

"That shows how keen he is on you, Glo," I say kindly.

"It's really nice, Amy. I feel very comfortable with him. After the last few years of being alone, it's so nice to have someone just to go to dinner and places with. I had forgotten what it's like when someone takes an interest. Maybe I'm fooling myself, but I honestly think Stanley would approve," she notes sadly.

"Oh, Gloria, I'm sure Stanley would want you to continue with your life. You mustn't feel guilty."

Just at that point, from two basins along, we hear a familiar voice.

"Young lady, this tea is tepid. Kindly bring me another!"

Gloria and I freeze. It's Julay. We hadn't even noticed her entrance, which in itself is quite remarkable. Has she been there long enough to overhear our conversation? We'd lowered our voices, so I'm hopeful that what we said remains just between us.

If Julay knew Gloria's back-story, she would doubtlessly have an unfavourable opinion.

Karen, who is the culprit 'tepid tea' maker, takes Julay's cup and rushes back to the small kitchen with it.

"Hello, Julay," I say leaning forward, smiling.

"Oh hello there," she snootily says. "Didn't realise you were there. I thought only the shampoo girls would be that side of the basin."

I resist the urge to rise to her comment.

"Hello!" Gloria resonates.

"Ah, Gloria. Hah, didn't recognize you either, with your crowning glory caked in slime."

"A dose of deep conditioning and my crowning glory shall be restored!" Gloria is not one to rise to snide put-downs either.

"Be with you in a minute, Julay," I continue in a bright professional manner. Returning my attention to Gloria, I wrap cling film around her hair to seal in the conditioning treatment and then wrap a towel around that to trap the heat.

"Can I get you a drink?" I ask.

Out of the corner of her mouth Gloria smirks. "Tepid tea please!"

We both giggle.

"Coming up," I smile, touching her shoulder. "Karen, cup of tea for Gloria, please."

I walk over to Julay.

"Would you like to come over and take a seat?"

Grumbling about being sat at the basins, as there were no other free seats, Julay gets up and follows me to a chair.

Sometimes I do think that handling scissors whilst dealing with customers like Julay is a risky business.

I look at her in the mirror and smile sweetly.

"Now then, what can I do for you? More tea perhaps?"

Chapter 12

Here's a new game I've invented. Every time I think of Steve and the tears start to form, I think of ballet. I'm hoping it will become automatic if I practise enough. It's a Pavlov's dog kind of thing. Of an evening, if I'm snuggled up on the sofa with Basil (Steve would never let him on the sofa, so it's our regular act of defiance), and my mind wanders into a melancholy state, I mentally replay the exercises at the barre or the steps in the centre. I consider writing a brain-training book, as it seems to work quite well. (Though I do wonder about its sale-ability as it wouldn't have mass appeal.) I do commend myself, however, as it has been a couple of days since I shed a tear – with the exception of stubbing my toe on the coffee table, but that's a different matter.

The changing room at the village hall can be quite chilly, so tonight I decide to put my leotard on at home and my jeans on top. As I'm checking my appearance in the mirror, my phone bleeps. It's Steve.

Hi Ames...

He is the only person to call me that. Does he really have the right to anymore?

...are you free tomorrow night? We need to sort out the house/bils etc...

Doesn't he have autocorrect?

Let me know. X

Ah look - the return of the kiss – well, well. I shoot back a text.

Fine. Let's meet after work. Expresso High at 6pm OK?

Keeping it in the public domain means that it should be civilized. A few weeks ago, I wouldn't have trusted myself not to scream, shout or cry, but I can manage it now...just about. He replies.

See you then.

Ah - and the kiss has gone again.

***

Class is energetic, fun and as mentally exhausting as ever. We are definitely gelling as a group. Even Julay, whose standoffish manner tends to set her apart, seems to be making inroads. It's starting to feel like a family. Everyone is their own person with their own idiosyncrasies and, in the main, there's an acceptance of each other. Often I find that I am one or two (or six) beats behind the group, and consequently collisions can occur. We are all relaxed enough to laugh at such mistakes. In professional classes, the competitiveness is rife but in our merry little band, it just doesn't seem to exist. I'm very aware that I am growing very fond of these people.

"Right, guys!" Helena addresses us. "There's something I want to talk to you about."

"Argh, we're a hopeless cause and you're leaving us?" Lucia jokes.

"Nope." Helena smiles. "Quite the opposite!"

"OK, don't keep us in suspenders then!" Lucia adds.

"OK, you probably all know that on New Year's Eve there's the annual 'Dixbury Does Talent' show..."

I can guess where this is heading and I am filled with dread.

"...and I would like us to enter!" Helena beams at us expectantly.

"Marvellous idea," Julay burrs.

"Really, Helena?" Gloria queries. "You really think we're good enough?"

"Yes, I really do! The beauty of ballet is that there are many roles. I can choreograph trickier parts for those with more experience and for those who haven't been dancing as long, they can 'frame' the ones that have. Have you been to the ballet? Have you seen how the 'players,minstrels,courtiers' are around the edges watching the soloists?"

Blank faces stare back at her.

"You have been to the ballet, haven't you?" she asks incredulously.

"My mother took me to Giselle when I was about thirteen, trying to instil some culture into me and my sister," Lucia speaks out. "But all I remember is us giggling at the bulges in the male dancers' tights! It was a great night, don't get me wrong!" she guffaws.

We all join in her laughter.

"I'm familiar with a few ballets," Gloria says.

"I saw a ballet when I was a child," I chip in.

"Many years since I went," Marion adds.

"Me too," Brian says.

"Well, People, this needs to be rectified. As part of your learning, I think we should all take a trip to the ballet. I was going to get myself a ticket to see Swan Lake next month at the Theatre Royal. Shall we all go?"

"Yes indeed, that would be splendid," says Brian.

I shoot a glance at Samantha who has remained quiet throughout.

"Are you OK with all this, Sam?" I whisper.

"Erm, sorry everyone," she timidly starts. "I don't want to be a killjoy but I'm just not sure. I suffer with nerves and really don't know about performing."

"Of course it's not compulsory," Helena interjects kindly. "But I can help you with the nerves, Sam. I have looked at the calendar and if we start rehearsing now, we have thirteen weeks. Now this doesn't seem long, does it...so how about we do an extra session a week starting next week? It'll be a free class.

We'll have two nights a week to work on the piece and you'll know it inside out, and hopefully that'll give you the confidence to perform."

Sam looks partially persuaded.

"I tell you what, I could choreograph it so that if it gets nearer the time and you really don't want to do it, your role can easily be dropped. I won't put pressure on you, but really hope that you'll want to do it. The feeling of performing is wonderful and I would love you to experience it."

All eyes are on Sam.

"OK, alright, I'm in."

We all make 'yay' noises.

"So that's everyone?" Helena scans the group with raised eyebrows.

"Erm ..." my voice is so small it's barely audible. "As one of the newest members, I really don't feel I can dance – let alone be on stage."

"I promise that I will not make a spectacle of you, Amy. I will choreograph carefully and give you movements that are well within your range - "

"Like walking?"

There's a ripple of laughter.

"You are more capable than you think, you've picked it up really quickly and very well too." Her kind eyes implore me to believe.

"OK then, I'm in," I reluctantly agree. I push the inner dread of making a complete fool of myself to the side for now. Let's see what she's expecting me to do before I default into worry mode.

"And Brian, if you're concerned too, being a beginner, you must trust me that the man's role in this production will be mostly to support the beautiful ballerinas around him."

Brian looks suitably pleased with that.

"Fantastic! We'll start rehearsals next week. If we stick to Wednesdays can we also meet on Friday evenings?" Helena asks.

We agree unanimously.

Looks like we are going to be performing!

Isn't it funny how life goes? One minute you - and by 'you' I mean 'I' - are in what you consider to be a happy marriage. You're planning a future of family bliss. You're content to be, in the main, sedentary, with no desire to move any muscles. The only kind of stretching you are involved in is your waistband and you never watch ballets, let alone perform in one.

Do you ever stop for a moment and think 'how did I get to *this* moment?'

Yep - that is exactly where you find me now.

Chapter 13

The changing room is bursting with jabbering dancers.

"I wonder *what* we'll be performing," says Marion.

"And we didn't ask how long we'll be on stage for," Gloria chips in.

"What about costumes? What do you think we'll be wearing?" I ask.

"Oooh, I hope it's pink and sparkly!" Lucia says wistfully.

"What are you - five?" Julay peers at her disdainfully.

"Oh relax, Stuffy Knickers, we get to dress up!" Lucia retorts. Julay shakes her head.

"I've never been to Dixbury Does Talent. What do we win? *If* we win, that is!" I quickly add.

"I think it's two hundred and fifty pounds, but it's more the honour of winning," Gloria answers.

"Well, if we have to organise costumes then that money might cover our costs," I say.

"Indeed," Gloria continues. "In fact, once we know what we're performing, and what kind of costumes we need, we could have a planning meeting. Between us, I bet we could cover everything. I have a sewing machine."

"I'm good at dying fabrics," Marion says.

"And, of course, I can sort out hair," I offer.

"Right then," says Gloria. "Once we know, we'll put the action committee into action!"

The buzz continues around the room. We wonder if our dance will be an excerpt from a ballet. Will it be Swan Lake? Will we be ghostly as in Giselle? If it's Don Quixote, will we be Spanish señoritas? Lucia likes this last idea and spontaneously treats us to some flamenco dancing. The excitement is contagious and soon some of us are dancing with fiery Spanish attitudes around the changing room. Marion is slipping out of her leotard and about to put her blouse on when Lucia grabs her to join in the dance.

"Ole, Marion!" Lucia squeals and spins her around.

Marion yelps like an animal in pain and, covering her arms over her body, she stands with her head lowered. We all stop. She is exposed and vulnerable. Her bra is grey and lifeless, and a large amount of her sagging flesh is mottled yellow and blue. Angry red marks at the top of her arm add to her shocking appearance. It's impossible not to notice, and we have all stared far too long now to turn away.

"Marion, you look like you've been in the wars," Gloria says with kindness. Marion twitches.

"I fell down the stairs a couple of weeks ago. I think maybe I blacked out. Silly thing to do really! I did hurt myself, but I'm on the mend now. It was lucky that Jack was there to help," she says, with a look that begs us not to challenge her. "Who knows what would've happened if he hadn't have been there." She tries to convey an air of levity in an obvious attempt to dissipate the gravity of what we are seeing.

Her story might be feasible if I didn't already know about Jack frog-marching her out of the pub. To also add doubt to her explanation, her bruises look like they were caused at different times, and judging from her response and the look in her eyes, she's not about to tell us the truth.

"Oooh, looks like you took quite a tumble," Sam says.

"I'll survive," says Marion, but the sadness in her eyes is palpable.

I want to reach out and put my arms around her. I want to take her home with me and move her into the safety of my spare bedroom. I want to cook her a good meal and care for her. I want her never to have to set eyes on Jack again. There are meaner things I want to do to Jack, but my primary concern is the safety of Marion rather than the retribution to Jack.

Marion inches back to where her clothes are and, in an air of sadness, we all continue to dress in silence.

The others are showered and out before me. Deliberately, I hang back to be able to take a longer shower. Having to cope with wet wipes and a newly acquired flannel does not cut the mustard, so I seize this opportunity to have the best shower I can with the facilities available. It's hot water dribbling over my body but beggars cannot be choosers.

Feeling refreshed, I make my way out of the changing room to see Joshua carrying a bucket into the hall.

"Hi there!" I call.

He spins around, spilling some of the liquid from the bucket.

"Now look what you made me do....more work!" His eyes sparkle. He looks genuinely pleased to see me.

"No rest for the wicked."

"And I am a very wicked fellow," he flirts. His broad smile forms creases at his eyes.

Don't blush, don't blush, don't blush... I blush.

Struggling for composure, I try to think of something to say that won't cause further embarrassment.

"I wonder if you would look at my shower?" I blurt.

What! How could I say that?

"Sorry, come again?" he looks amused by the effect he's clearly having on me.

"My husband left me," I sigh. "He left me with a breaking shower and now it's broken. Not a drop of water. Nothing. That's why I'm still here, I've spent ages in the shower cubicle in there," I jerk my thumb backwards towards the changing room. "Trying to get clean. Would you help me, please?"

"Help you shower?" he roguishly grins.

"No! Help me by *looking* at my broken shower!"

He laughs and I look down, hiding my embarrassed smile.

"Yes, Amy the new ballerina, I'll help you. Of course, I'll take a look at your shower."

"Thank you so much," I say. "When would be a good time?"

"How about Sunday morning?"

"Yes, that would be perfect! Excellent"

"You gonna let me know where you live, then?" he raises his eyebrows.

He thinks I'm stupid...or besotted...or both?

I scrabble in my bag for a pen and paper, and jot down my address and pass it to him. He reads it.

"Yep, I know where that is. See you Sunday, say 10am? Mine's white with one sugar!"

"No problem – see you then."

I watch him walk away.

Be still my beating heart!

For goodness sake, Amy, act your age. Or more importantly, act your marital status.

Chapter 14

It's ten minutes to six and I'm sitting in Expresso High with a skinny latte and a jittery stomach. The light outside is starting to dim, and a slight patter of rain is starting to fall, trickling down the large windows. Sometimes, in life, we have moments that can change the course of our lives and this feels like one of them. I've had a busy day at work but, in all honesty, I've been distracted. Firstly, my distraction came in the shape of pondering why I become a twelve-year-old girl around Joshua. But, as the day wore on, it was due to my imminent meeting with Steve. I can't claim to have clarity but I am thinking straighter than in the past few weeks and I'm ready for this discussion with Steve - there will be no histrionics.

Nursing my latte, I recall how I used to think that some relationships were not designed to last the course. In some ways, it makes a mockery of marriage, but maybe, in life, we are only supposed to be with a person for a certain time and then we're meant to move on? Wouldn't it be wonderful if we could appreciate all that we have learnt from that person, the personal growth we have achieved by their presence, and then civilly shake hands and say goodbye?

'It's been great, thanks, moving on now, see you around (or not!)'

Sadly, intimate relationships by their very nature make this nigh on impossible to do. Highly charged emotions prevent us from shaking hands and quietly walking away. My feelings are still raw from Steve's betrayal but I'm hopeful that this meeting will inch me towards finding a measure of peace.

At that moment, the door opens and Steve walks in, looking around. He looks so familiar but at the same time so alien. With his shock of dark hair and tall, slender frame, he's still a good-looking man but my heart doesn't leap at the sight of him.

Seeing me, he nods and heads over.

"Want a coffee?" he asks.

I point to my cup. He must be as nervous as I am and, despite myself, I find this endearing.

"It's waitress service, she'll be over in a minute," I tell him.

He smiles weakly and sits opposite me.

"Right, c'mon then, let's talk," I keep my tone light and playful. If we cross swords, we'll get nowhere.

"OK where do we start?" he nervously asks.

"I suppose there are two things I'd like to discuss. One is how we got to where we are now and second is the practicalities of what happens next, finances, the house etc."

Warming to my calm manner he says.

"Which do we do first?"

The waitress appears and takes his order. As she walks away, I say.

"Let's do the tough stuff first...tell me how you ended up falling out of love with me and in love with someone else."

He takes a deep breath and momentarily looks away. I think my words have hurt him.

"OK. We were plodding, Amy. We didn't do much together anymore. You seemed to find fault with me all the time. I felt I couldn't do anything right. Bit by bit, you weren't really bothering with me. We were just living together, not really as a couple anymore. You've been distant. It just wasn't working anymore. I'm a bloke, Ames. Justine started paying me attention and before I knew it ..." he trails off.

His honesty and weakness pain me in equal measure.

"But, Steve, you could've talked to me. We could have tried to get back on track. You just gave up without discussing anything with me."

"You're so involved with the shop all the time, and if it wasn't the shop, it was Basil. I was left out. I'm not very good at talking, you know that, and it just happened." He looks genuinely sad. "And," he says, fixing me square in the eyes, "I never said that I have stopped loving you."

"Oh please, Steve, don't say that," I say, pierced by the poignancy. "You walked out and left me – it's doesn't exactly scream undying love!"

"Or Endless Love?" he smiles, alluding to our old private joke.

In our younger days, we would drive listening to a mixed CD of eighties songs, and when it came to the Diana Ross and Lionel Ritchie classic, we would duet. Invariably he would be Diana and I would be Lionel. It was us in our love-soaked silly days. I reluctantly smile at the memory.

A softness fills the air.

"I do miss you, Ames," he says quietly, tenderly.

I look down, feeling sadness in the core of my being. I don't know whether to say that I miss him too, or whether I should remind him that he is the reason that we are in this situation. I look at him sadly.

"Are you happy, Steve?"

"Err, well, yes I suppose so," he falters.

I'm not convinced, but I don't want to start holding out hope for a reconciliation. Sentimentality is par for the course. We've been through so much together, but that shouldn't cloud the fact that things have changed: he left.

The waitress appears with his coffee and I change tack.

'OK – let's talk practicalities – what's going to happen to the house, Steve?"

"Well, I'm living above the pub, but I will want to settle somewhere soon, so I'd like it to go up for sale - if that's OK with you?"

I don't know what I was expecting, but I feel like I've been punched in the stomach.

"Seriously, Steve! You up and walk out of our marriage and now I'm supposed to up sticks and move too? This is so unfair!"

"Well, it's not like we have children and it's their family home or anything."

I look at him bitterly. That's a low blow. Of course we don't have children and whose fault is that? His cruel words hit me hard. The Steve I know wouldn't have said this. Is this really how he thinks now?

"You're right, Steve, we don't have children," I spit the words. "And can I add that it's wonderful how quickly you've forgotten Basil! You haven't even asked about him!"

"Look, you know I'd take Basil, but I can't. Justine has a miniature Staffy who doesn't like other dogs. They just couldn't live together." The tension in his jaw is showing.

Is he really one of those men who has a family and then neatly moves on to the next, forgetting every trace of the original one? Is my Steve this man?

I then remember that he's not 'my Steve' any longer.

"Right, well...thank you for making me feel so monumentally replaced and in record-breaking time too!" The hurt and anger is burning through my eyes. He has the decency to lower his head.

"I want to stay in the house, Steve, it's my home and I love it."

"Then you'll have to buy me out...sorry," he says.

"You know I can't afford that!"

There's an empty uneasy silence between us.

"I don't want things to get nasty, Ames – but we need to move on," he states.

Moving on – it's all about moving on these days. But it's such a miserable thing to have to do when, for me, staying still was working just fine.

"Steve, what's the rush? Are you so sure that we're over and that you're ready to end everything? No going back?"

I'm not sure I want to hear the answer.

He doesn't reply with words. He just looks at me with an agonizingly sorrowful expression. I feel my heart plummet to the floor. I want to shake him, to remind him of everything we've shared. I want to take away his pitiful appearance and replace it with one of hope.

Feeling resolute in my determination not to cry, I take a deep sigh.

"OK, I'll get the house valued. Three different agents and then we meet to review," I say, sounding briskly professional. "Until we sell, you pay your share of the mortgage and I'll take care of the bills. The upkeep of the house - if anything needs doing, should be fifty-fifty as we'll be splitting the proceeds when we sell."

"That sounds fine. I did transfer some money to the joint account for someone to have a look at the shower. Just let me know how much the repair is, if it's not enough."

I look at him, my eyes accusing. He's guilt-ridden but paying for our temperamental shower doesn't redeem him to me now. I don't even know if he wants redemption. He's royally dumped Basil and me and it seems that he wants us out of the house tomorrow. Was he always this hard-hearted? What on earth happened to the man I loved? I'm guessing he wants to sever all ties with me, pack 'us' away in a box, and start anew.

He looks at his watch.

"Supposed to be somewhere?" I ask.

"Err, I have to be at The Dog and Trumpet for a darts match," he says, squirming.

No doubt with Justine.

I search in my bag for my purse. Guessing my actions, he stops me.

"Don't worry, Ames, I'll get this."

I rise from my chair and put on my coat. I look down at him.

"Thank you. And stop calling me that. It's Amy."

Before he can see the tears forming in my eyes, I hold my head high and walk out of the café.

Chapter 15

Samantha is just leaving Dalton's when the text comes through from her mother.

Fancy popping in for a cuppa and chat when you finish? Lol mum x

Samantha doesn't know how many times she has told her mother that 'lol' doesn't stand for 'lots of love'. With no immediate plans for herself, she texts back.

Sure. 'Lol'. Be there in ten mins or so. Xx

She hopes nothing is wrong. Thinking about it, she remembers that if something is wrong, her mother calls rather than texts. So with no urgent panic, she picks up her coat, shouts goodbye to her colleagues, and leaves.

She drives through the town, slowing down at regular intervals to avoid the last of the Saturday shoppers who seem to think that the road is their extended pavement. She listens to Frank Turner singing.

"We can get better 'cos we're not dead yet."

It resonates in her ears and in her heart. She can't bear to think about death. The not knowing how much longer her mother will be around evokes a sad gnawing feeling deep in her stomach. She will face the time when it comes – it's all she can do. Many years earlier, her mother had talked to her about the futility of worrying; it's what they now refer to as "The Cat Story". The story goes that there's a cat that sits in the garden enjoying the sun. Every day, at around five o' clock, the neighbour returns home and lets his Alsatian dog out into his garden. The Alsatian barks madly over the fence and the cat runs for cover. The cat knows that this happens on a daily basis but doesn't let the thought of it spoil the afternoons spent happily sitting in the sun.

Samantha is trying desperately not to fret over her mother's imminent death. Her mother always tells her to be 'the cat.'

Some days it's easier than others.

Pulling into her mother's drive, she looks at her childhood home. It's a pretty nineteen sixties bungalow with old majestic trees lining the edges of the sweeping lawn. Sam and her friends used to enjoy long innocent summers of fun in this garden. Her eyes are drawn to the tree house where they had drunk homemade lemonade and then to the brick weave drive that, one year, they turned into a rather dangerous roller skating slalom course. Looking at the garden now it's in need of a little attention and she makes a mental note to offer her help.

"Hello, Darling," her mother says, ushering her in.

Sam looks at the thin ghost of a woman. She was never big but she has lost every ounce of fat possible. Her hair is thinned from the chemotherapy and her hands, feet and nose look disproportionately big for her body. Accentuated by her hollowed cheeks, her beautiful grey blue eyes appear wide and bulging. Nevertheless they still shine. This alone gives Sam hope that they still have time; that her mother isn't giving up.

"How are you, Mum?" she asks, gently.

"Not bad, Sweetheart. The doctor gave me something extra to help me sleep and it certainly did the job last night. Tea?"

"That's good. Thanks, yes please. You sit down, Mum, I'll make it."

Her mother smiles wearily and goes to sit on one of the pretty chintz chairs in the conservatory.

Minutes later, Sam brings the tray replete with teapot, milk jug, sugar bowl and chocolate biscuits.

"Thought you wouldn't mind me opening these," Sam smiles, nodding towards the biscuits.

"Of course not, Love – let's enjoy them. How are things with you then?"

"Good, actually," Sam says, pouring the tea. "You know the ballet class I go to? Well, the teacher, Helena, wants us to take part in Dixbury Does Talent. To be honest, I'm petrified. But Helena's lovely and has promised that if I feel I really can't do it, then I can drop out at any time."

"Oh, that's very kind of her. Difficult to do that when you're organizing a show, I would think," her mother says, dunking a biscuit into her tea. "You know, Sammie, you always were so nervous of performing, and I never really understood why. You're such a beautiful dancer. Your old teacher used to say that all you needed was the confidence, and you could be a top dancer."

"I know, Mum, I know." Sam is tired of hearing this. "I can't help it though. The thought of performing scares me!" Sam doesn't mean to snap.

"OK, Dear, I'm only saying." She holds up her hands.

Her mother's disappointment sits heavily on her shoulders, and Sam wishes that she'd never mentioned the competition.

"Was there any particular reason you wanted to see me, Mum?" she asks, anxious for a change of topic.

Sam's mother leans forward and carefully places her teacup and saucer onto the table. She clears her throat.

"Yes, Dear."

Sam feels a sense of uneasiness.

"With all the recent events and the doctor's latest prognosis, I thought I needed to sort out some things." Sam can hear a tremor in her voice. "I know you have friends but I'm your only family and I don't like leaving things like that. For everything that happened, you still have a father and..."

"Oh, Mum, what have you done?" Sam asks with dread filling her voice.

"I found him on Facebook, would you believe?" her mother says brightly with pride.

"Mum? You? On Facebook? I didn't know you even knew about Facebook!"

"Hush now – don't look so amazed, I'm not a dinosaur. The nice young nurse, Maisy, helped me. Anyway, the point is that I found him and have been in touch. He's coming round later this afternoon and I just wanted to talk to you before I see him."

Sam is at a loss for what to say. She has vague memories of her father, John. He was a distant solitary type of man. He found it difficult to show love and affection and, although Sam knew that on some level he had loved her, he certainly never showed it. Sam's mother had done everything for her. If Sam's friends wanted permission for something they would have to ask both their parents but in her family it was only ever her mother. There was not a single decision she remembered that was made by her father. Her parents had lived in a cold silent impasse for some years and when Sam was ten years old, her father had quietly upped and left. It had been difficult for her to miss him, as he had never really been present.

"What do you want me to say, Mum?" Sam asks.

"I'll be honest, Sammie, I want you and him to reunite. He's not a bad man – he's just a closed man. He has, or rather *had*, an inability to express his feelings. He might be totally different now, who knows? It was all a very long time ago and I needed more. I couldn't live with second guessing how he was feeling all the time. I wanted someone to show me love." Her will to convince Sam is painfully evident.

"Mum, this is a bit of a bolt out of the blue for me. What time is he coming?" Sam asks, unable to conceal her alarm.

"Around five thirty."

"I don't really know what to think. I'm not cross or anything, but I really want to leave before he turns up," Sam says, looking quickly at her watch. "I'm sorry, Mum, I'm just not ready for this. Not yet."

"That's fine, Dear, just think on it, please. For me."

"I will, Mum, I promise."

"It means a lot to me." Her mother's eyes are watering.

"Don't worry, Mum, I will come round to the idea, I'm sure. It's just a bit of a surprise. Give me a bit of time and I'll be fine. I'll text you later, OK?"

With that, Sam kisses her mother affectionately on the cheek, gives her a quick hug and without a second look back, makes for the door.

Rushing for the car Sam quickly unlocks it and climbs in. As she is waiting to pull away, she sees in her rear-view mirror a dark green hatchback pull up. She peers hard at the man getting out of the car and knows full well that he is her father.

As she drives away, she is relieved that, for today anyway, she doesn't have to open that can of worms.

Chapter 16

I am lighting the pretty pink and lilac candles on the mantelpiece. I love my lounge as the nights draw in, it is just the right size of cosiness. Actually, I just love this house. I can't believe that I am going to have to leave as I truly believed that Steve and I would stay here until our own family outgrew it. We had such hopes and dreams. When we had moved in, Steve decorated it and I lovingly bought soft furnishings to make it ours. This was our love nest, our happy home. After finishing our week's work, we would double bolt the wooden front door and I would feel enshrouded by a warm blanket of security. Nothing and no one could infiltrate our bubble of happily-togetherness. This week, estate agents will come in with their clipboards and their critical eyes, and will tell us what it is all worth. At the other end of that road, we will pay off our mortgage, take our cash and walk away in separate directions.

Feeling overwhelming melancholy, I decide to open a bottle of wine. It may not be the answer, but it is my answer for now. My phone chimes a text. I wonder if it's Steve – although there's no reason that it should be.

Hi Amy, it's Sam. Any chance I could come over? Sorry. I understand if you're busy. Xxx

Not Steve then. And really not busy either. She might just be saving me from an evening that could easily end in drunken dribbling and tears. I wonder what's going on with Sam. I hope she's OK. In such a short space of time, I've grown very fond of her. Maybe we are troubled kindred spirits as she has the sadness of her mother and I have my dilapidated marriage.

Not busy at all. Perfect timing. I'm just opening a bottle of wine! Was thinking of Chinese takeaway too. So come over, you're more than welcome! x

I hit send, pull the curtains and start plumping cushions in case she does come round.

Lovely. Thanks. Send me your address and I'll be there. Xxx

I quickly send back my address and shoot around the house making sure it's all reasonably clean and tidy. I open the Rioja to breathe and tip some roasted vegetable nibbles into a bowl. Basil looks hopeful. Stroking his head, I treat him to a roasted parsnip. After a moment of it being in his mouth, he releases it back on to the rug. "Not a fan of the roasted parsnip huh, Bas?" I pick up the half soggy crisp and put it in the bin.

Fifteens minutes later, there's a knock at the door and just in case I hadn't heard it, Basil barks furiously.

"OK, OK Basil – it's only Sam!" I say, opening the door. "Hi!"

"Hi, Amy. Thanks ever so for letting me come over." She looks a bit shaken.

"No worries at all, my lovely. Come in, come in. Wine?"

"Sounds great!" she beams.

We ensconce ourselves on the large striped baggy sofa with our drinks and nibbles.

"Do you watch Strictly? It's on tonight," I say.

"Ooh yes, I love Strictly!"

"Shall we watch it and then get Chinese afterwards? Or are you hungry now?"

"I'm fine at the moment," she smiles, holding up her wine glass. "In fact, I've just come from my mum's..."

"Oh, Sam, is she OK?" I jump in.

"Oh yes, yes, nothing like that. No, the thing is she's been thinking about the future and she's decided that she doesn't want to leave me without any family. So she found my dad on Facebook – I tell you, Amy, I had no idea she was aware of the

Internet, let alone Facebook! And she invited him to her house today," she grimaces.

"Did you see him?"

"No, well, yes, kind of..."

"Wow, Sam – 'no', 'yes', 'kind of' – ha ha, which is it?" I gently tease her.

She laughs. "Well, as I was leaving, I saw him pull up. So I drove off quick smart!"

"Did you not get on with him?" I ask, taking some nibbles. "Help yourself," I point to the bowl. She nods and proceeds to tell me about her parents' marriage and what kind of a father he was. I listen, chipping in here and there.

"Can't have been easy growing up with a man like that," I sympathise.

"I didn't know any different. I remember visiting friends and their parents spoke to each other, and I was amazed. I thought all parents didn't talk to each other. The thing was, Amy, he wasn't an abusive man, not aggressive or overly critical. He just wasn't there. I know he loved me. Though how I know that, I have no idea, as I have no proof," she casts her eyes down, pushing a fair wispy curl behind her ear.

"Maybe your mum is right to reintroduce him into your life. Don't you think that things happen at different times in life, and maybe now is the time for you to reconnect with your dad? He may be very different now."

"That's what she said," she sighs, staring into the distance.

She takes a sip of her wine. Shaking herself from her thoughts, she eyes her glass.

"This is going down very nicely," she smiles. "Anyway, enough of me, how about you? How are things?"

I fill her in on the latest with Steve. She is suitably horrified that I am going to have to leave my lovely little cottage. As friends do, she backs me up with my grievances against him and sympathises with my situation.

"This *is* a gorgeous cottage," she says looking around. "I can certainly see why you wouldn't want to leave, but a lot of it is what you've made of it. The furnishings, the decoration, the objet d'arts..." We both giggle. "...are what you've put here. And you could do it again in another home. You obviously have a gift for creating a beautiful, comfortable home – and that's come from you, not the house!"

She's right. When we first bought this cottage, I loved having the project of styling it. I read home magazines for ideas and cut out pictures of furnishings that I liked and made a mood board. I coordinated and planned every room. I enjoyed every moment of it. I quite often reflect that I am a person who enjoys the journey, the process, more than the finished result. If I were to get a new place, I could enjoy the inventiveness all over again, a new canvas to create on. And maybe the memories attached to the dream of my life here are better to be left right here. There's an easy silence in the room.

"What are you going to do about your dad, Sam?" I ask.

"No idea. What are you going to do about your house?"

"What a pair we are!" We both laugh.

"More wine?" I ask, waving the bottle at her.

"I'm driving." Her mouth turns down in mock sadness.

"Stay over! I have a spare bed! Let's get ratted!"

She laughs. "Pour me another!"

Chapter 17

My mouth feels dry and scratchy. I move my tongue over my lips but all moisture seems to have departed. My head is stone heavy on the pillow, and is filled with pulsing aches. I tentatively open one eye. The light is streaming in the window with no curtains pulled to block it. I wince. Then I spot a foot in front of my nose – a small foot. Flashes of memories start to form. We had finished the bottle of wine, opened a second, called for Chinese food to be delivered, and then enthusiastically ventured on to a third bottle. I was neither in a fit state nor inclined to make up the spare bed with fresh bedding. I refused to let Sam sleep in used bedding, and so, rather illogically it would appear, insisted that she 'top to tail' with me.

"Urgh," Sam groans.

"Indeed, dehydration. I'm dying from dehydration," I wail.

"I'm just dying," she moans.

The doorbell's ring makes my head shoot up from the pillow. I immediately regret the sudden action and then frown, trying to imagine who might be calling at this time on a Sunday morning.

Even the frown hurts.

As a small light bulb goes on, I start to panic - oh no, oh no no no no! What's the time? I fumble for the bedside clock. It can't be ten thirty! No! It'll be Joshua! Damn it, damn it, damn it - how could I have forgotten?

"Sam! Sam!" I say, nudging her legs as I heave myself out of the bed. "It's that guy from the hall, Joshua!"

"Eh? Why's he here?"

"I have a shower that doesn't work and he said he'd have a look. Oh God, look at me!" I say, catching a glimpse of myself in the mirror.

Sam pulls the covers over her head and moans something inaudible.

I grab my dressing gown and shout in the direction of the door.

"Be with you in a mo!"

My skull spasms in pain. I race to the bathroom and survey the damage. My hair is in knots, my skin blotchy, eyes are barely visible and I must reek of wine. The house, itself, has the aroma of last night's food, and even though we only sat and talked, it looks like we have had some kind of rave. I splash water on my face and quickly brush my teeth. My hair and skin are a lost cause, so in lieu of a sixty-second makeover, I adopt a remorseful expression.

I open the door to find him smiling widely.

"Good morning, Angelina Ballerina." He is positively perky. "And how are we this gorgeous morn?" From looking at me, he can tell full well how I am.

"Come in," is all I can muster.

"A bit of a party last night was it?" he asks, looking around the lounge.

"Not really." I don't feel particularly stable so I cross the room to a chair. "You know Sam from the class? Petite? Looks like a proper ballerina?"

He nods.

"She came over and we had a few drinks and a takeaway. We might have had more than a few..."

"Ah gotcha. Should I be whispering?" he says in a low voice. He is clearly finding this highly amusing. "Tell you what, you sit there and I'll make some coffee, and get you some water and tablets."

"Thank you, that'd be nice," I say, putting my head in my

hands. "Tablets are in the cupboard, coffee and stuff near the kettle."

I am pitiful.

He goes off to the kitchen and whistles a cheery tune whilst fixing the drinks.

"Would you like some stomach-settling toast?"

"Eurgh – just the coffee for now, thanks," I weakly call back.

He enters the room and I look at him properly. He is in light blue jeans, t-shirt and a grey hoodie. He has some weekend stubble that rather suits him. He is undoubtedly handsome. I, on the other hand, am hideous.

He takes a seat on the Queen Anne chair and studies me.

"How many bottles exactly?" I can hear the smile in his voice.

"Two...maybe three."

"Each?"

"No! Between the two of us!" I wonder if I have the right to be indignant.

"Well I guess it's still no surprise that you're..." he searches for the right word. "...poorly."

At least he didn't plump for 'rough.'

I'm finding his proximity to me and my ghastly appearance too much to bear. Being a lush is definitely not the impression I wanted to create.

"Would you like to have a look at the shower then?" I ask, trying desperately to put an end to our uncomfortable dialogue.

"Sure, sure."

He follows me to the bathroom and I explain the events leading up to its demise. He starts to investigate further and I take this opportunity to scamper back to my bedroom in an attempt to rectify my unsightly appearance. Fortunately, the wet wipes are on my dressing table, so I quickly strip off and wipe myself all over. I don't have to worry about Sam witnessing any of this as she is clearly out for the count. I overuse the deodorant; spray my favourite cologne and slip into jeans and a soft pale pink jumper that usually brings colour to my face. I can't style my hair so I grab a headband to cover it. I quickly brush some powder over my face and add mascara. I look in my oval glass mirror and know that, for today, this is as good as it gets.

"How's it going?" I stand at the bathroom door.

He is just stepping out of the shower cubicle. His eyes glint as he registers my appearance.

"I think I know your problem," he says, leaning against the cubicle, sipping his coffee.

"Yeah? What's that then?" I feel my confidence starting to return now I'm half decently attired.

"Your shower doesn't work."

"Oh, very funny!"

"OK seriously, your pump isn't working. I think it might be in your loft. OK to take a look?"

"Sure."

I take him to the loft hatch in the spare bedroom, open it and pull the retractable steps down. I stand at the bottom and watch the back view of him disappearing up them. I idly wonder what the etiquette is for manhandling the handy man?

Good grief, Amy, it's like you're in a Carry On film - calm down!

"Yep," I hear his muffled tones. "It's definitely the pump."

"Eurgh, how much is that gonna cost?" I whine.

"Hold on, coming down." He springs to the bottom of the steps. "They aren't too much. I can get you one at trade, so that'll be cheaper."

"OK, thanks, how much?"

"I'll have to check the exact price but I'd say you're looking at around ninety pounds."

"OK and then labour on top obviously."

"Don't worry about that, Amy Ballerina, I'll fit it for you, no charge."

"That's very kind of you, Joshua Handyman, I really appreciate it."

Once again we are smiling at each other, neither breaking the gaze.

There is a groaning from the other room. We raise our eyebrows and wander into the hall.

"Sam, you OK?" I call, only to see a flash of person race through the hall into the bathroom. We stand there listening to the familiar sounds of a body rejecting too much red wine.

"I think I'll leave you to it," he winks.

Oh my – don't wink at me!

"Thanks ever so much, I really appreciate you coming over."

"No problem, I'll look into the pump, let you know, and we can fix up a time for me to fit it."

He turns to leave. "What you doing the rest of the day?"

"First thing? Go back to bed for a nap!" I say.

"Do you know that's one thing I can't do – once I'm awake I'm awake. No going back to bed for me."

"Urgh, couldn't live with you then!" I joke.

"Fair enough, but thank you for briefly considering it."

I laugh out loud and then wince, raising a hand to my fragile hung-over head.

"Careful now." He gently places his hand on my shoulders and brushes past me to the door. My body zings from the electricity between us. Opening the door, the autumnal sun streams in and I groan at the brightness.

"Later, Amy Drunken Ballerina!" he laughs.

See you, Joshua Dishy Handyman.

I head to the bathroom to check up on my friend, cringing that the nineteen-seventies word, 'dishy', is in my vocabulary. I solemnly vow that it can stay there and that I will never utter it aloud ever.

Chapter 18

"OK, OK, gather round People," Helena says. "Tonight we're going to start rehearsals! The piece I've chosen is...drum roll please... Dance of the Mirlitons from The Nutcracker!"

'Oohs' and 'ahs' fill the room.

I join in with the cooing but, quite frankly, I don't have a clue.

"I've brought my laptop so we can all have a look at it. Now, don't panic – I will be modifying the steps so it's do-able. It won't be professional level, but I'm confident you can present a poised beautiful dance." Helena smiles at us.

She is a marvellous teacher, kindly in her corrections and knowledgeable of her art, but I think that her greatest gift is instilling confidence in us.

"I truly believe," she continues. "That good solid technique wins every time. We don't all have perfect turn out with penguin feet." We laugh as she waddles penguin-style. "But we can work with what we've got."

"Hello?" a voice comes from the door. "Is this the ballet class?"

We all turn to see a woman in her mid thirties with a teenage girl. Both with long blonde hair tied up in ponytails. I would bet they are mother and daughter.

"Yes, come in, please!" Helena welcomes them. "I'm Helena, and you must be Josie and Catherine?"

"Yes, I'm Josie," the older woman says, "and this is my daughter, Catherine."

"As I said on the phone, it's a mixed ability adult ballet class – that is what you were looking for?"

"Oh yes it is." Josie says, smiling shyly. "One thing I didn't say is that Catherine is studying at The Dance Studio and has exams coming up and would really benefit from another class...but she's only fourteen, is that OK?"

"Yes, that's absolutely fine. And you have some experience, don't you, Josie?"

"Well, I used to dance as a child, but haven't for many years. I'm very rusty," she admits, self-consciously.

"OK, don't worry about that. As I said, we're all abilities here, and I like to think we're a friendly supportive bunch, aren't we?"

Murmurs of agreement resound. The only non-consenting person seems to be Julay who is eyeing Catherine as serious competition.

"We're just starting to prepare our entry dance for Dixbury Does Talent in December. It's the Dance of the Mirlitons from The Nutcracker. Perhaps tonight you could join in the class and decide whether you'd like to be a part of it?"

They both nod and smile.

"Changing rooms are through the hall but bring your bags back in here," says Helena, pointing to the pile of clothes, shoes and bags in the corner.

"Oh we're dressed already," Catherine smiles, revealing thick metal braces. They take off their coats and place their belongings with ours.

"Wonderful," Helena says. "Let's watch a clip of the Kirov Ballet in action, then. Get ready to be inspired, People!"

We all gather round the laptop and Tchaikovsky's music starts. Oddly, the lead dancers are children but my classmates are more preoccupied with the music that they say is from an old television advert for fruit and nut chocolate. We watch two girls and a boy dance (a 'pas de trois,' Julay delights in enlightening us), with the rest of the dancers around the edges of the stage, pulling facial expressions and watching them.

I'm feeling heartened. I can stand and watch and pull faces.

It lasts around three minutes and as it ends, we break into a smatter of spontaneous applause.

"I'm liking that!" Lucia enthuses.

"It's beautiful," Sam sighs.

"I presume I'm to be the fine male figure in between the two beautiful ballerinas?" Brian asks.

"Yes, Brian, you'll be holding and guiding your leading ladies. Now, I know that children are in the lead roles, but we're going to apply artistic licence and loosely base our performance on this piece. It'll be our interpretation."

"Fab, then those ballet know-it-alls in the audience won't be able to compare it with the real thing," Lucia throws in.

Helena laughs, nods in agreement and continues.

"So you saw the other dancers were just observing the three main characters? In our version, this will not be the case, but, saying that, I will choreograph to your abilities, so no need to worry."

I preferred the idea of standing and watching.

"Who will be taking the leads?" Julay enquires.

It's a simple question, but one look at her taut expression, and it's obvious that the answer could have serious repercussions.

"I think it's only fair that, for the next couple of classes, those who fancy a lead role can learn the steps. After a few sessions, I can make a decision. But be aware, I won't necessarily be choosing the most accomplished dancers. I have to take height, looks etc. into account. There are other ways to shine in this production too. I'll choreograph extra parts for those who wish to take their turn in centre stage. Please think of it as an ensemble piece, everybody contributes something to the dance."

Julay is clearly not appeased, but decides to hold her tongue for now. I am guessing she is mightily keen to bag a leading role.

"Right," Helena clasps her hands. "Let's get started with our barre work. We'll warm up nicely and then move on to the dance."

As we run through our exercises, I glance at our two new members. Josie has wonderful posture but it is her daughter who catches my eye. She is tall, lithe with long slender limbs and an ease of grace. I would imagine that she started dancing from a very early age. To me, she looks not that dissimilar to the dancers we have just been watching on YouTube, though that probably says more about my lack of knowledge than her ability. After forty minutes of barre work, we stretch out and drink water.

"Right - those who would like to learn the steps for the leads please stand on this side." Helena says pointing to her left. Julay, Gloria and Catherine step over. Julay glares at her perceived opponents.

"Do I automatically qualify for that side of the room?" Brian quips.

"Ha ha, well you're in the centre, all on your own, Brian," says Helena.

Marion, Lucia, Josie, Sam and myself are left. I look at Sam questioningly.

"What?" she whispers.

"Why aren't you on the other side?" I say through clenched teeth.

"Because I don't want to be," she mouths back.

I roll my eyes at her and she breaks eye contact, half smiling, she knows I'm itching to say more. She's blessed with such talent. It's a shame she's unwilling to step into the limelight.

Helena starts running through some steps with the prospective leads and then turns to us.

"Whilst I'm working with this group, can you be practising your pirouettes please?"

And so we are off like drunken spinning tops again.

***

95

At the end of class, Josie and Catherine bid their farewells whilst the rest of us head to the changing room where the atmosphere is noticeably cooler than usual. Out of the three aspiring leads, Catherine is the most proficient dancer which has clearly riled Julay.

"I like our two new additions," Lucia says, innocently, unaware of Julay's disdain.

"Huh, this is an adult ballet class, and that young girl is not an adult!" Julay harrumphs.

"We're hardly full to capacity here," Gloria tries to calm the waters. "The more the merrier, I say."

"Do you? That's what you say, is it?" Julay turns on Gloria.

"And what does that mean?" Gloria is taken aback.

"So big hearted, aren't you, Gloria? It doesn't matter if a fourteen-year-old steals our show!"

"What?" Gloria laughs. "What do you mean, 'steals our show'? She's a lovely dancer – why shouldn't she be in it? Makes us look better!"

"And that's what it's all about for you, Gloria, isn't it? How it looks! You are all about how things *look,* aren't you. But it's not always the truth is it?" There's venom in Julay's voice.

I know where this is heading, and looking at Gloria's face, I think she does too.

"What do you mean?"

"You present yourself as this perfect person," Julay's eyes are wild. "A high and mighty woman, this almost widowed soul who lovingly cares for her husband. But tell us, Gloria, how long has it been going on with Brian?"

Gloria takes a sharp intake of breath at the realisation that Julay overheard our conversation in the shop. I have profound sympathy for my friend and bewilderment at Julay. How could I have believed that she was starting to blend with the group?

"Julay that's enough!" I snap.

Gloria is visibly defeated.

"I don't have to explain myself to you, Julay. Not to you or anybody else for that matter." Her voice is shaking and her eyes are cast down. With that, she picks up her bag and coat, and rushes out of the room.

Julay has the look of knowing she has crossed a line. Her stance is high and mighty, but her eyes are unsure.

"Unbelievable!" I spit at her as I leave in pursuit of Gloria.

How can Julay be so vicious? Yes, Gloria is still married technically, but her story is not one of adultery. There are other factors at play here. It also seems to me that Julay's intended target tonight was Catherine, but Gloria ended up as the scapegoat in the firing line.

I run out to the car park just in time to see Gloria's car lurch away.

"Gloria!" I yell to no avail.

As I turn to go back inside I come face to face with Joshua who is rushing out of the building.

"Hi!" I say.

"Hi, Amy. You OK? I'm waiting for a price on that pump...I'll let you know," he says, heading quickly to his van. "Sorry, gotta dash, catch ya later!" he says over his shoulder.

I stand alone in the car park, feeling deeply troubled.

This evening started off so promisingly and now I'm deflated. Joshua couldn't get away from me quickly enough, and I'm sure that poor Gloria will be hurting from Julay's attack.

I like to believe that most things in life can be settled in gentle conversation over a cup of tea. Confrontation is an unnecessary distress. There are usually more important things to worry about, and, as a splotch of rain falls on my head, I acknowledge that me getting home tonight is one of them.

Chapter 19

I traipse back into the changing room. Lucia seems to be conducting a monologue; relaying details about her burgeoning relationship with the deaf fellow, James.

"It's fascinating you know," she says, regardless of anyone listening. "Sign language is amazing! When he's with me, he uses his voice which I'm starting to get, but when he's with his mates he just signs and I don't understand a flipping word! Or should that be a flipping 'sign'? Anyways, he's rather lovely, and I think we've got it sorted – forget talking or signing...we've got the language of lurve!" she cackles.

Julay passes me on her way out and fixes me with a stare. I ignore her. I don't want to be her opponent in Round Two. I just want to get home.

"Did you catch up with her?" Marion asks me.

"No, she's gone, and I have no lift home. Does anyone pass by Beacon Lane or know of a local taxi company?"

"Dearie, I can take you," Marion kindly offers.

"Oh that would be lovely, thank you. Is it terribly out of your way?"

"No it's fine. Come on."

We walk outside and climb into Marion's old Smart car. It's battered and in need of some tender loving care, and I wonder if the same could be said of Marion.

"Thank you so much, Marion, I really appreciate this."

I look across at her. She is hunched over the wheel and she reminds me of a tiny, delicate crab. She cuts a sorrowful figure, her bones are visible and her skin hangs loose. Her hair is dry from too many permanent waves and too much dye. She has yellowy frizzed curls with an orangey hue. I would love to get my hands on it.

"It's not far out of my way and I'd like to help," she smiles across at me, displaying badly fitting false teeth. There is something endearingly amiable about Marion.

"I do hope Gloria will be OK." I worry aloud.

"I don't really understand what the fuss is all about, to be honest. I knew about Gloria's husband and I think the sweet lady has a right to have a new friend if she wants one."

"I agree. It's not really anything to do with anybody else anyway, is it?"

"Julay needs to calm down a bit. She shouldn't take it so seriously. We're a bunch of folk, performing a bit of a jig. Where's the bother in that?" Marion smiles and twitches – both of which she tends to do quite often.

"I like your thinking, Marion – 'a bit of a jig,' ha, I like that!"

A phone rings and I take mine out of my bag, hoping it's Gloria, but it's not mine that's ringing.

"Is that your phone, Marion?"

"Probably," she says. Her face has dropped and she keeps her eyes deliberately forward.

"Do you want me to get it?" I offer.

"I know who it is, Dear, it'll be Jack just checking that I'm OK. I usually get in at this time," she says, glancing at the clock face on the dashboard. "He'll just be worried about me."

"Does he worry about you a lot?"

"He likes to know where I am."

It's evident that Marion doesn't want to talk about this and I certainly don't want to pry.

"Men, eh!" I say, attempting to lighten the mood.

"Can't live with them, not allowed to kill them," she says.

We laugh, but I can't help feeling there's an element of sincerity in Marion's words.

We travel the next ten minutes listening to Classic FM and chatting generally about ballet. Our conversation is punctuated by the ringing of Marion's phone. She resolutely ignores it.

We pull up outside my cottage and my phone bleeps a text.

"It's Gloria," I say. "Ah, she's OK and she's just saying sorry for running off without me."

"I'm glad she's OK," Marion replies.

Her phone rings again. She rolls her eyes and taking a deep breath, she reaches behind the chair into her bag and pulls out her phone.

"Hi Jack……..yes Dear………I'm heading home……….I'm just dropping off a………OK, Dear, see you soon."

From what I can hear, he sounds tetchy, verging on angry. Her final words linger in the air as he's obviously hung up. Marion's cheeks tinge pink with embarrassment.

"Marion, is everything OK?" I softly ask.

She gives a deep sigh.

"I've looked after him too well. He's a big baby and he relies on me too much. He doesn't cope well when I'm not there."

"Do you tend to go out a lot?"

"Only this ballet class. But now we have the extra night, he's getting antsy."

"Doesn't he have any of his own interests?"

"I am his interest," she rubs her arms as if she's cold and appears even smaller.

I want to say so much, but I can't. Equally I don't want to detain her any further and risk her incurring the wrath of Jack.

"Right, I'd better get inside. I have a Cocker Spaniel that gets antsy too!"

Marion giggles and twitches.

"Go on, Dearie, off you go. See you Friday evening, then."

"Thanks ever so much for the lift. You know Marion, if you ever need me, you know exactly where I am now," I say, nodding towards my cottage.

"Thank you, Amy," she says, giving me a look of understanding.

I squeeze her hand, jump out of the car and wave goodbye.

Once inside, I quickly phone Gloria. When she picks up, her voice sounds strained.

"Oh Gloria, are you OK?"

"She's right, you know," she holds back tears. "I am being unfaithful to Stanley."

"Gloria, it's not black and white like that, and you know it. Julay was being mean and spiteful. She was just miffed that young Catherine is the better dancer, and she took it out on you. It's unforgiveable. You mustn't let her get to you," I try to persuade.

"It's given me a lot to think about, Amy. I'm not sure this dalliance with Brian is wise." Her voice quivers. "I'm not one to be influenced by others' opinions...but I'm just not sure anymore. You have to be able to sleep at night don't you?"

I can't argue with that. But I also believe that people should embrace their opportunities for happiness. Following a short contemplative silence, Gloria exhales wearily.

"Darling Amy, thank you for phoning me, but I'm going to have a cup of tea, a headache pill and go to bed."

"OK Gloria. I'll speak to you tomorrow, OK? You take care."

"I will, my dear, thank you, goodnight."

As I reluctantly hang up, a text comes through from Steve. Urgh, what does he want?

Hi Ames,

He clearly wasn't listening to me, was he?

..any luck with the estate agents? S.

Yes I have had luck. The agreed three have been round and I'm waiting for their quotes and their rates of commission to come through. I could easily text that to him, but I don't.

"C'mon Bas," I say. "Let's call it a night. I've just about had enough of some people for today."

Chapter 20

I get into work early the next morning, as I really want to give the place a good clean before we open. It's actually Karen, the apprentice's, job but let's just say that she's not as conscientious as she could be. And anyway, oddly enough, I quite enjoy cleaning. Eventually, with fifteen minutes to spare before we open, I make a pot of coffee and sit down in the staff room. The moment I have my coffee mug in my hand, I hear Gina coming in.

"Mornin' Babe," she says, heading straight for the freshly brewed coffee.

"Morning G. How you doing?"

"Not bad, not bad. How 'bout you? You still likin' all that prancing abou' in a tutu?" she teases.

"Ha ha – very funny! I really like it. Certainly takes my mind off Steve and all that. We've started to learn a dance for the Dixbury Does Talent competition. I'm going to be on the stage, Dahling!" I theatrically joke. "Will you come and watch?"

"If it don't clash wiv me darts night!"

"How's that going?" Gina is a keen 'pub and darts' type. She's been known to win little statuette trophies.

Uncharacteristically, she goes quiet.

"Fine," is all she answers. Usually, Gina can't stop talking about the minutiae of her life. I have learnt things about this woman that I really haven't needed to know. But at this moment, it appears that she is struck dumb. Gina can never hide what is going on in her head. Something is troubling her.

"G, what's going on?" I follow my hunch.

"Whaddya mean?"

She fidgets and flushes.

"Gina, there's something you're not telling me, isn't there?"

She sighs, seating herself carefully in the chair opposite me.

"Now don't be upset..."

Apprehension starts to rise.

"I wanted to tell ya, honest I did," she nervously rushes on.

"So tell me now."

I sound controlled, but my heart is beating so wildly that I wonder if it's visible.

"I know Justine from the darts, right, and I knew she woz seeing someone but honest, Amy, I didn't know it woz your fella. Honest!"

At that moment, I wonder whether she's my friend and confidante, or someone who has betrayed me by her silence. Her eyes exude honesty but I'm struggling to think clearly.

"So you've seen them together?" I ask.

"Yeah, I saw 'em last week at The Dog and Trumpet." She looks down.

"I wozn't s'pposed to tell ya this an' all – but I fink you should know," she swallows hard and looks up at me. "She's up the duff."

I can feel a rush of pressure in my ears and my focus fuzzes.

"Amy?" I vaguely hear Gina's voice.

I wonder if I'm going to black out and consider that it would be a welcome escape, albeit temporarily, from this grim moment. My mouth has run dry, yet beads of sweat form all over my body, and my mind is ready to explode under the weight of it all.

"She's pregnant?" is all I can say. I'm bewildered.

"I'm so sorry." She moves to sit beside me and puts an arm around my shoulders. "Like I said, I fought you 'ad a right to know. Ain't right them sneakin' abou' and you in the dark. I told Steve as much when I saw 'im. Said that he'd tell ya in 'is own time. I 'ope I've done the right fing 'ere."

"Yes, you have." My voice squeaks.

On the day Steve left, I thought that what I'd experienced was shock, but that wasn't a patch on what I'm feeling now.

She's pregnant!

That was my dream - that was our dream - what we had talked about! We had always planned to start a family. In the early days, we had dreamed of two children; a boy and a girl, in that order. We discussed names. He liked 'Matthew' and 'James' whereas I liked something more Victorian such as 'Edgar' or 'Albert'. For a girl, we both agreed on 'Libby'. We laughed about how I would become plumper. We discussed how I would keep Hip Snips but temporarily promote Gina to oversee the day-to-day business. We even discussed the right age gap between our pre-conceived children.

Frantically, my mind switches to Steve and Justine's relationship. Wasn't she supposed to be his transitional person? A prop to get him out of a marriage that he wasn't happy in? Maybe my thinking has been all wrong. Maybe they had wanted a baby. Oh no, were they trying for a baby? Was all this planned? No wonder he shot me down in flames when I brought up the topic of making a baby recently. He had already started that process, with someone else.

Strangely, no tears have fallen but I feel broken.

I can't work today.

I ask Gina to either take over my clients or contact them to let them know I'm unwell. She agrees and so she should. I am niggled that she kept a silence. I have the overwhelming feeling that I am, yet again, the last person to know and this leaves me feeling incredibly hurt and foolish.

Dazed and saddened beyond belief, I leave the shop and return home. Once there, I bolt the door and close the curtains. I plonk down on my familiar sofa and cocoon myself in my favourite pastel fluffy blanket.

And then I weep.

Awaking, I find the room in darkness. I shiver underneath the blanket and instinctively know that I've been asleep for quite a few hours. I get up from the sofa and switch a light on. The wall clock says it's nine thirty. Basil is fussing at my feet. Poor Basil, he's missed his walk and his dinner. I let him out into the garden, and head to the kitchen to prepare his food. I catch sight of myself in the mirror and see exactly what I would expect. Crying myself to sleep has left me with streaked eye make-up, patterned cushion marks on my cheek and my hair in a tangled knot.

Studying my reflection I utter wryly. 'Bet he'd take you back in an instant if he could see you now, you gorgeous thing!'

I pull a strand of kinked hair away from my face and watch as my eyes fill with tears once again.

I am desperately unhinged, but I'm also experiencing the first flutters of closure. If he is to be a father then there really is no going back. If he could do all of this without talking to me, then we really have no place to be together. It truly is over. I cross the room to my handbag and retrieve my phone.

The estate agents valued house at 161k, 165k and 170k. Best deal is 165k at 1.5% commission. Will put it on market. Would appreciate you picking up rest of your things asap. You can pick up when I'm working. Heard your news – nothing more to say.

I hit send before even checking it. Even though he physically left a few weeks ago, it is only now that I feel he has finally gone.

Chapter 21

Thursday morning and Dalton's Garage is open for business bright and early. Sam pulls on her drab grey overalls, and begins setting up the till for the day. Her mind is preoccupied with the previous evening's spat in the changing room. They are, in the main, such a friendly group that Julay's aggression is disappointingly out of place. The 'Dixbury Dollies', as she affectionately calls them, shouldn't be concerned with who the better dancer is. She knows only too well that, had she entered into professional dance training, then being 'the best' would have been paramount, but the Dollies are far from professional. Their dancing is supposed to be fun! She hopes that in-fighting won't trigger the group's demise.

The petrol pump button beeps. Sam resets it and continues setting up the counter. She is refilling the air freshener stand when the doorbell signals an incoming customer. Sam looks up smiling and immediately does a double take. His is a familiar face - only this man has additional wrinkles and a smattering of grey hair. His skin is now leathery tanned but his tired green eyes are unmistakable. She knows that he is the person in the framed photograph that she keeps at home in a drawer. She is face to face with her estranged father, and he looks as alarmed as she feels.

"Hello Samantha!" he says.

She is surprised that upon hearing his recognisable Derbyshire lilt her stomach flips.

"Hello," she gulps.

"Didn't know you worked here. Your mum said you had a job in a garage, but I didn't know it was this one." His nerves shake through his voice. "How are you?"

"I'm alright," she answers. "You saw Mum, then?" She already knows the answer but small talk keeps emotions at bay.

"Yes I did, it's really good to see her again."

Sam had seen her mother since that day but had chickened out of asking how their meeting had gone. The thought of it makes her feel uncomfortably queasy. Someone else embarking on a close relationship with her mother brings about pangs of jealousy. For most of her life, it has been just the two of them; is her father going to come between them and change the family dynamic? It perturbs her that she could be usurped as *the one* whom her mother relies on. She has a bond with her mother that she wants to keep, literally, until death do they part.

Another customer enters the shop.

"I see," she says dismissively. She looks at the other customer and then turns back to her father. "Sorry," she says curtly. "But can I take your payment now, please?"

He takes a card from his wallet and hands it to her. Their hands brush but Sam defiantly ignores it. As she processes his payment, she is guarded. She keeps her focus down. As she passes him the receipt, he hands her his business card.

"When you're ready, give me a call." Nerves control the sides of his mouth that make his smile twitchy and awkward.

She takes the card and, flicking it with her fingers, she eyes him sullenly.

"*If* I'm ever ready, OK."

Visibly hurt, he nods, and turns to leave.

She watches him climb into his car and looks at the card. She'd like to be that person who rips it up and throws it resolutely into the bin. But she's not that person; she is Sam, good, quiet, easy-going Sam. She tucks it into her trouser pocket and serves the waiting customer.

Later that day, as if her mother subconsciously knows of the chance meeting, Sam receives a text from her.

Hi Sam, Making your favourite tonight – fancy joining me? Lol mum x

Depends what you think my favourite is!

Shepherds pie of course! ☺

It's their joke. When Sam was little, her mother could never remember if her daughter liked shepherds pie. She would make it every few months and be surprised when Sam expressed her dislike by pushing the meat and potato dish around the plate. Her mother's mental block became their long running family joke.

Sure, Mum. I'll be round when I finish xxxx

***

She arrives to find her mother in a cheery mood.

"Sammie, lovely to see you." Her mother kisses her firmly on the cheek and hugs her tightly.

"Hi, Mum, good to see you too."

"I'm making fish and chips, just like I used to," her mother chirps as she heads to the kitchen.

Sam considers that she hasn't seen her this upbeat for months.

"You're looking well, Mum," she smiles.

"I'm feeling great!" her mother enthuses.

"Doctor put you on some wacky pills?"

"Ha ha ha, no, Love! I'm just feeling well!"

Sam wonders whether the reappearance of her father has anything to do with this resurgence of energy. Upon closer inspection, her mother's clothes are neatly pressed and she's even wearing make-up – is this all in his honour? Despite her mother's shrunken body, she is looking quite gorgeous. The paradox of this dying woman standing before her looking vibrantly alive is not lost on Sam.

Tucking into a delicious supper of crispy coated fish and plump chips, they chat amiably. "Mum – that was delicious, thank-you. I feel absolutely stuffed!" Sam groans, putting down her knife and fork.

"Good, glad you enjoyed it." Her mother smooths her skirt, beaming with pride.

Sam looks at her mother across the table and takes a deep breath.

"Mum, I saw Dad," she says cautiously.

Her mother is surprised, caught off guard.

"Really, Love? Where did you see him? How did that happen?"

"He came into the garage this morning for petrol. I think we were both as surprised as each other. What was he doing around this neck of the woods again?"

Her mother shifts uncomfortably in her seat. She coughs, clearing her throat.

"Well you know we met the day you were here, remember? Well, I tell you, Sammie, we talked and talked, and he ended up popping back the next day. We've sorted out a few things and we're getting along very nicely." Her mother's eyes are shining. "It was supposed to be about *you*. I wanted to contact him for *you* to reunite with him for when...well, you know." We exchange a sad knowing look. "I certainly wasn't expecting to reunite with him! He wants to be here for me and it seems silly him travelling back and forth to Derby, so he's staying here for a while." Her smile is Cheshire cat broad.

"Mum! Seriously? Really?"

People are shocked when their parents announce their intended separation, but Sam feels exasperated at the idea of hers reuniting. The thought also creeps into her mind of whether there's a soul alive who likes to think of their parents 'having relations.' It makes her feel slightly bilious.

Her mother continues.

"Times change, Sammie, and I always loved him. We had our problems back in the day, of course we did, but there are still feelings there...on both sides," she adds quickly. "He's really changed – he's more open. I mean we're actually talking - the last time we did that was in the last century! I feel like we've been given this chance to end our story so to speak. Can you be happy for us? Well, for me?" she implores.

Sam's fears are confirmed. Her father is galloping in on his white steed and Sam is being put out in the cold, surplus to requirements. It's a childish reaction, but this is how she feels. However, saying that, there is something about seeing her mother looking happier than she has in months that influences Sam's response.

"Of course I'm happy for you, Mum. It's going to take some getting used to – but if you're happy, I'm happy. You deserve it."

"Thank-you, Sammie, that means so much to me. He has to go back to Derby next week for some work things, but he's planning to be back here for a few days the following week. Will you have dinner with us?"

"Can I meet him on my own first, please, Mum, if you don't mind?"

"Certainly, darling." Her mother looks completely contented, like her chickens have come home to roost. "Oh, do you know how to get hold of him?"

"Yes, Mum, I do."

Surreptitiously Sam touches her trouser pocket. Guess she will be needing that business card after all.

Chapter 22

He wasn't even technically running late the other night. He was only meeting his friend in the pub. So why did he race away from Amy like some silly teenage boy?

'What a coward you are, Joshua Antony Milne,' he thinks to himself.

But what is he so scared of? She can't cast a spell on him to rob him of his future plans to set up a new life on the other side of the world. Or can she? Her whole manner is charming. He could quite happily while away time watching her animatedly speak with her funny little hand movements. He could lose himself in her sumptuous green eyes. Even last Sunday morning, when she was hung-over and, quite frankly, dog rough, he had found her irresistible. It troubles him that she has the power to overwhelmingly disarm him. He still has to return to her home, as promised, to fit the shower pump. He decides to do that as quickly as possible so he can then untangle himself from her life.

Then, the thought that he constantly tries to suppress pops into his mind. What if they are meant to be together? How do you know when you have met the right person? He reflects that Sophia had presented as the perfectly 'right' person. They had shared a love of long walks, sailing, old films and Italian meals. Their love was passionate and all-consuming. They adored each other. He would have staked his life that, one day, they would be drawing their pensions together. He could not have been further from the truth.

Their relationship had been thriving until Sophia was promoted to Telefutures' Events Manager for the South of England. Her new role meant that she was required to travel extensively. They had discussed the opportunity and both agreed that she should take it: confident that theirs was a love that could withstand distance. It quickly transpired that she was away more often than home. Joshua was the patient, understanding boyfriend, but over time, it prickled that she seemed to be wholeheartedly enjoying her nights away. The phone calls from hotels became brief and increasingly infrequent. Sometimes there would be a drunkenly slurred late night call, but these also became few and far between. Eventually they sat down and had 'the talk.' There was a certain sales rep in the company that Sophia had 'tried to resist' but, as things turned out, ultimately failed to. A few harsh words, the divvying up of possessions and Joshua was a single, albeit broken, man once more.

Joshua shudders at the thought of how damaged he'd felt. He believed that he would never trust another woman and vowed he would never get involved again past a certain point. Fun dating is one thing but letting someone have access to his heart was a no-go area. And anyway, if he became involved with Amy, she has her own marriage baggage. Is it wise to get involved with a recently separated woman, no matter how beguiling she is? He could end up as her transitional man, ultimately discarded and broken again. And to rub salt into his wounds, he would still be residing and working in Dixbury.

No. The plan of new beginnings stays determinedly in place. In fact, he feels that his temptation for Amy is edging him towards fixing a date for his big adventure. His tenancy agreement for the apartment in Wellington came through two weeks ago. So what is he waiting for? He is going to Google flight prices to New Zealand and begin the planning process. He will leave before he can miss her.

Tomorrow evening, he is opening and closing the village hall for the additional Friday ballet class. He will stay true to his word and agree a time with Amy to fix her shower. After that, on ballet class evenings, he will endeavour to make himself scarce.

Maybe if they had met at a different time, he wouldn't need to be running away, but they did and he does. He laughs to himself, realising he's behaving like some resistant hypnotist's subject.

'I must not look into her eyes, I must not look into her eyes.'

Those beautiful clear shining eyes.

OK. Before he leaves, maybe he will allow himself to glance into them just once or twice...

Chapter 23

Late Thursday evening, I text Gloria, asking how she is and whether she's going to the Friday evening class. I hear nothing back. I try not to worry. Maybe she is sorting things out with Brian. I do hope that she decides to take some breathing space rather then end the relationship altogether. Julay's cruel attack has sparked Gloria's conscience. I understand that, but I hope Gloria doesn't do anything rash. Any fool can see that Brian and Gloria have genuine feelings for one another. And at this moment, I, more than anyone, understand the importance of treasuring love.

By Friday morning, I still haven't heard from Gloria. Putting my worries to one side, I realise that if she isn't going tonight, then I have no way of getting there and back. It's only a walk away, but not in the pitch black of night. Mmmm, I could leave Basil extra food and go straight to ballet from work and then, maybe I could ask Marion to give me a lift home. It sounds like a workable plan. I pack my ballet clothes into my rucksack, explain what I'm doing to Basil – not totally confident that he's grasped it - and head off to the salon.

***

At the end of the working day, I jump off the bus near the village hall and realise that I don't have that long to wait until class. I can easily fill the time by snacking on fruit and nuts, and then by warming up. I wander in hoping that Joshua might be around. Unfortunately, the hall is empty and there's no sign of him. I'm a little deflated; it would have been a perfect opportunity to chat with him. 'Don't be daft, Amy,' I chide, 'there's nothing between us and I really need to keep my overactive imagination under control.'

Sam and Lucia are the first to arrive, followed by Julay, who I'm not going to ignore. I'm thirty-two, not twelve.

"Hello," I say flatly.

"Hello, Amy." She looks twitchy as she approaches me. "Is Gloria coming tonight?"

"No, she's not. In fact I haven't heard from her."

"Oh." She looks crestfallen. She's on the verge of saying something, but doesn't. Instead she walks away. Is she sorry? I hope so.

We're all gathered in the hall. Gloria and Marion are absent, and without them, it feels like an incredibly small gathering. Helena' s face registers slight disappointment.

"OK, People, we'll start with Prayers and Pains, and then do a fairly swift barre, and then on to the dance. Anyone know if Marion and Gloria are coming?"

Murmurs of 'don't know' resound, and I notice Julay look away. It is of some comfort that she appears to have a conscience.

When we break into our separate groups, Catherine, Brian and Julay are left to practise their parts. Helena walks over to teach us our steps. True to her word, she gives us choreography that we can do and, if done in unison, should be impressively graceful.

We are practising individually to master the moves when Brian approaches me.

"Have you heard from Gloria at all?" he asks in a low tone.

"No, Brian, I was hoping you might have?"

"I know what happened in here the other evening, but she hasn't answered her phone to me since." His brow is furrowed and my heart goes out to him.

116

"Don't worry, Brian, I'm sure she's just taking some time. I'll let you know if I hear from her, OK?" I squeeze his arm.

He doesn't look any happier, but nods gratefully and goes back to working with Julay and Catherine.

I resume dancing and lose myself in effort and concentration. I am completely absorbed and with quick glances in the mirror I see myself, at times, looking like a *real* dancer. A thrill of accomplishment runs through me.

Afterwards, I quickly change and skip out of the hall, literally bumping straight into Joshua.

"Oh hold up there, Missy, mind where you're going!" he teases.

"Oh, sorry!" I try to pull some hairs away from my face but they seem to be stuck to the sweat. Definitely not my best look. "Didn't see you there!"

"Clearly," he grins. "I wanted to catch you anyway, is Sunday morning OK to fit that pump? It's ninety-two pounds."

"Oh yes, that'll be fine. Thank you so much, I really do appreciate you helping me."

"Try not to drink too much on Saturday night, OK?" he jibes.

"Ha ha, very funny! No, I'm having a night in with Basil. Oh shoot!"

"What's up?"

"Aaargh, Marion's not here!"

"Not making a lot sense here."

"Sorry, sorry, Gloria usually gives me a lift here and back, and she's not here, so I got the bus and was going to ask Marion for a lift home, but..."

"Marion's not here," we both say together.

"Oh dear, Amy Ballerina, hope you've got a torch?" he smiles wickedly.

"I'm going to try and catch the others in the changing room, and beg one of them for a lift. Better go! Thanks again and I'll see you Sunday," I say, turning away.

"Whoa whoa, hold up, I'll drop you off," he offers.

"Really? I don't want to put you out."

"No trouble, no trouble at all."

We walk into the car park and I'm expecting to see his white van, but he leads me to a beaten up old Skoda. He opens the passenger door.

"Please take a seat in Sheila."

"Sheila? Great name for a car!" I smile.

"Sheila Skoda. She's a fine motor. Bits keep falling off of her but she keeps going. My kinda gal!"

I laugh. He is such easy company.

"How are things?" he asks, as we drive through the dark lanes.

"Not bad. Found out my miserable excuse for an ex has managed to get his bit-of-stuff-barmaid pregnant."

"Ouch, that must hurt. Was it on the cards that you and him would have children?"

"Yup. But I suppose I could look at this as dodging a bullet; I mean if we had had children and then he'd decided his feet should be under her table, then I'd be in a worse situation now, wouldn't I? I'd be having to deal with abandoned children, plus the stress of being a single parent."

"Yes, you can look at it that way. Very philosophical, Amy." There's a gentle playfulness in his voice. "So are you going to divorce?"

"Eurgh, that's a big question. I'm certainly getting nearer to that decision. Her being pregnant has made the end of our marriage more definite. For the first few weeks, I just wished him back. I'm not feeling that so much now. I know it's not going to happen."

I suddenly become conscious that I'm doing all the talking, and it's all about my pitiful love life.

"Enough about me, what about you? Are you married?"

"No, no, I went through a painful break-up myself a while ago."

"Oh, I'm sorry. No going back for you either, eh?"

"No, that is not going to happen," he says resolutely.

Pulling up outside Rose Cottage, he wrenches the handbrake on. Leaving the engine running, he turns in his seat to face me.

"My future is about travel!" he announces.

My heart descends to my boots.

"Really, where you off to?" I aim for a light tone.

"Well, I was born in New Zealand. My parents brought me here when I was a baby. So, I have a right to live there and that's what I'm gonna do! Well, I'm gonna give it a go. See if I like it. I'm due to take up a post at Victoria University, lecturing in plumbing, but that's not for a couple of months, so I thought I'd get out there and have some chill and relax time."

The wind has truly been taken out of my sails. I know I have no right or reason to be disappointed, but I am.

"That sounds like a marvellous plan, Joshua. I bet it's beautiful out there," I force sincerity.

"It's a new beginning," he replies, keeping his focus forward.

There is silence. He slowly turns to look at me. Regardless of logic, there is undeniable chemistry between us, and my nerve endings are buzzing alive. He leans in. I'm panicked, as I don't know what to do or what to expect. My heart is thudding through my shirt. He gently kisses me on the cheek.

"Goodnight, Amy Ballerina, see you on Sunday."

Trying to regain some calm, I thank him for the lift and bid him goodnight.

As I leave his car, I am grateful that my quivering legs manage to successfully transport me to my door. It's only once inside that I can breathe normally again.

Chapter 24

Saturday morning brings a buzz of customers into the salon. We work non-stop. The general atmosphere is babbling liveliness with clients lined up on the seats by reception, chattering while they wait. We have one client waiting for her colour to take, whilst another is being styled, whilst another is being shampooed in preparation for a cut. It's a carousel of hairdressing.

I pride myself on my staff as they show an interest in the clientele, and are happy, in turn, to share stories of their own lives with them. I am cutting a young girl's hair, and next to me Gina is blow-drying Mrs. Fitzherbert. Above the racket of blow driers and general hubbub, I catch snippets of their conversation. Gina is relaying the details of her latest darts match. She mentions Justine's name and it's like a knife stabbing my gut. I know that I will have to get used to this, but am irked by her insensitivity. It is only weeks since Steve left. My wounds are still fresh.

Not all of our clients are sweetness and light and just before lunch, Gina is preparing to shampoo the inimitable Pamela Cox. Pamela is a scratchy type who suffers persistent back pain that manifests itself in perpetual bad temper. Gina being Gina is enjoying light-hearted banter with another customer when she absent-mindedly directs the hot water nozzle over Pamela's hair.

"Aaaargh!" Pamela shoots up from the basin. "What do you think you're doing?" she shrieks.

"Oh blimey, sorry, Pam!"

"Sorry? Sorry?" Pamela is apoplectic. "You've scalded my head, young lady!"

"Lemme 'ave a look."

"Keep away from me, you've done enough damage." Pamela's eyes are scathing and wild. "Amy! Amy!" she screeches, summoning me.

I immediately switch into damage limitation mode and pamper her, checking her scalp and reassuring her that everything is fine. Gina sulkily stands behind the basin, chewing gum.

"Let me wash your hair, Pamela," I soothe her. "Gina, go and take over Mrs. Lambert's blow dry," I hiss.

Gina pulls a sarcastic face and flounces up the shop like a reprimanded teenager.

Later, way past lunchtime, Gina, Karen and I are seated in the small staff room, gobbling down sandwiches before the next onslaught of customers arrive.

"Wot abou' that ol' cow, Pam, today, anyone would fink I did it on purpose! I mean, I said sorry." Gina justifies her actions.

"You didn't sound very sorry though," I bite.

"I ain't lickin' 'er boots!"

"I don't want you to, but equally I don't want to be sued!"

"Nah that won't 'appen, she's all mouf and no trousers 'er!" she smirks.

"Gina!" I snap. "It isn't you who would be sued, it would be me! It's my business! You weren't watching what you were doing and you put scalding water on her head!"

"Blimey, calm down!"

"No! I won't, you messed up!"

"And I've messed up before and you ain't bollocked me like this! You sure this is abou' Pam? Cos you've 'ad the right 'ump wiv me lately. Isn't this really abou' your fella and Justine? I fink you're still pissed off wiv me abou' that!" Her eyes are challenging, "OK, I 'old me 'ands up, I kept it from ya, but I did tell ya though didn't I? I did the right fing in the end!"

Karen, open-mouthed, is watching our exchanges like the finals match at Wimbledon.

Gina is right. I am rankled by her association with Steve and Justine. I want to ask her if they have a sense of permanence; whether they irritate others with their private jokes and furtive glances...whether they are in love? But it would be unfair to, as she shares an allegiance with them as well as with me. Unfortunately though, the rather large elephant in the room now taints the open and honest relationship Gina and I used to share.

I sigh. For all her faults, I love her. She's brash and uncompromising, and she did make an error of judgment by keeping their news from me, but is it worth potentially losing a friend and valuable colleague over?

The telephone rings and I jump up, grateful to escape for now.

Gina and I work the afternoon with, mostly, a cold silence between us. We speak only out of necessity. I don't care for the discomfiture of it. I am not one for holding grudges, and so I decide to resolve our troubles. I wait for the shop to quieten before I ask her to join me in the staff room. She huffs and follows me.

"Gina, I don't like falling out with you. I think you're right. I am hurt about you not telling me about Steve, but I hope we can get through this. I'm sorry that I went for you earlier, if nothing else, it was unprofessional."

"Nah, Amy, it's me - I'm the one wots sorry. I did feel really bad keepin' it from ya."

"If I'm honest, it's not just that. You see them both and that bugs me. In the past, you and I could talk about anything, but now I want to ask you things about them, and I can't. You're Justine's friend and that leaves you and me on a sticky wicket." I feel the old familiar tears forming.

"Blimey, is that wot this is abou'? Of course you can ask me! I'm your mate aren't I? I don't even 'ave that much to do wiv Justine. Babe, we ain't gonna fall out over this, come 'ere." She pulls me to her, wraps her arms around me and the scent of Vera Wang once again engulfs me to the point of choking. I think she's never going to let me go.

"I ain't sorry abou' that ol' bag though."

We pull apart laughing.

"Gina!" I mock admonish.

Karen enters as our cackling fills the small room. She raises her eyebrows, shakes her head and leaves us to our laughter.

Chapter 25

This time, I am up and waiting. I have wet wiped myself to an inch of my life, liberally applied deodorant and walked naked into a spritz of Coco Chanel. I carefully spend much time creating the illusion that I have taken a casual five minutes to get ready. I deliberate over grey or red hoodie; hair clipped back or loose; whether slippers are considered casual cosy or 'old biddy' dowdy. I do stop and question why I'm doing this for a man who has fixed plans for his future that clearly do not include me, but I plough on regardless.

Just after ten, Basil's barking alerts me to the doorbell.

"Good morning!" I say brightly, swinging open the door.

"Good morning, " he beams, carrying a toolbox and a cardboard box.

"Come in, come in."

"Hold on, there's one more thing." He places the boxes in the hall and races back to his van. He appears seconds later carrying a bag of croissants. "I thought we'd go posh," he says, handing them to me.

"Yum! Thanks! Coffee or tea?"

"Coffee, white, one sugar, please."

I get a glowing satisfied feeling about him being here, in my house. I know that he'll be out of my life soon enough, so why not embrace the moments and just enjoy the time that I have with him? This whole attraction is probably all in my head anyway.

I am in the kitchen, placing the croissants on a plate, when he appears at the door.

"Are we doing coffee and croissants first or would you like me to get on with the job?" he twinkles.

I have no words...

"Let's be civilized and dine first," I say, smiling.

We sit at my old dining table. Basil sits near Joshua's feet hoping for falling crumbs.

"Hello, buddy," he says, stroking Basil's long ears. "You're a handsome fella aren't you?"

"You like dogs?"

"Yep, grew up with them. My parents always kept a couple of retrievers. It's harder to have a dog when you're working and you live alone, don't you find?"

Yay – he lives alone.

"Yes, I'm lucky that Basil is quite content to stay at home. Some might call him lazy, but I think he's just happy in his all-day bed. Saying that though, he's always pleased to see me."

"Who wouldn't be?"

He quickly looks away. I don't think he meant to say that out loud. Was that a polite compliment, an off-the-cuff remark, or are there grounds to my romantic imaginings?

I clear my throat nervously. "So how long do you think it will take to fix the pump?"

Oh no, why did I say that? He's going to think that I want him to fix the shower and go, when the truth is that I want more time in his company.

"Oh I'll be out of your hair in an hour or so," he says, smiling.

He did take it that way...

We continue to chat amiably until he finishes the last of his croissant, picks up his coffee and heads to the bathroom.

I can't loiter in the bathroom engaging him in conversation whilst he works, might seem too clingy. So I opt for telling him that if he needs anything he can give me a shout. I wander back into the lounge and decide to put some music on. Thumbing through my CD collection, the internal debate strikes up again. Do I choose something modern that indicates, I am 'up with the times' (or undesirably 'down wiv da kidz')? A little known indie band to show I'm cool? A touch of classical to demonstrate my refined tastes? Some ironic Perry Como? Nineteen-nineties Madchester? The Beatles? Classic Sinatra? I have to say that this internal monologue is frying my brain! I opt for The Beatles. I hold a belief that if someone doesn't like any Beatles' music, then there must be something fundamentally wrong with them. It's a theory that generally holds true.

Just then, Basil starts barking again. I'm not expecting anyone and I don't particularly want anyone to interrupt my time alone with Joshua.

Hoping it's just a cold-caller or a religious zealot (it's not often I wish for either of those!), I open the door to find Gloria looking pale and dishevelled.

"Gloria, come in. Oh my, what's happened?"

Her normally smooth straight hair is uneven with frizzy waves. Her clothes, which are usually pristine, are crumpled. She has no make-up on and her eyes are red sore. We go into the lounge where she drops onto the sofa and fumbles for a tissue from her handbag.

"I hope you don't mind me just turning up like this?"

"Gloria, of course not! Tell me – what's happened?"

"I had a call from the home, Stanley's home. It was Friday evening. They said he had taken a turn for the worse and I should be there."

She takes a deep breath.

"By the time I arrived, he'd lost consciousness. He did open his eyes once. I doubt he knew I was there, but he half smiled at me. I sat with him through the night." She stares into the middle distance. "I held his hand as tightly as I could, hoping that somehow he could feel it...or at least sense it. They told me that his organs were starting to pack up. They were giving him oxygen, and keeping him comfortable, but really it was just a matter of waiting."

My heart goes out to her as a solitary tear rolls down her cheek.

She continues.

"I didn't really sleep; I just sat watching him. I thought of our life together and how happy we've been. I thought how lucky I was to have met him, to be blessed with all the days I've spent with him." She heaves a deep sigh.

"Anyway, by the morning, my neck and back were stiff from the recliner chair. The nurses suggested I get some air and stretch out a bit. They assured me that he didn't seem ready to go yet. They know these things don't they?"

"They do," I say softly.

"You know that cream I use on my muscles?" I nod. "I wanted that to ease my neck and back, plus I fancied a change of top. I estimated a half hour round trip home. I had driven for no more than ten minutes when they called me. I pulled over and they told me that two minutes after I had left he had drawn his last breath." Gloria erupts into a fountain of tears. I move to her side and put my arm around her.

"Oh, I'm so sorry, Gloria."

"I wasn't even there at the end! You see, that's me isn't it. Always thinking of myself! Why was it so bloody important to get the cream? Why did I need a change of top? He was dying for goodness sake!"

She is beside herself.

"But you'd spent the whole night awake. You weren't thinking straight," I say. "And anyway the nurses usually do have a feel for these things and they told you it would be a safe time to go." I want to ease her pain, alleviate her guilt.

"I should've stayed. What kind of a wife did I turn out to be, Amy? Out enjoying myself whilst Stanley was in the home, not being with him in his last moments? I can't bear myself." She is wretched.

"Gloria, please don't be so hard on yourself. You're grieving and that is enough for now. Don't hurt yourself more."

We are huddled together on the sofa. She is crying long shuddering sobs. I hold her. I am silent. At this moment, words are meaningless.

I look up to see Joshua's head around the door.

"Sorry to interrupt..."

Gloria jumps in surprise.

"Sorry, Gloria, Joshua is here fixing my shower," I say.

"I see," she says with embarrassment. She buries her head in her tissue, wiping her nose, trying to regain her dignity.

"It's all done, Amy. You stay where you are, I'll let myself out," he says.

"No, no, let me pay you." I rush to fetch my purse and he follows me to the kitchen.

"Is your friend OK?" he asks.

"Her husband has just died."

"Ah, sorry, give her my sympathies."

"Sure, thanks, I will."

I count the money in twenty and ten pound notes into his hand. I add an extra note.

"Please buy yourself a drink, and thank-you so much, Joshua, I really do appreciate your help."

"No problem, Amy." He smiles a lingering smile.

He picks up his toolbox. He is almost at the door when he slowly turns on his heels. Waving the last note thoughtfully, he says.

"Hey, how about you and me split this and I buy you a drink?"

"That would be lovely."

"How about Thursday? Say I pick you up around seven?"

"That would be lovely."

"Don't forget to shower!" he jests.

"Ha! I won't! And thanks for the croissants."

"Well, thank you for the coffee and for The Beatles – I love 'em!"

He winks as he turns to leave.

Chapter 26

I return to the lounge. Gloria is reclining on the sofa with her eyes closed. I have only been absent for a couple of minutes and she has drifted off. Looking at my beautiful friend, I consider how, at present, life is dealing her a harsh hand. I pull a throw from the armchair and place it over her. I creep to the CD player and switch off The Beatles. I suddenly appreciate that I have a working shower and take the opportunity to sneak away and cleanse myself in the way that wet wipes cannot.

Feeling utterly refreshed I change into my baggy Sunday clothes and put the kettle on. I pop my head around the lounge door to find Gloria just waking up.

"Hello there, sleepy-head," I say.

"Oh dear, Amy, I'm so sorry, I must have nodded off."

"No need for apologies. You're exhausted, Gloria. Anyone would be. Did you sleep at all last night?"

"No, I spent it with my sister, Roberta. She came over and we sat up most of the night. She's a dear. She was very fond of Stanley, so we just grieved quietly together. I came here this morning because you're the only person I have talked to about...Brian." She struggles to say his name. "I couldn't tell Bobbie about him. I'm not sure she would approve...or understand. I suddenly find myself shamed. I'm not proud of my connection with him." Her eyes are downcast.

"Oh, Gloria, you haven't done anything wrong!"

She eyes me doubtfully. "Haven't I? So why do I feel so guilt-ridden? It's ironic, isn't it, that whilst Stanley was alive, I thought little of it but now that he's gone, and I am free to do whatever I please, I'm weighted down with remorse."

"I suppose it's not simple, Gloria. I think you should talk to Brian when you're ready. He is a lovely man and a great companion for you. Don't throw the baby out with the bathwater. You have just lost your husband. Brian will understand and give you time to grieve, I'm sure of it," I reassure.

"I can't contemplate seeing him at the moment," she says sadly. "But talking of seeing things, I certainly wasn't expecting to see Prince Charming here on a Sunday morning!"

"Gloria!" I say, half glad that she is teasing me, even though it's not a conversation I really want to have. "Don't go getting any ideas! He came round to fix my shower, that's all."

"Mmm, a euphemism if ever I heard one."

It's lovely to see the sparkle in her eyes again.

"Gloria! You were the one who suggested I ask him. So I did, and he came today to fix it for me. End of story!"

"Me thinks my lady doth protest too much," she hams it up.

I have to laugh.

"Cup of tea?"

She smiles. "That would be much appreciated, My Dear."

***

Despite suggestions that Gloria should stay with me for a few nights, she insists that she wants to be in her own home. After a light lunch together, I walk her out to her car.

"Will you be alright?"

"Yes, or course, Darling, don't worry about me. I think I've cried sufficiently to exhaust me into sleep."

"You know where I am if you need me, OK? Just call me, anytime."

"You're very kind."

She kisses me and we warmly hug before she drives away.

I decide that the rest of the day calls for loafing on the sofa with Basil. First, I need another caffeine boost. It's been quite a day so far. I haven't allowed myself to think about Joshua's invitation. He really did ask me to go for a drink, didn't he? Is this as friends or is something more happening between us? He's heading off to the other side of the world. Why would he start something now? I choose not to dwell on it and instead plan to enjoy whatever time we have together. It's a man and a woman going out for a drink, it's hardly a betrothal of marriage!

Just as I'm snuggling down on the sofa, Basil signals that someone is at the door again. 'What is this? Piccadilly Circus?' I mumble as I traipse up the hall. Opening the door, I am astonished to find Steve standing there.

"Hi, Ames," he says.

"Steve, what can I do for you?" I am sharper in tone than I mean to be.

"That's not a great welcome!"

"What were you expecting?"

He sighs, lowering his defences. "How are you, Amy?"

"Just great, thanks." Sarcasm oozes through my words.

We reach an impasse as I stay square on the doorstep.

"Can I come in, please?"

"Why?"

"There are a couple of DVDs that I want to pick up, and I left my fishing rod."

"You want to go fishing?" I roll my eyes and sigh.

Reluctantly I step aside to let him through.

He goes through to the lounge and immediately starts making a big fuss of Basil. I stand to one side watching as Basil laps up the attention. Dogs! They are so forgiving, and even if they do bear a grudge, they can't remember it long enough to act upon it. In an ideal world, Basil would spurn Steve's attention and run to my feet in a mark of solidarity. In reality, Basil is rolling on his back and drooling, clearly in seventh heaven.

"Which DVDs did you want?" I ask, refocusing his attention.

"I don't know exactly," he says, looking up at me. "I thought I could have a nose through and pick some out, if that's OK with you?"

"Sure."

"Don't worry I won't be taking Mamma Mia," he quips.

I allow myself a small smile, he always hated that film with a passion and yet it didn't deter me from imposing it on him regularly.

A poignant silence fills the air.

"I am sorry, Ames," he says seriously. "That you found out through Gina. I was going to tell you, honestly."

"Well of course you were! You'd have had to at some point!" I retort.

"It wasn't planned, you know. But when she found out that she was pregnant, it just seemed right that I should go. I was going to tell you, but breaking up was hard enough without making things worse."

"I still think you should have told me everything all in one go. But you didn't, did you? You were cowardly. You didn't stay and talk at all, you just ran off! And you left me to find out from someone else. How do you think that made me feel?" My voice is cracking.

"I was trying to protect you..."

"Protect me, Steve? You weren't thinking of me! You were thinking of yourself!"

" ...I thought you needed time, so I delayed telling you. I know now that I was wrong."

He sighs deeply. He runs his fingers through his hair. He looks imploringly into my eyes,

"I am so sorry, Ames. I never meant to hurt you like this. I will always regret it."

This man shattered my life - he deceived and betrayed me. He has shown little kindness to me in recent weeks and appears to be nothing but a coward. There is no reason to believe his remorse, and yet I do. His sincerity is touching and it stirs old feelings within me. I am catching a glimpse of the man I married.

A sad stillness exists between us.

Basil is still on his back and he paws Steve's arm to remind him that he is supposed to be stroking him. We both chuckle quietly.

"Sorry to you too, Bas," Steve says, resuming the stroking.

"I had a call from the estate agents and a couple are coming over to view next week," I say gently.

"OK, that's good. Let me know how it goes."

I nod.

"Right, do you want to get your DVDs and fishing rod?" I say, prompting him. He looks surprised, as if he's forgotten his reason for being here.

"Sure, sure, then I'll be out of your way."

He spends five minutes rifling through the drawer of DVDs, picking out action films that I would never watch in a million years.

"I'm not sure where the fishing rod is, so I'll come back for it another time," he says.

I don't think he ever intended to pick it up. The fishing rod and the DVDs were merely false pretences to visit.

"Please take it now, Steve, I'm pretty sure it's out the back in the shed. I don't mean this unkindly, but I don't want to keep seeing you, it just hurts too much."

He nods and I'm moved to see tears in his eyes. He lowers his head and makes for the back door.

"I won't come back in, I'll go out round the side, OK?"

"OK, thank you."

"Bye, Ames."

The back door closes behind him.

"Bye, Steve."

Chapter 27

Sam is sitting in Expresso Coffee. She's pleased that Amy introduced her to the delights of their skinny cappuccino. Coffee helps with indecision. She is toying with her father's business card. It is plain and simple, in black and white. Does a business card say anything about the person? If it does, this says very little about her father. Is he straightforward? Are there no hidden depths to him? This isn't how she remembers him, but her memories are that of a ten-year-old girl. Through a child's eyes, he was guarded, detached with seemingly no urge to cuddle or make a fuss of her. She longed for him to play-wrestle as she'd seen her friends do with their fathers. Hers had solemnly sat hidden behind a broadsheet newspaper, not contributing much of worth to her upbringing.

Her parents had struggled to make ends meet so they had taken a job-share in a pub, splitting the evening shifts between them. Sam loved the nights alone with her mother but found the ones with her father difficult to navigate. One particular night, Sam had gone to bed with a glass of water. She had drunk it all but then awoke an hour later feeling thirsty. She summoned all her courage to call out for her father. (Once in bed she wasn't allowed to get up.) He entered her room and asked what she wanted.

"Can I have a glass of water please, Dad?"

In the darkness of her room, he could see that she had a glass next to her bed.

"You've got one there."

Calling him to her room had used up all her bravery and now there was simply none left.

"Oh yes, I have. Sorry."

He turned on his heels and Sam was left still needing a drink.

Why hadn't she told him? Why was he so difficult to communicate with? He wasn't an angry man, just an imposing one. Something made her want to please him but something also made her nervous to be around him.

She looks again at the business card. Things could be different now. She is no longer ten-years-old – she's twenty-three. She can be her own person with no need to bow to him. The fathering years are passed as far as she's concerned, but maybe he could be a supportive friend, if that were something he wanted too.

She dials his number and can feel her heartbeat quicken as she hears the ringing tone.

"Hello?"

"Hi, it's Samantha," she says, trying to quell her nerves.

"Samantha, hello, how are you?"

His voice is so familiar.

"I'm OK, thanks. Have you seen Mum?"

"I'm just leaving her house now. She's very keen for us all to get together, but she mentioned that you'd like to see me first?"

He doesn't beat around the bush.

"Yes, I just thought if we have a coffee and a chat, clear the air, and then we could all get together."

"I think that's a grand idea." He sounds genuinely pleased. "When can we meet? Sooner the better for me."

Gosh, when did he become so keen?

"Are you heading back to Derby now?"

"No, I'm staying at Mum's for a few nights again. I'm just popping to the supermarket to pick up some groceries."

"Oh, OK. Well, I'm in Expresso Café, if you want to meet for a quick coffee now?"

She can't believe she just said that! But maybe it's better to face him now than delay and run the risk of changing her mind.

"OK, I know that place. I'll come right over, see you in a bit."

She hangs up and, with nerves more jittery than ever, she catches the waitress' eye to order another cappuccino, this time with a double shot.

By the time her father arrives, Sam is buzzing. From a child's perspective, he was a large looming figure but in reality, he's barely five feet seven and of slight build. This man, nearly in his sixties, looks mild and unthreatening. His greying wispy hair is thinning and he's slightly hunched. He wears chinos and a brown sweatshirt with his trademark dirty white trainers. What happened to the man who intimidated Sam?

He pulls up a chair and sits in front of her.

"Would you like another drink?" he asks.

She drily notes how that question is about fifteen years too late.

"No, thank you, I'm fine."

Her father signals to the waitress who immediately comes over to take his order.

Their unexpected meeting, in the garage, had been fraught with nerves. She'd been totally unprepared, but now, face-to-face, she wonders what to say to a father whom she hasn't seen for thirteen years? The man who walked out of her life just as teenage years were beckoning and a father's input could have been much needed?

"Mum tells me you're dancing again," he says.

"Yes, I'm in an adult ballet class and the teacher wants us to enter a local competition. We're dancing a piece from The Nutcracker."

"Argh, you know me, never cared for all that ballet stuff, but if it makes you happy..." He checks himself. "You always were a lovely little dancer."

Sam is itching to retort that he wouldn't have known what kind of dancer she was, as he paid no interest, but that sort of talk will not mend bridges.

"So, thank-you for sending cards on my birthdays and at Christmas. I know Mum appreciated it too," she says, out of not knowing what to say.

"No trouble, Love. You know I would've come to see you, but things between me and your mother, they just weren't good." He barely looks Sam in the eye. "It was difficult times."

She feels that this is the perfect moment to be brave.

"But it wasn't just about Mum, it was about me too. Couldn't you have just come to see me?"

He shifts in his seat.

"Money was tight, I just couldn't afford the travel, and I would've had to stay somewhere. Money doesn't grow on trees y'know," he says, defensively. "And you know I've worked hard at my job. Did you see I'm regional rep for the company now?"

"I know," Sam concedes, feeling her courage sapping away.

"And then I had my bad back, laid up for a long time with that, y'know. Quacks didn't know what it was for ages. I'm lucky I wasn't paralysed, they told me. Took a long time to get back on my feet."

And so his monologue continues, excuse after excuse, justifying his absence for the past thirteen years. Eventually, the excuses dry up, and he then just drones on about himself. Samantha wishes he came with an 'off' button. She nods and makes noises in agreement but her mind has already wandered far.

She now understands that this is the relationship that never was and never will be. What kind of a person doesn't want to see their child? What kind of a person has a string of excuses that trip off the tongue for not seeing their child? It's not about affording travel and accommodation or about work or health, it's about priorities. If he had wanted to see her he would have, it's as simple as that. He has a job and that means he has money. If he has money he can put a little aside each week to accumulate enough for a trip, even if it was only once a year. And if he were bed-ridden, he could have maintained contact by phone. No, she will not accept his lame excuses.

With a heavy heart, she realises that they have not spent ten minutes together and she already knows exactly who this man is. But where does that leave her? How can any kind of relationship be built between them on such shaky foundations? It suddenly occurs to her that maybe this *is* all about her mother. It's her mother's happiness that has to be paramount and if re-engaging with her father induces that, then Sam will go along with it purely for her sake. When the tragic inevitable happens, and her mother is no longer around, then Sam will be the one to cut the ties with her father once and for all.

With this in mind, Sam chooses light, safe topics and now, at points when she waits for her father to instigate conversation, nothing but awkward silence ensues. Increasingly, as Sam is talking, his eyes dart away in a fidgety manner and there are even moments when he positively glazes over. Deciding that she's suffered enough torture for one day, Sam throws in the towel and proffers her excuses to leave.

"Let's do that meal with Mum sometime," she says, fetching her purse from her bag.

"Yes, Love, that'd be nice." Her father starts patting his breast and trouser pockets. Sam cringes knowing what's coming next. She chooses to pre-empt the pathetic 'left my wallet somewhere' plea and magnanimously offers to settle the bill.

Once outside, they shelter awkwardly from the drizzling rain underneath the café's narrow striped canopy.

"Nice seeing you, Love," her father says.

"Yes. See you again."

He hops from one foot to another and opts for a friendly punch on the arm as a means of an affectionate goodbye.

Sam pulls up her collar and walks away wondering what exactly her mother sees or ever saw in him and, vowing that should she ever choose a life partner, then that person will be the polar opposite of her father.

Chapter 28

Joshua is sitting at his kitchen table looking out at the grey skies; it's a typically British sight. He's no fool to believe that it won't rain in New Zealand, but one temptation of going is the hope of a sunnier clime. He opens his laptop and goes immediately to the airline sites that he's bookmarked in anticipation of deciding a date. He runs his finger down the screen checking the different prices and dates. They all seem suddenly very expensive!

Oh I know what you're doing here, matey – you're looking for an excuse not to go, and you can stop that right now!

He wonders whether he should redefine his self-image as he used to think he made decisions and saw them through with unwavering determination. He used to have the confidence to trust his sensible inner voice, and not deviate from what it told him. But herein lies the problem. His inner voice is now having a two-way debate of its own. The head and heart are at war.

The last thing he had wanted was to be going out on a date with Amy. He had been resolute to fix her shower pump and be gone. Or at least he believed he was resolute. Alas, it seems that no matter how he preps or programmes himself before they meet, the moment he sets eyes on her, he goes completely off script.

"Hey, how about you and me split this and I buy you a drink?" he had said. Where had that come from? No matter which

way it's viewed, it's definitely not the same as *'now I've fixed your shower pump, I will never see you again!'*

He can't explain it. She's like an inevitable disease that he doesn't want, an addiction he's trying to dodge. He could easily blame her eyes, her cream complexion, her soft round hips, her infectious laugh, the way she talks, those funny hand movements, or a multitude of other qualities, but in truth, it's everything about her - it is just Amy.

He scans the Air New Zealand site and finds a discounted so-early-in-the-morning-that-not-even-the-larks-will-be-up flight and begins completing his details. Already, he is bargaining in his head that he will suffer eternal remorse if he doesn't at least go to New Zealand and try out his plan. And anyway, let's say he goes and doesn't like it, he can always return. Besides, it doesn't have to be forever. Maybe he could go for a few years? Or only a few months, if it doesn't live up to his expectations? Nothing has to be set in stone. The important thing is to stay focussed on the plan. The plan is New Zealand, not Amy.

He stares at the screen. He checks the details again.

Hitting the 'Buy' button, he leaves for Wellington in under a month.

Chapter 29

With the exception of Gloria, we are dressed and ready at the barre for Wednesday's class. Helena calls for 'Prayers and Pains'. It's in 'Pains' that I explain Gloria's absence to the group.

"Gloria has asked me to let you all know that her beloved Stanley passed away peacefully at the end of last week. I wonder if we could all chip in for some flowers for his funeral – it's being held next Friday."

Everyone murmurs in agreement.

"Poor Gloria," Marion says.

I look at Brian, and I can't read from his expression whether he already knew this or not. He stares blankly at the floor.

"Is she going to be coming back?" Lucia asks.

"I'm sure she plans to at some point, but not for the time being," I say.

"Right, thank you for that, Amy," Helena says. "I think we should indeed arrange some flowers and a card, and I also think we shouldn't bank on Gloria being in the performance. I don't want her to feel under pressure. If she comes back in the next couple of weeks, she can pick up the steps of the corps de ballet – that is you," she says pointing to the non-lead characters. "But we'll preclude her from a lead role for now."

Julay, by default, now has one of the lead roles, yet she looks on the verge of tears. Did she get what she wished for and now doesn't want it? For all her competitiveness, I'm sure she wouldn't have wished for the death of Gloria's husband.

The mood in the room is understandably low.

"Our thoughts are with Gloria," Helena continues. "But the best thing we can do is dance *with* our feelings. We take the sadness, the emotions from within and put them into our dancing. We dance for her!"

Helena motivates us once again and her sentiment is right. She has just said, in the kindest possible way that 'the show must go on'.

Even though we have only learnt half of the dance, Helena insists that we watch each other to get used to 'the feel of an audience'. We watch Julay and Catherine's opening piece, and what strikes me is the depth of emotion Julay conveys. Who would have thought that, behind all those airs and graces and general bluster, there would be such a wealth of feeling? In fact, I witness some of the most poignant dancing I have ever seen in all of my classmates. Even Josie and Catherine, who have only met Gloria briefly, are caught up in the melancholy mood of class. It's only me who is having an off night. I am a beat behind and then three steps ahead. I'm sure I must look like I am being remote-controlled by someone with a perverse sense of humour.

Recouping energy, leaning against the wall, sipping water, I watch Sam practising a pirouette. She is exquisitely precise, and she possesses the much sought after combination of core strength and perpetual grace. Her head whips around and around spotting a focal point in the corner of the room.

She suddenly stops and holds her neck.

"Oooh, you OK, Sam?" I ask.

"Argh, I've been having a lot of tension in my neck and shoulders, and just felt it go. Flippin' 'eck it hurts!" she says, rubbing her neck. Helena overhears and rushes over. She asks Sam to move her head in different directions, which highlights the limited movement on her right side.

"OK, you might want to put some heat on your neck when you get home, one of those lavender wheat bags are good. But for now, just take it easy."

"It's been like this, on and off, for quite a while. I used to get massages but I've stopped going recently."

"You might want to get some physio. I see a wonderful man in town, Philip Lee. I've been going to him for years. Might be worth getting an appointment. He can treat you and advise you about which exercises will help. In this day and age of bending over computers and phones, upper back, neck and shoulder issues are really common. "

"OK, I'll look him up. Thanks."

"But, like I said, in the meantime, just be careful. I don't want to lose another of my dancers!"

Samantha has been dancing for so many years that she returns to her pirouettes without further thought. She dances through the pain like a real pro. I can't imagine doing that. I'm far too much of a coward. Pain hurts! I vaguely consider that maybe I will never make a true dancer.

***

"Guys, before you all leave," Helena says, rounding up class. "I'd like to have a quick chat about costumes. Now, we don't need to be traditional, but I'd like to get a feel for what you'd be comfortable in."

"Pink and sparkly all the way!" Lucia grins.

Julay grimaces. "Something adult!"

"How about the leads in matching costumes and the rest of us in normal ballet wear, just colour co-ordinated?" I chip in.

"It's not my decision," Helena says. "But I like that idea."

"The Nutcracker is so Christmassy, why not Christmas colours?" Josie says.

"Red, green, gold?" Marion asks.

"But I want pink!" Lucia whines.

"OK, OK, there's a compromise to be had here," Helena intervenes. "How about the leads in gold and the corps de ballet in splashes of pink? I know how some of you are keen on your black, so you could wear skirts and leotards with pink tights and maybe something in your hair that's pink too?"

Everyone seems quite keen on this idea.

"Now for the gold outfits," she carries on. "We can get lighter coloured skirts and leotards and dye them. Anyone good at dyeing, so to speak?"

Laughter ripples around the room.

"Me. I have dyed plenty of clothes in my time," Marion pipes up.

"Marvellous! Are we all happy then? I'm going to Chappelle's tomorrow, so I can rummage in their bargain box for anything decent," says Helena.

"I probably have the largest lounge," Julay says, looking around the group. "So why don't we all meet at my house Sunday after next, to work on our outfits, try out hairstyles, etc.?"

I inwardly chuckle at how she manages to combine loftiness with a kindly offer.

"I live on Mountbank Road, number 22. Follow the road past the church and over the level crossing and mine is the first big house on the left."

Well of course it is. We wouldn't have expected anything less.

Chapter 30

Things have settled between Gina and me, so as soon as I have finished my last customer, knowing that I'm going out with Joshua, she ushers me out of the shop.

"Go, go, I'll lock up!" she says. "You deserve a night ou', Babe – go and 'ave some fun!"

"Thanks, Gina," I say, grabbing my coat and bag, heading for the door.

"Oi, don't forget to put yer sexy gear on!" Her dirty laugh rings out.

"Bye, Gina!"

As I'm sitting on the bus, I consider that she's got a point. I'm certainly not going to be putting on my 'sexy gear', but what *do* I wear? This brings my internal debating to a whole new level. It's tricky to gauge without knowing where we're going. He didn't mention dinner, so for just drinks, a dress is a bit much, and trousers too formal - maybe jeans and a pretty top will suffice?

Since Joshua fixed the shower I'm in the lap of luxury. I bring out the big guns shower gel and spend far too long replacing human scent with a gorgeous expensive fragrance. I opt for light makeup and soft curls. 'Oh no,' I think appraising my appearance in the mirror, 'this white high collar cotton blouse makes me look a little choirboy-ish.' Ah well, too late as Basil heralds Joshua's arrival.

"Hi!" I say opening the door, trying to rein in my widest smile.

"Hi, Amy," he twinkles.

My, he's drop-dead gorgeous! He's wearing grey jeans, traditional red Doc Martens, a printed blue t-shirt and a casual jacket. As he leans in to kiss my cheek, I catch an appealing scent that I can't place. At that very moment, all I want to do is rugby tackle him to the hall floor and spend the night there.

Uh-oh 'Carry On Amy' is back...

"You look very nice," he says.

"Why, thank you! And so do you."

"Are we ready then?"

"Absolutely."

We drive out into the countryside to a quaint old pub with low ceilings and beams everywhere. Steve and I visited it once but tonight is not the night to be thinking of him. We pick a table in a quiet corner, and Joshua goes to the bar to order a pint and a white wine for me. As if by telepathy, he brings back a menu.

"Are you hungry? I didn't have time for dinner."

"I'd love something light to nibble, yeah."

Agreeing on a sharing platter of ham, cheeses and breads, he returns to the bar to order. Settling back next to me, he says nothing, he simply looks and smiles.

"What?" I ask, blushing.

"Nothing, nothing, it's just nice being here." I flush further. "So, how's life treating you?"

"Oh, OK, I suppose. Steve popped over out of the blue. I think he's feeling guilty. He found a flimsy excuse to come round..." What is wrong with me? Why am I talking about him? Joshua's faded smile confirms that this isn't the conversation to be having. "Look," I say quickly changing tack. "Why don't we have an evening of me not mentioning my ex and you tell me nothing of yours?"

He brightens. "That sounds an excellent plan! It'll save the evening from being a sob-fest. I tell you what, why don't we tell each other random facts about ourselves? It'll be fun, you'll see.

You can have one minute to tell me as many random things about yourself as you like. You can say anything. You game?"

"What kind of things?"

"Anything! The randomer the better!"

"Is that even a word?"

"It is now," he laughs. "You can tell me anything: your shoe size, your first pet's name, anything!"

I think of possible answers.

"Go on then, I like a game. Bring it on!"

Our platter arrives.

"Nah-ah," he shakes his head. "No food 'til your one minute of randomness is up!"

"Argh, right, OK...my favourite colour is blue. I hate UHT milk. I don't like beach holidays. My mother instilled in me that people who drive white cars are bigheads..." He sniggers. "I had my first kiss at fourteen. Err, mustard makes me sweat. Gin makes me fall asleep. My favourite season is spring. I'm scared of cobwebs – walking into them – eurgh!" He laughs again. "As a child, I wanted to be an ice skater, but never leant to skate. I don't watch films that are for adults, don't like all that sex and violence. I was once sick on the Waltzers. New Year makes me sad. I have never broken a bone in my body and...um...um...is that a minute yet?"

"Dunno, I wasn't timing you!"

We both collapse laughing.

"Can I eat now?"

"Yes you can. You deserve it. And whilst you tuck in, let me just say I don't want to be around you at new year's if you're on the mustard and gin, and yep, it's official, I'm a bighead, my van is white."

We laugh more.

"OK, Mr. Smarty Pants, your turn. And I will be timing you!"

"Oh crikey, OK, erm, I can't stand Adele's warbling and I don't like reality TV. I love pork pies, especially those ones with the egg in them..."

"Ditto."

"Hush your mouth, woman, it's my minute, " he deadpans. "My favourite film is The Godfather - I do violence but not so much sex. I have seen Elbow in concert five times. I can't eat beetroot – it makes my pee red…"

"It makes everyone's pee red!"

He signals to zip it. I giggle.

"I don't like lemon meringue pie. I've only been fired from one job. One of my pinkies is shorter than the other," he says holding up his little fingers to demonstrate. "It's from playing the guitar. I used to have a crush on Angellica from CBBC. I have never been to Norway but I want to go. I wear boxers, never tighties. My grandmother went on a date with Ronald Reagan…"

"Whoa whoa, wait - what? Your grandmother went on a date with Ronald Reagan?"

"Did I not mention the rule that you're allowed one fib?" he grins mischievously.

"Ha ha, what I particularly enjoyed was how you segued from your 'tighties' to your grandmother so seamlessly!"

"That's a natural progression, don't you think?"

We dissolve into fits of laughter. This is the most fun I've had in a long time.

Conversation flows effortlessly as we clean up the ham, cheese and bread. In true gentlemanly fashion, he offers me the last breadstick, and I graciously accept. There are no awkward silences; no moments of tension, we are delightfully comfortable. I check the time and it's like the clock hands have secretly crept forward.

"Wow, time flies when you're having fun!" I say.

"Don't I know it," he replies, suddenly looking distant.

"You OK?"

"Just thinking that I won't be around here for much longer - I booked my flight to New Zealand."

For the first time a heavy atmosphere descends.

"Ah, I see. Not having second thoughts are you?"

"I need to go, I've been planning it for so long."

"You didn't answer my question."

He smiles sadly. "I have an apartment in Wellington and the job is terrific – it's the opportunity of a lifetime. I just need to focus on winding things down here."

"It does sound like a great opportunity. You must go... and anyway, don't worry I'm sure they'll have plenty of pork pie there," I tease. "And Adele CDs."

He looks down laughing and the tension eases.

"Another drink?" he asks.

I'm feeling the effects of the two large glasses of wine, so I decline. We agree to make tracks, but then lose ourselves in conversation again until the landlord shouts 'time' and directs us to go home.

Pulling up outside my door, we are discussing the plethora of annoying Facebook posts.

"You know the one that gets me?" he says, switching off the engine and turning to face me. "'Like' if you love your mother with all your heart'. I'm always tempted to put 'meh – she's OK'.

We set off giggling again.

As the laughter quells I sigh happily.

"Joshua, this has been such fun."

"Yes, Amy Ballerina, it has indeed."

He reaches for my hand. He sits there, looking at our entwined fingers, deep in thought. His thumb strokes the side of my hand and it is in this perfect moment that I feel my heart happily flutter. It's a bitter-sweet feeling as the joy of the evening is undoubtedly shrouded in a poignant sadness. There's a true connection between us, but as he needs to follow his dreams, our paths are crossing, not joining. I wonder if our attraction is made stronger for knowing that there's a definite end date? 'Unobtainable' always has an allure that 'readily available' doesn't.

"What date are you leaving?" I shyly ask.

"10th December."

"Ah...not long at all."

We exchange sad smiles and he pulls me into a hug. I breathe deeply into the scent of him and then it happens - the discernible moment when the dynamic shifts. We move slightly apart but then he lowers his face to mine. I can almost hear his thinking, that he knows he shouldn't do this, but is beyond resisting. We kiss - a long sweet, gentle pressing of lips. Our bodies mould together with not a millimetre of space between us. My insides turn into gooey schmaltz whilst electricity bounces all around us. It's beautiful, heady. I am lost. I have a feeling of being home, of belonging. I have never been kissed like this, ever. We reluctantly disentangle.

"Thanks for a lovely evening," he says softly, moving a hair back from my face.
His eyes are glistening in the dashboard reflection.

"I had a great time, thanks," I manage to say. And I have. I sense that our feelings for each other are genuine, but so is his desire to live the life he had planned. I definitely don't want to unpick this dichotomy now, not tonight. Tonight, I want to leave with my head in the clouds and the perfect evening intact.

"Goodnight, Joshua," I say, climbing out of the car.

"Goodnight, Amy," he says, watching me.

I walk to my front door and pause with the keys in my hand.

He starts the car and pulls away.

I stand and watch until his rear lights disappear from view.

Chapter 31

Ballet classes come and go, and our dancing is incrementally improving. We repeat the same steps again and again until they are firmly embedded in our minds and bodies. Gloria isn't present, which is no surprise as Stanley's funeral was only last Friday, and Joshua is sadly nowhere to be bumped into either. The night out with him had been immense fun and I remained on quite a high, but gradually I have been drawn back down to earth. Each ballet class I wonder if I will see him, but I don't. He must be opening the hall especially early and closing it after we leave. Is he staying out of my way? Maybe I misread his feelings? Or is he concerned that if we have more evenings like that one, filled with laughter and kisses, he might be tempted to stay? If he did and our attraction turned out to be short lived (especially if the deadline of being separated is eliminated), he would have passed up a great opportunity. The only thing I know for sure is that, in his absence, I have reverted back to the self-pitying state that Steve left me in.

This afternoon I will head over to Julay's 'big house' for our costume making session. For now, I sit at my table watching the half naked trees in the garden blowing their dying leaves to the ground. Basil is spooked by strong winds and he sits at my feet looking up at me for protection.

"Don't worry, Bas, I'll look after you. And why didn't you do this when Steve was here, eh? You must try to remember who feeds you these days," I chide. We begin the ritual tickling-the-

153

tummy session that will last as long as I allow. Two minutes in and my phone beeps. Ah, wonderful, it's Gloria.

Hello dear Amy. Thank you so much for the card and flowers from the ballet girls. And thanks for your text. Stanley's funeral did go well; it was quite beautiful. Would love to see you sometime, if you're free. G xx

Hello there! So lovely to hear from you. Glad the funeral went well. This afternoon we're all meeting at Julay's house to run through costumes and hair etc. Why not join us? It'll be fun. ☺

I wait, wondering whether the mention of Julay will spark a reaction.

Yes, why not! I can pick you up if you like? Love G

So pleased ☺ She lives on Mountbank Road and we're meeting at 2pm. So see you here around 1.30pm? x

Perfect. G xxx

I idly wonder whether I should alert Julay that Gloria is coming but decide better of it. They can sort out their differences without any interference from me.

***

Out of the window, I see Gloria's car and I gesture for her to stay there. I throw on my coat, grab my hairdressing kit and join her. We greet each other warmly with hugs and kisses on both cheeks.

"How are you, Gloria?"

"Oh, you know, getting there," she says, slowly pulling away.

She looks tired but her impeccable choice of clothing colours and the right make-up disguises it well.

"I suppose I did a lot of my grieving after the accident." She sighs, keeping her eyes on the road. "To all intents and purposes my Stanley had gone, so now it's an unusual grief I find myself in. I already longed for him, already missed him, already grieved for him, so nothing much has changed. I wasn't foolish enough to believe that he would 'come back' to me, but there again, where there's life there's hope, and so maybe, in a tiny

154

corner of my heart, I *did* dare to dream that it might be possible, that one day they would call to say he was miraculously fully functioning again."

"We put a lot of stock in our dreams, don't we? Even if they are unrealistic."

"Yes we do, until reality gets in the way. Tell me, how's it going with Steve? Heard any more?"

"Eurgh, yes I have. He turned up out of the blue under the pretext of wanting to pick up DVDs and his fishing rod, of all things!"

She raises her eyebrows. "How inventive!"

"I know. Oh, I don't think you know about the baby, do you?"

"What?" She turns to me in shock and then has to swerve quickly to avoid a central bollard.

"Sorry, probably should've saved that news 'til we were stationary."

"A baby? She's pregnant?"

"'Fraid so. Gina told me. She plays darts with them. It's the old cliché of 'the wife's always the last to know.' Anyway, he turned up at mine and I really didn't want to see him."

"I'm sure you didn't!"

"But, you know what, Gloria, there was something about him. For the first time, he showed real remorse. I think he thought that ending our marriage first and then later, much later, telling me about the baby would somehow soften the blow. Of course it didn't. It worked the other way. Finding out through Gina was just awful and I don't know if I'll ever forgive him for the way he's gone about things. But on that Sunday, when he was at mine...I don't know...I just saw the old Steve. The one who wouldn't hurt me. I'm pathetic aren't I?"

"I think you want to believe that he's the same, good man that you married. Sometimes it's hard to accept that someone has changed. We assume that in life we learn and grow and change for the better. Maybe some people change for the worse?"

Gloria holds wise counsel.

'I do think if you'd told me even a year ago that this would happen, I wouldn't have believed you," I say. "He was always so constant, you know, trustworthy and kind. I never dreamt he would do this. I wonder if I could've done something to stop it happening..."

"Amy," she pulls me up short. "I don't ever want to hear you say that. Believe me, you could torture yourself endlessly with that question and no good will come of it! There's nothing you could or couldn't have done. It is what it is, and having regrets won't solve anything. He's the one who went behind your back. How could you do anything when you had no idea that anything was askew?

"I know, I know, you're right. I'm pathetic," I whine.

"And stop saying that! You'll believe it soon!"

"Well you see, I was doing OK...but then I had a night out with Joshua..."

"Amy?"

I must stop scandalizing her whilst she's driving...

" ...yes, that day you were round, he kind of asked me to go for a drink. So we went out the other Thursday. Gloria, it was lovely - relaxing, flirty, funny, and it finished with a kiss that I felt all the way down to my boots!"

Gloria gives a deep chuckle.

"Well that sounds like fun!"

"Yes it was, it really was, but since then I've not seen hide nor hair of him. I'm so glad that we didn't take things any further or else I'd be feeling properly used. The thing is that he's all booked and ready to start a new life in New Zealand. I fear we're 'right people, wrong time'."

"When does he leave?"

"Two weeks' time. 10th December."

"Oh dear, that isn't very long is it?" She inhales and exhales deeply. "I think if I've learnt anything in these recent weeks, it's that some things you just have no control over. My darling Amy, if it's meant to be, it will be, and if not...I suggest you stalk him all the way to New Zealand."

I adore Gloria's wicked sense of humour.

Still laughing, we arrive outside the first big house on the left. And you know what, it's really not so big.

Chapter 32

Julay swings open the front door with a look of mild panic at seeing Gloria at my side.

"Hello, come in," she smiles nervously.

We file into a narrow hall with deep carpets and tiny rosebud patterned wallpaper. There are framed cross-stitches of birds lining the walls. Julay takes our coats and leads us into the lounge. A crazy bricked fireplace lines the full length of the room and paintings of landscapes and churches adorn the walls. Marion, Josie and Catherine are already there, seated on a camel velour three-piece sofa situated around a low glass coffee table.

"Right, we're just waiting for Lucia, Samantha, and Marion," Julay says. "Can I offer you tea or coffee?"

"Tea, please," I say.

"For me too," Gloria adds. Julay smiles warmly at Gloria, nods and disappears to the kitchen. Do I sense a calming of the waters? Let's hope that they have a chance to settle differences as, in my opinion, Julay definitely has some humble pie to eat.

Marion pulls out garments from her bag.

"These are the leotards and skirts that Helena gave me to dye gold. We just have to check if they fit you and Julay," she directs to Catherine. "And these…" she says, holding up various pink items. "…are totally up for grabs."

We all pick up various clothes and hold them up for size.

"Helena has also provided some braiding, lengths of sequins and lace for us to use as we like. Apart from the colour

159

co-ordination, she really doesn't mind how we decorate the outfits. Brian's getting a specific costume that Helena is borrowing from a friend, so it wasn't worth him coming today."

I sense Gloria exhale a subtle sigh of relief.

The doorbell rings and our remaining classmates join us. Cheerful greetings sound out in an excited hubbub. Julay appears with a trolley of delights consisting of a three-tiered silver cake stand housing fruit scones, fairy cakes, fondant fancies and mini cherry Bakewells. Alongside are two large willow patterned china pots of tea, matching sugar bowl, milk jug, cups, saucers and side plates. Murmurs of approval fill the room and very soon we are sipping tea and relishing delicious cakes. Chatter around our impending performance and the steps we are unsure of dominate the conversation. After an hour or so, we have to remind ourselves why we're gathered.

Duties are undertaken voluntarily with Marion, Catherine and Julay in the bathroom hand dying leotards, skirts and tights, Josie and Gloria pinning adornments to the pink garb and Lucia, Samantha and I, in the kitchen, creating hairstyles.

Whilst curling Sam's long hair, I ask, "How's your mum doing?"

"How long have you got?" she half laughs.

"We've got all the time in the world," Lucia says, admiring her new hair-do in a hand mirror.

"Well...don't know how much you know," she directs at Lucia. "But my mum is terminally ill and had the wisdom to contact my estranged father who has now turned up in my life."

"Oh, I'm sorry, I didn't know about your mum and, err, you don't sound thrilled about your dad."

"I'm not. I didn't really know him as a child, and from what I've seen of him recently, I'm not sure I like him all that much. The problem is that my mum really does like him, and they're playing happy couples."

"The Oldies getting jiggy with it, eh?"

"Eurgh, Lucia!" Sam laughs, throwing a soft hair roller at her. "It makes my stomach turn."

"There's not going to be a bedside wedding is there?" Lucia asks.

"No need, they never divorced." Sam falls silent, seemingly computing this for the first time.

"They're still married?" I ask.

"Yes, they are."

Lucia and I exchange questioning looks.

"Wanna know about me and Deaf Danny?" Lucia then asks brightly. We both turn to look at her.

"Please tell me you don't call him that to his face!" I say, aghast.

"Well if I did, he wouldn't know, he's not that good at lip reading," she cackles. "Of course I don't, I'm only joking! Well, he's luvverly, a real gent. I found one of those online things that teach you some signs. "See this, this is 'hello,'" she waves her hand in an obvious 'hello' manner. "And this…" she puts her hand to her chin and lowers it. "This is 'thank you'. And this…" she makes two fists and repeatedly bounces her forearms.

"Oooh, being cold?" I guess.

"Nah – it's rumpy pumpy!" Her filthy guffaw sounds out, sending us into fits of giggles.

"'Hello', 'rumpy pumpy' and 'thank you' – guess that's all you need for a happy relationship," I say. "Although a 'please' might be nice too." Our laughter continues.

"You not got a fella, Sam?" Lucia asks.

Sam doesn't answer at once. I lean around to see her face.

"Sam? *Do* you have a fella?"

"No, no, no. But I might have met someone this week who's rather nice."

"Oooh, tell us more!"

"Well, you know Helena told me about Philip Lee, the Physio? I went along for an appointment but he was off ill, so they put me in with his son, Jason, who is *lovely*…but so lovely I don't think I can go back to him again."

"Kind of embarrassing taking your kit off with a handsome dude, eh?" Lucia asks.

"Yep. I'll have to book his father and just hope to bump into him there."

"Did you get the vibes that he liked you?" I question.

"You know, it's funny, I did."

"You should trust those vibes," I say, considering how I should take my own advice. Last week, I would have sworn that Joshua was reciprocating my feelings and yet his noticeable absence has made me doubt myself. "Well, one thing's for sure, Sam, he can't make a move on you if he's treating you, it'd be against his code of ethics. Don't go back to him, but yeah, just hang around the waiting room!"

We're all laughing as Gloria wanders into the kitchen.

"What are you girls talking about in here?"

"Sexy physios and Deaf Danny," Lucia guffaws.

"Now that sounds like fun! I'm afraid we've done what we can with the frills and bits and pieces for the mo, so we're taking a break."

"There you go," I say to Sam, holding a mirror to show her wavy hair in a pretty chignon with a pale pink flower to the side.

"Oh, it's lovely, thanks, Amy, spot on first time!" she says, tilting her head, admiring my handy work. "I'd like it just like this on the night, please."

"Not a problem. Shall I try putting your hair up now, Gloria?"

"Yes, Darling, that would be marvellous."

Sam and Lucia sit at the kitchen table whilst I start pinning up Gloria's luscious sleek hair.

"Hey Glo, we were all so sorry to hear about your Stanley," Lucia says.

"Thank you, Dear, even though I knew it would happen sometime, it was still a shock."

"I don't think we can ever prepare ourselves for the death of someone we love," I sympathise. "And did the funeral go OK?"

"It was lovely. Quite a few people came, which heartened me – he was a popular fellow. They all had various tales to tell about him. Most talked of his wit and his humour; many spoke of his kindness. He was known for his generosity – he gave his time and himself freely. He was such a good soul."

"You get the measure of a man through others' eyes, don't you?"

"Yes, you do." Her voice is tight. "But you know what? I was utterly blessed to be married to him. We had the will reading and there was a letter for me that he must've written about a year before the accident. In it, he says how grateful he was to share his life with me, his only love."

"That's beautiful," Sam wistfully sighs.

"It also turns out that my Stanley was a bit of a squirrel. He had been secretly depositing money in a Building Society account for many years. I mean, we were quite comfortable already, but this was for our retirement, to enjoy our last years together without any financial burden. But of course, that isn't to be. Instead, he's just lightened my load. He did well by me, right to the end. It's strange isn't it, inheriting money. How many people would rather have the person they love still there, than a healthy bank balance?"

I see a strange look in Sam's eyes and her usual soft pink complexion has turned pale.

"Are you OK?" I ask her.

"Fine...yes, yes, I'm fine."

I haven't known my friend for long, but it's most apparent from her look that she is most definitely not fine.

Chapter 33

Luckily, having found a friend to sublet to, Joshua is depersonalising his flat ahead of his departure. He's put aside the things he wants to take with him and the rest of his belongings are to be packed and stored at his mother's house for when he returns. He finds photographs and mementos of Sophia. With a surge of resolute determination, he tosses them into a black plastic rubbish sack. Why would he keep those reminders for when he returns? Why is his return at the forefront of his mind when he hasn't even left yet! There's a one-word answer for that – Amy.

Taking a coffee break, he sits in his favourite battered leather chair. His mind wanders back to their evening together. He smiles at the thought of the Random Facts game in the pub. He pictures her throwing her head back, in a fit of giggles. He closes his eyes and remembers the kiss, the electricity crackling between them. It's not possible that it was only him who felt it. It takes two to make chemistry like that. They haven't laid eyes on each other since that night and he wonders how she feels. Is she nonchalant? Disappointed? Angry? Hurt? He can't bear the thought of her being hurt. She is still vulnerable from the break with the idiot who let her go, and he really doesn't want to add to her pain. And that is why the best option is to persist with avoidance. But can he leave without saying goodbye? Isn't that kind of rude? Didn't his mother teach him better than that?

With a head full of conflicting urgings, Joshua sighs, and with a heavy heart continues to pack. The only indisputable fact is that meeting Amy when he did has been the worst case of bad timing ever.

Chapter 34

Pulling up outside her mother's house, Sam takes a deep breath, pulls on the handbrake and exhales slowly. She would give anything to restart the car, drive away and spend the evening doing something else, anything else. Instead, when her mother contacted her and asked her to join them for dinner, Sam had duty-bound agreed, and now she has to follow through.

Standing on the doorstep, she feels uneasy, her finger hovers before pressing the doorbell. After a moment, her father appears and immediately territorial instincts gnaw at her insides.

"Hi," she says. She will not call him 'Dad'.

"Hello, Love, come in, come in." He looks like the cat that got the cream and another cat's cream too. "We were just laughing about the time your mum and me tried ice skating. We weren't very good at it..." He fails to finish his sentence as he is laughing too much. Sam fakes a laugh. She presumes that this will be the first of many throughout the evening. He, uncharacteristically, moves forward for an embrace but Sam quickly hands him her coat.

He's going to have to be quicker than that.

Best plates and cutlery are beautifully laid out on a pretty floral tablecloth. Her mother enters the room appearing perky and bright, and Sam concedes gloomily that she does have the look of a smitten woman. Despite Sam's misgivings towards her father, she has to accept that he does have a positive effect on her mother.

"Sam, Dear, look what your father brought," her mother says, displaying a cheap bottle of red wine that looks half drunk already.

"Lovely. I'll have a sniff of that." She tries to smile naturally, she wants to be happy for her mother but something just doesn't sit right.

Her mother pours her a glass. "Dinner will be ten minutes," she calls over her shoulder en route to the kitchen.

From where she's seated in the lounge, Sam has a bird's eye view of her parents in the kitchen. Her father is leaning around her mother pouring himself another glass of wine. He is jiggling up against her and in turn she giggles girlishly.

"Oooh John!" she shrieks.

'Oh yuk,' Sam says under her breath.

"Come on now, Cherry Baby, we used to dance!" he says, pulling at her arm.

"I haven't danced in years!"

"C'mon girl!" He spins her around and they start jiving in an uncoordinated fashion. Breathless after a few moments, her mother puts her hand to head.

"OK, that's me done!"

"You go and sit down, Pet. I'll carry on here." He winks at her and, as she turns to join me, he gives her bottom a hearty slap. She giggles more and fans herself with her hand. Flopping into the armchair beside me, she wipes beads of sweat from her forehead.

"You alright there, Mum?"

"Yes absolutely," she puffs. "I'm just fine, Dear."

Her mother's eyes are shining and Sam feels a rush of love for this special woman. As a child, Sam had believed her mother to be the most attractive woman in the world, and despite the ravages of cancer, her beauty is still apparent. Her mother rests her head back on the chair and sighs.

"Sam, do you think it is possible to be dying and yet to feel *so* alive?"

"I do, Mum. We are alive until the moment we die." Sam feels insensitive saying the 'D' word but her mother seems unaffected.

"That's very deep, Dear, and very true." She smiles. There's a small silence. Her mother leans across. "He does make me very happy, you know."

"I know."

They exchange small smiles.

"Grub's up!" her father shouts.

Seated around the table, the public display of affection between her parents makes Sam want to vomit into her prawn cocktail. Trying to swallow small mouthfuls, she studies her father. His red nose and slightly slurred speech signal that he's fairly drunk already. He looks at her mother with puppy dog eyes. He continually touches her cheek and squeezes her knee, and her normally level-headed mother laps it up like a kitten would milk. Sam feels invisible. This is not a family meal, it's a courting couple and an onlooker, and she can't help but wonder if this is her father's intention. Is he trying to replace Sam in her mother's affections or are his intentions even more deceitful than that?

The conversation at Julay's house has planted seeds of doubt. Her father possesses certain attributes but generosity, warmth and fondness to others are not among them. From where she is sitting, she sees a man who is falling over himself to garner affection and it looks like an elaborate charade. Her parents are still married and this would make her father the next of kin. They may have discussed many things but Sam doesn't actually know the contents of her mother's will, or even, for that matter, if she has one. In the absence of a will, Sam's father would be the main beneficiary. Sam isn't concerned about the financial side of things, the house or chattels, but she is worried that her father can just waltz in, at the eleventh hour, and claim everything that is not rightfully his. Watching her parents in their mating dance ritual, she wonders how she can expose this man's true intentions. And if she manages to do that, she will only end up hurting the one person she loves most, her mother.

At the end of an evening endured in slow motion, Sam sees her mother is flagging.

"Go to bed, Mum, you're wiped out," she says.

"Nonsense, Dear, I'm fine."

"C'mon, Cheryl love, you trot off to bed and I'll finish up down here," her father cajoles.

"Oh, alright then, thanks."

Sam is irritated beyond belief. She suggests that her mother should rest and is rebuked, but when *he* says the same, her mother immediately obeys. Her mother rises and kisses them both.

"Be up in a while, Love," her father calls after her, as she heads upstairs.   Sam and her father are left with nothing but a tension-filled silence between them. Sam starts transporting dishes into the kitchen. As she returns to the dining room, her father blocks the doorway.

"You alright, Love?" His tone is stern, his manner altered. No more Mr Nice Guy, it would seem.

"Yes, why?"

"I dunno, I just get the feeling you don't approve of me and your mum."

She can feel herself tremble. "Not really my business, is it?"

"Well, you're right about that. You seem to look down on me though, like I'm doing something wrong, but believe me, I'm only here thinking of your mum's happiness. That's what's important to me."

"Really? So if that's true, why's it taken you this long to reappear? If you care so much about her happiness, where have you been all these years?"

"Look, Love, I told you, things were difficult between us. We were young back then, didn't know what we were doing. Then when we split, I was down on my luck financially..."

"Mmmm...down on your luck financially...and now?"

"What's that supposed to mean? You know I've had it rough over the years." He thinks for a second. He fixes her with a steady gaze. "Oh, I see where this is heading, you think I'm here for a hand-out?"

With pulsing temples and a look of defiance, Sam holds his stare until he looks away to the floor. Sam wonders if her words have hurt him.

"I can't believe a daughter of mine would think such a thing! You should be ashamed of yourself, my girl!"

"I tell you something, *John*," she spits. "There's one thing I do know, and that is that I'm not and never have been YOUR GIRL!"

Sam grabs her coat and bag, and, with angry tears streaming down her face, runs out of the house, slamming the door in her wake.

Upstairs, Cheryl rouses from her sleep, intuitively knowing the reason for the crashing door. As she drifts back off to sleep, she makes a mental note to have a talk with her daughter soon.

Chapter 35

It's a measure of how keen we all are that we're in the changing room thirty minutes earlier than necessary. Gloria is back in the fold and the atmosphere is buoyant. Conversations fly as we change into our ballet wear.

"It's the trip to Swan Lake tomorrow, isn't it?" Marion says.

"Yes it is," I reply. "Is anyone taking partners or is it just us lot? I'm not sure how many tickets Helena bought."

"I think it's just us lot," Lucia adds. "But anyway if it is with partners, I'd still be on my own. Deaf Danny dumped me."

Cries of 'oh no' and 'what happened?' ring out.

"He said it was 'communication'. But I think it was more that his ex came sniffing around when she found out he was seeing me. She's deaf too, y'see, and signs perfectly. They have great 'communication', she says, enunciating the word with derision.

"Are you OK Dear?" Gloria asks.

"Yeah, but tell you something, I finally found a sign of my own I could use to him." We all laugh. "Guess it just wasn't meant to be. It was fine when it was just us two, but in a crowd, I couldn't understand a bloody thing anyone said. I'd end up just looking into my drink. Not fair to ask him to tell me what they were going on about all the time. It's a shame. But if we had really loved each other, we could have found a place somewhere between sound and silence." She stifles a giggle.

"Lucia, have you been watching 'Children of a Lesser God'?" I ask. She throws her head back laughing.

"Wondered if you'd spot the quote! Ha ha ha. What a load of old crap, eh? Folk are folk, and if the chemistry were right, then Deaf Danny and me would be together, and it wouldn't matter whether our ears worked or not. Nah, he just wanted to be back with his ex. I'm moving on, anyway, I'd like a nice blind fella next."

Behind the humour, I suspect Lucia is hurt, but she's not the type to welcome pity.

"Working your way through the disabilities, eh?" I chuckle.

"Then it's on to race, religion, gender. I'm open to anyone! Just call me Ms Equal Opportunities." Her filthy laugh fills the room.

"Lucia, you are terrible!" Marion titters.

"I'm all about equality, Mazza," she winks.

***

"Right, with under four weeks left, I would like to run through the dance," Helena says. "Don't worry if you're not fully up to speed, I just want to see how it's coming together and which parts we need to work on. By the end of the night, I'll've put all the final changes in place and then that's it, no more changes. This'll give you all a clear idea of the finished dance. Is that OK with everyone?"

We all nod our agreement and get into our starting positions. I am stood in a pose at the side of the stage, 'framing' the others and I have the chance to watch my dancing friends. The choreography suits their strengths well and the overall dance is quite impressive. We reach the part of the dance that consists of coordinated arm movements, when Helena claps her hands.

"Sorry, can I stop it there, please. Your arms are lovely, People. You're perfectly in time, but there's one thing missing - the foundation of life – the breath! I know you're all

174

concentrating, and that makes us automatically hold our breath, but we must breathe, it transforms the dance!"

She demonstrates moving her arms whilst holding her breath and then repeats the movements with purposeful breathing. It does indeed come alive.

"So I know it sounds odd, but I will give you times to breath. First I'll call them out as you dance and then after a while it'll become second nature."

"Gosh, I've been doing it my whole life and never thought I'd have to be taught to breathe," quips Lucia under her breath.

Helena continues, "The art of ballet is to achieve impossibly difficult steps whilst giving the impression of it all being effortless. Your body may be screaming but your face must be joyously calm. The breath is vital in producing a look of serenity. If we tense up, we lose the breath and then we lose the beauty. We must relax and breathe, but believe me, Folks, I do know it's harder said than done." She laughs. "Dance training taught me to hide the pain, to keep it within. It used to amuse me that we'd be on stage, smiling throughout, and then as soon as we hit the wings we'd be bent double, gasping for breath and, ironically, gagging for a cigarette."

"You smoke?" Catherine asks.

"Not any more. There's a myth that dancers take care of themselves and lead a monk-like existence. Couldn't be further from the truth! I ate rubbish, smoked too much and many a time, in morning class, I was still drunk from the night before. See, your teacher was no saint!"

We all laugh in shock at her admissions. She looks the model of good health so it's surprising, and entertaining, to learn of her not-so-squeaky-clean past.

Within the dance, there are natural moments to breathe and our task now is to learn when they are. I am starting to feel a little exasperated. I'm already struggling with choreography, timing and expression, and now I have to remember to breathe! I have a sinking feeling that, even with four weeks left to rehearse, I'm not going to be performance-ready. At the end of class, I approach Helena.

"Can I have a word, please?"

"Of course, Amy. You OK?"

"I'm just worried that I'm not going to be ready for the competition. The others are miles ahead of me and I don't want to be the one to let the team down."

"Right, firstly you're not going to let the team down at all." She reassuringly touches my arm. "Everyone's at different levels and there's no point comparing yourself to them. Each dancer is unique and I really do believe that everyone brings something special to this piece. Now, if you're worried about not having enough practice, then why don't you see if you can book the hall for some time on your own? I know for a fact that no one uses this place on a Sunday. You already know the steps, you could just run through them at your own pace."

"That's a great idea. Might help my confidence as well."

"I do think confidence, or rather a lack of it, is what's troubling you. If you spend some time practising on your own, or with a couple of the others, you should feel better. It's a lot to do with preparation, but if you're still unsure of any part, please just ask, OK?"

"OK, thanks."

"You know you really are dancing well and you've picked up the steps amazingly quickly." I blush, feeling humbled by her praise.

She pats me on the shoulder. "Good luck, Amy. See you tomorrow at the theatre."

"Thanks, yep, see you then." I start to walk away but quickly turn back. "Oh, who do I see about booking the hall?"

"Oh, err, just see the caretaker handyman chap, Joshua, he'll sort you out."

Chapter 36

We are assembled outside the Theatre Royal waiting for the last of our party, Marion, to arrive. Helena hands out tickets and takes our money.

"I'm going to get a programme," Julay announces.

"I want some sweeties," Lucia says. The rest decide they want either one or the other, and so we traipse inside leaving Helena outside to wait for Marion.

I love the smell of the theatre. I always have. The Theatre Royal is old and desperately in need of refurbishment and yet there is something intrinsically charming about it. At one time, the carpets would have been thick and deep and the wallpaper would have been in fashion. There are magnificent ornate pillars rising up to the off-white artexed ceiling. The front of house staff wear black waistcoats and burgundy bow ties, and if it weren't for the smell of popcorn, I could easily believe that I am in another era. With confectionery and programmes purchased, Helena and Marion join us as we enter the auditorium.

We have seats on the end of the seventh and eighth rows. Gloria is in front of me with Julay beside her. I cannot help overhear their exchanges. Both women are reserved and polite, and after one particularly prolonged silence, Julay clears her throat.

"Gloria, I do hope we can put all that business behind us?"

"Julay," Gloria speaks steadily. "Is that an apology?"

"I might have said a little too much. It really is none of my business what you do in your private life."

"I couldn't agree more."

"Can we put it behind us?"

"Yes, I think so. And Julay," Gloria says touching her arm. "I am genuinely pleased that you have one of the lead parts."

"That's very kind, thank you."

The two women smile at each other. I feel my heart swell. Gloria is so benevolent. After a moment, Julay looks over her shoulder.

"Excuse me," she says to Gloria. Turning to Brian, she says, "Brian, could I be a dreadful nuisance and ask to swap seats? I'm just not comfortable here and would prefer an end seat. Would you be a dear and swap with me?"

Ever the obliging gentleman, Brian, clueless to motif, gets up and swaps seats. Julay joins the end of my row and winks at me.

Well, well, who would have thought?

I am now in the best seat to listen to Gloria and Brian's conversation, and do so intently until I become aware that Helena is asking me a question.

"Amy? Did you manage to fix up a time for the caretaker chappy to open the hall for you?"

Dragging my attention away, I start to answer but then the lights lower. Helena shakes her head for me not to answer, gives me the thumbs up and sits back in her seat.

Yes, I did fix up a time and I'm still cringing from our conversation. I had found the hall contact number, aka Joshua's mobile number, on the notice board, and punched it into my phone. I decided to wait until I was home to call him as I needed mental preparation. Finally, I summoned up the nerve, took a deep breath.

"Hi Joshua, it's Amy."

Aaargh silence.

"Amy, hi, how are you?" he said, surprise showing in his voice.

"Good thanks. You?"

"I'm fine."

"Erm, I got your number from the hall notice board…"

I cursed the quiver in my voice.

"…and I'm feeling like a bit of a fairy elephant on stage…well, you've seen me dance, and I really need to improve. So, basically, I need more time in the hall…" I was babbling. "…so I wondered if you would mind opening it up for me? Sorry if it's inconvenient, and how much is it to hire? I really do need to practise. You see the others, they're so good. And then there's me. They're all slim and I don't even look like a ballerina, more like a belly-rina!…" I had snorted with laughter and silently smacked my forehead, not believing what was coming out of my mouth. "…so could you, please?"

"Could I what? Help you with your belly?"

I could tell that he wanted to laugh.

"No, yes, no, I mean…help me by letting me book the hall on Sunday for an hour or so."

"Yeah, of course, no problem. I've got a few jobs I need to do there anyway, so how about…say…two 'til four?"

"That would be marvellous. Thank you so much!"

"You're welcome. And by the way, 'Belly-rina' should be the name of your autobiography."

We laugh, that easy laugh we share together. Although he is leaving the country next week, and we are therefore not likely to be lovers, we are definitely friends.

"Thanks, Joshua Handyman. See you Sunday!"

"Bye, Amy."

We hung up and I sat there, on my sofa, hugging my phone to my chest, smiling. Whether I'm nervously talking gibberish or am completely lucid, it doesn't seem to matter, we just click.

I am broken from my reverie by the fifty-six 'swans' on the stage. They are breathtakingly stunning in their grace and poise. I can hear the patter of their pointe shoes on the stage, and I thrill to watch them in perfect formation. In truth, I don't really care about the story as I'm completely entranced by the dancing. I watch their steps and try to recognise something, anything, that

I can do (albeit at an elementary level), and I'm disappointed to say I find nothing, not one step. I shrug and comfort myself with a big handful of Samantha's popcorn.

Seated around the bar at the interval, Gloria starts to confide.

"Julay apologised to me you know, well, in a manner of sorts."

"I'll come clean, Gloria, I heard every word, I was right behind you!"

She laughs gently. "You eavesdropper, you!"

"Sorry, couldn't resist." I chuckle. "You OK with her now?"

"My motto is that life's too short, and that pretty much covers everything. I don't think she's a bad person. I think she carries hurt or an injustice around with her, and that's not healthy. I would guess that something or someone hurt her in the past. I kind of feel sorry for her, cos she's really only torturing herself."

"You're such a kind and sensible person, Gloria, you're my role model, you know," I say, squeezing her hand. "The one thing I didn't hear though is your conversation with Brian..."

"Ha! You're as subtle as a brick," she laughs. "Well, we chatted and that's a start. He's such a sweet man. He says he's missed my company, so I think we're friends for now and see where it goes."

"Friends with potential. Sounds like a good plan. You never know what the future brings, eh?"

"Friends with potential? That's a new one on me. Is it the same as friends with benefits?"

"No Gloria, it really isn't!" I choke, spluttering on my drink.

"Ah, well from that reaction, I don't think I want to know what that means!"

"No, you don't." I raise my glass to hers. "Here's to the future, Gloria, and whatever it holds."

"My Dear, I will certainly drink to that!"

Chapter 37

Throughout the following day, the exhilaration of the ballet stays with me. I'm gliding up and down the salon, aware of my arms and posture, and have the music of Swan Lake reverberating in my head. The nearer it gets to Christmas, the more fun and lively the salon becomes, and I'm floating around having a wonderful time. To all the cynics who claim that Christmas is merely an exercise in consumerism, all I can say is that they haven't been to Hip Snips. There's an excitement in the air. People, in genial moods, being nicer, friendlier to each other, are buzzing in anticipation. If people can be like this at Christmas, why can't they be like it all year round? Kindness breeds kindness. The day flies by in a whirl of hard work, laughter, coffee and mince pies, and before I know it, I have bid goodbye to clients and staff, and am closing up.

I walk to the front of the shop to make a last check on reception when there's a knock at the door. Peering in through the tinted glass is Steve.

Oh no, what does he want?

I unlock the door.

"Hi, Steve."

"Hi, Ames, how are things?"

"Good, all good, thanks."

He is shifting from one foot to the other and with a dishevelled appearance and pallid face, he looks totally frayed around the edges.

181

"Is everything OK with you?"

"Not really." With that, he bursts into tears. Despite all the hurt he has laden on me, I instantly feel sorry for him. I've seen him cry twice in our years together; once when his beloved grandmother died and once when we had to leave Basil at the vets for an operation. I lead him to the staff room and put the coffee pot back on.

"OK, talk to me," I say kindly.

"I'm confused, Amy. I thought I had everything sorted, but I'm not so sure now. I keep thinking about us, about what we had. Some days I wake up and can't believe that I left you." He looks pitiful raking his fingers through his hair.

"Well, you did." I want to show empathy but it's not easy.

He looks down at his shaking hands.

"Steve, maybe it's just this time of year, eh? You're thinking back to the Christmases we shared. It's a nostalgic time. It doesn't mean that we should be together, does it?"

"I don't know. Do you remember our first Christmas?"

I nod and smile.

"We spent it on our own, didn't we?" he continues. "We bought far too much food and drink for just the two of us, and didn't get around to cooking much of it either, remember?" He half-smiles suggestively. "We learnt a lot about each other that Christmas, didn't we?"

"Yes, mainly that nakedness and pine needles aren't a good combination."

We both laugh softly at the memory. I look at him closely. He's familiar in the way that brushing your teeth or waking up is – it's an automatic familiarity. I don't have to wonder what he feels like to touch or how he smells, I know him completely. I used to think that I knew his entire thoughts (sometimes even before he had them) but that part has gone. His reasons for leaving, and the way he left, forged a change within me. It's odd though that, in this moment, I feel the old bond between us again. I once read an article saying that in long-term relationships, when the tingling excitement of the first throes of passion dies, we *choose* to love our partner. I used to choose him on a daily basis. Sadly, he chose someone else.

"Has something happened with Justine?" I ask, wanting to deflect from dwelling on our past.

"Sort of, it's nothing really." He shakes his head. "Maybe you're right, it's just the time of year." Despite the words coming out of his mouth, his eyes send out a different message. He gives me a look that I recognise from back in the days when he loved me. I don't want it to affect me, to penetrate my armour, but it does. I find myself softening.

"I'm not being funny, but why don't we go out one night?" he asks. As his question hangs in the air, I realise that I'm going to be late for ballet class and, as I do want to talk with him more, I hastily agree.

"Sure, we still have things to sort out anyway."

"How about Tuesday evening? I'll come by about seven?"

"Fine."

We get up and walk the length of the shop. Just before the door, he stops and turns to me. I look up at him and I see him again, my husband, this handsome man who has loved me for more years than he hasn't. I think he's going to kiss me, but he just pulls me close for a warm, enveloping hug. It feels so natural. Our bodies know this moment so well. I can feel that he wants me and I know that if I instigated a kiss it would be welcomed. I don't. He is with Justine, and she is expecting his baby; those are big hurdles to overcome in the race to happy ever after.

As we draw back from each other, he shoots me his beautiful lazy smile.

"I still love you, Ames."

With a brush of my cheek, he turns and walks away, leaving me utterly troubled.

Chapter 38

Sunday is a cold crisp wintery day with clear skies, so I decide to cycle to the hall. Checking my lights are attached for the return trip in the evening's dusk, I mount my faithful sit-up-and-beg bike and head out along the country lanes. My face is being whipped by the biting wind and I'm grateful to have a woolly hat on under my helmet. Hardly a fashion statement, but it stops my ears from dropping off. Once the blood gets pumping around my body, I start to enjoy the ride. My mind flits between Steve and Joshua. With Steve, I wonder if he's just having a wobble, thinking that he loves me again, but I doubt he'll walk out on his pregnant girlfriend. And Joshua, well, he ticks all the right boxes, but is New Zealand-bound before the week is out. As neither are likely suitors, I'm just wasting my energy analysing and overthinking. I need to stop my mind's constant chatter.

Arriving at the hall, I realise that I've left my bike lock at home. Joshua pulls up in his van.

"Good afternoon!" he calls, as he walks towards me.

"Hiya. I've left my lock at home, can I put my bike in the hall, please?"

"Sure, leave it in the corridor," he says, unlocking the door.

"How are ya?" he smiles.

I kid ye not, my knees tremble.

"I'm fine, thanks. I'm ready to nail this dance."

"Good for you! I like a woman with determination. And I promise I won't watch." He closes one eye in jest.

"You have jobs to do!" I reprimand.

"I do indeed, no time to be watching a beautiful ballerina."

I blush under his gaze as we stand together awkwardly not speaking. I'm acutely aware of my thudding heart. I clear my throat.

"Right, best get on. A couple of hours you said, right?"

"Yeah, but no rush. You take your time."

"Thank you."

Once in the hall, I start going through the steps slowly and deliberately. I check the shapes my body is making in the mirror to adjust an arm, my feet, the tilt of my head. Some time later, I plug my iPod into the main speakers and begin the dance. With no one around to observe (I am presuming Joshua has kept to his promise), I allow myself to feel the music and let go totally. In my head, I am on stage performing to an enraptured audience. My technique is far from flawless, but what I lack in accuracy, I make up for in expression and emotion. My heart is in turmoil and this is the perfect outlet. I spin and twirl, losing myself completely in the movements. The music ends as I raise my head to face the mirror with tears falling silently down my face. I see the reflection of Joshua standing at the back of the hall behind me. He swiftly crosses the room and wraps his arms around me. With sobbing shoulders I cling to him.

"Shh shh, now," he comforts. "It's OK, it's alright, I'm here, shh shh..."

I cry harder, so grateful that he's here, so grateful to be cocooned in his arms. Why can't I stay here indefinitely? Even smelling the cleaning fluid on his overalls is somehow comforting. He holds me until my tears subside. As he releases me, I try to calm my juddering breath.

"Sorry. I'm really sorry. I don't know what came over me. I'll be fine really," I gasp, wiping my nose.

"No need for apologies," he says, thumbing away a tear from my cheek.

"I think it was just the hideousness of my dancing that did it," I attempt a joke.

He doesn't laugh.

"It certainly wasn't hideous from where I was standing. It was beautiful. Very moving. I tell you, Amy, if you dance like that on the night, you will do yourself proud."

I want to hug him again.

"Thank you," I reply shyly.

"Do you wanna talk?"

"I do...but do you really wanna listen?"

"Of course I do. Coffee?"

"Not many places open round here on a Sunday," I say thinking aloud. "My place?"

"Sounds good to me."

I pack away my things and retrieve my bike.

"You'll have to give me a head start," I say.

"Or a tow."

I laugh. "Give me ten minutes."

I have rarely pedalled so fast. It's fortunate that I am still warm from dancing and can push the pedals with such ferocity. I need at least two minutes at home alone. Once in, I fly around picking up cups, plumping cushions, hiding the tampon box in the cupboard, hanging up clothes and pulling the duvet over the bed. (The latter strikes me as unnecessary but I acknowledge that my subconscious is at work here.) I haven't time for a shower but I definitely need one, so I will wait for him to arrive and then disappear for a couple of minutes.

Right on cue, he rings the doorbell. I explain that if we are to sit in the same room, then I will need to shower, to which he laughs and offers to make the coffee whilst I cleanse. On my return, feeling scrubbed and shiny, I find him and Basil on the sofa with the sound of The Beatles coming from the stereo. Two coffee mugs and a plate of biscuits are on the side table.

"You found my secret stash of chocolate digestives, eh?"

"Putting them in the biscuit tin is not the best hiding place in the world."

I laugh. "I meant that the biscuit tin was hidden, you numpty!"

"Ah I see, well, just call me nosey 'cos I went in your cupboards. Very neat they are too."

"Inside the cupboards, yes, but outside, not so much. I had to race in here to get it respectable looking." I wonder to myself why I bother doing such things if, at the first given opportunity, I blab about it.

"Well, you didn't need to bother on my account, he says, passing me a coffee. He adjusts his stance to face me. "So what was that all about, back there?"

I take a deep sigh,

"Steve, ex husband, he with the pregnant wench, turned up at my work on Friday. He was in a right mess, crying and telling me that he's not sure he's done the right thing. He says he still loves me. I don't know if something happened with his new woman, but he was looking at me the way he used to look at me. It's just thrown me a bit, that's all."

He looks vaguely disappointed. Was he hoping that it might be his imminent departure that prompted my tears? I can't tell him that in part it is, that he is a factor in my troubled mind. I don't want to put that on him. He needs to be able to leave without being burdened down with my feelings.

"How do you feel about it?" he asks.

"I don't know. That's part of the problem, I suppose. When he left me, I was devastated and would have done anything to get him back. You know, if I could wipe away the past, make like none of it happened, I would be with him. Ignorance really was bliss being that guileless fool who thought everything was rosy in the garden."

"Well, we've all been there," he sighs.

We exchange sad half-smiles.

"But I can't wipe clean the past, can I? He did what he did. He had an affair, got someone else pregnant and left me." My voice wobbles. I don't want to cry any more, I've got no energy. Joshua places his hand on mine.

"Cry, Amy, it's OK," he says, taking my coffee cup and placing it on the side.

I look at his handsome caring face. I lean forward and he places his arms around me again. I cry gentle tears against his chest while he strokes my hair. We gradually recline together on the sofa.

Long after I have finished crying, we're still there, entwined, just listening to our own heartbeats and the sound of The Beatles.

Chapter 39

Opening my eyes, I am momentarily confused. I shift to sit up and rouse him. I have no idea how long we have been there, but from the fading light in the room, we must've been asleep a while.

"Wow, sorry, I didn't mean to fall asleep," I say, rubbing my face. I cannot begin to imagine the vision he sees before him. After so many tears, I must have red eyes and make-up everywhere.

"No worries. I fell asleep too, so I guess we needed it. Just think of us as a couple of toddlers needing their afternoon nap."

"Ha! More like old fogies who nod off in the afternoon."

"How you feeling now?" he asks.

"OK. Better actually. Sometimes a good cry is what you need. Just hope I don't do that in the competition. Nobody likes a cry baby."

He laughs. "What do you wanna do now? I don't know about you, but I'm starving."

"Yeah, me too. I can rustle up something if you like? Spag bol? I have plonk to wash it down with too."

"Now you're tempting me, " he grins.

"I'm just going to nip to the bathroom to freshen up."

"Want me to start chopping? Peeling? Boiling water?"

"All of those, please," I say over my shoulder as I leave the room.

In the kitchen, I find him with my apron on, chopping an onion. He has found another Beatles CD and is swaying in time to 'With A Little Help From My Friends'. I join in as we dance around the small kitchen island. He has already opened the wine, and we stop for a sip or two before restarting the dance and preparing the food. The atmosphere is light and carefree. We are friends, good friends. If he were staying in England then maybe there might be an opportunity to see where this could go, but sadly, that's not to be.

As we sit across from each other at the dining table, our conversation is easy-going. We tease each other, we laugh and I'm sure we're flirting. I am reminded of the age-old question of whether a man and a woman can be just friends. We certainly feel like friends, but didn't that kiss we shared cross a line?

I go to pour him another glass of wine.

"Better not, I'm driving."

"Ah, of course, sorry."

There is a lingering silence as he looks at me.

"I tell you something though, Amy, I don't want to go."

"Then don't." The words come out of my mouth before I have even thought about them. "We're not going to sleep together," I blurt out, back-tracking.

"Well, I don't want to sleep with you."

"Ouch, that hurts!"

"I want to stay awake with you. I'm Steven Tyler."

"Eh?"

"Skinny singer? Big lips?" I'm drawing a blank. "Aerosmith, you heathen!"

With that, he proceeds to sing out of tune. "Don't wanna close my eyes, I don't wanna fall asleep, cos I'd miss you babe, and I don't wanna miss a thing."

I clasp my hands to my ears laughing. "Right, right, I've got it, stop singing!"

Our laughter dies down and he looks at me quizzically.

"What's that look for?" he asks.

"I've finally found that you do have a flaw."

He leans across the table, smiles a sigh and takes my face in his hands. He kisses me softly and slowly. I wonder if the reverberation through my whole body is due to him being my forbidden fruit. Regardless of reason, I let myself enjoy this heady moment. I am disoriented and enchanted in equal part. As we pull away, he stands up, takes my hand, and leads me up to the bedroom. There, he lies down and pats the bed inviting me to join him. I slide next to him and we cuddle up. I pull the throw from the end of the bed up over us and we settle.

The sun sets and rises again as we talk, laugh and, at times, dose off. At one point, he wakes me with a poke in the ribs.

"Uh-oh, you're a blanket hogger."

"I am not!" I protest, but then look to see that I am in fact hogging the majority of the throw. I start to pull the cover over him. "Well at least I'm not a snorer," I harrumph.

"Hey! I have overactive adenoids that have plagued me all my days. It's a sensitive subject, so thanks for bringing it up."

I snort and giggle at him. In turn, he grabs the blanket and wraps himself in it. We tussle until I have regained my half and we settle back comfortably. He kisses my hair.

"What you gonna do, Amy?"

"Get some earplugs and a bigger throw."

He laughs. "You know what I mean."

"About Steve?" I exhale. "I honestly don't know. I spent many years with him. Do I just throw away all of that? I don't know if we can fix what's broken. I'm not even sure if I want to. I guess the main thing is I don't want to end up with regrets."

"D'you know, I don't do regret."

"And how do you manage that?" I ask, turning my face up to look at him.

"I believe that we make our decisions based on where we are at that precise moment in time. We make choices dependent on the situation, how we feel and the things we know to be true. To regret afterwards seems futile, as we couldn't have made a different decision. We can't rewind the clock and choose another option. 'Regret' and 'worry' are stable mates and they're both a complete waste of energy."

"Wow, profound!" I tease. "But you're right," I add seriously. "I do see what you mean, but I suppose my problem is that I really don't know what to do. I'm conflicted."

"Sit with it, Amy, you'll get there."

He squeezes me tightly and we fall silent. Within a few breaths, I hear his overactive adenoids once again.

The next time I awake, the room is bathed in morning sunlight. He is still sleeping and I am happily admiring his unruly hair splayed across the pillow when he opens his eyes.

"What you staring at, Mrs?"

"Something the cat dragged in," I joke.

"Very funny, so sue me...I need my morning beauty regime!" We laugh genially.

Basil, hearing voices, bounds into the room and jumps up at the side of the bed.

"Morning, Basil!" Joshua says, stroking his ears. "Is he allowed?" he asks, gesturing to the bed.

"Most definitely not, but that doesn't stop him. C'mon Bas." I pat the bed and Basil joins us. And there we are, the three of us together and I have a feeling of completeness, a family unit. Reality hits that this is not something that can or will last. As if reading my thoughts, Joshua kisses my forehead and starts to get up.

"Better get going. I still have packing to do."

"Of course. C'mon Bas, let's get up."

"Don't worry, you stay there and have some more kip. I'll see myself out."

He straightens his clothes and nips to the bathroom. A few minutes later, he comes back with his coat over his shoulder. He perches on the side of the bed.

"You know, Amy Ballerina, it's quite simple, you just have to listen to your heart. Take your time, there's no rush and if you really can't walk away from him, then give it another try. What do you have to lose?"

Tears prick my eyes.

"Sorry, please don't cry again," he says stroking my hair. "I know I'm not going to be around, and I wish I was, but you know I'll always be your friend." He smiles and gently play-punches me on the arm. "I've got your back, kiddo."

"I know, thank you."

With a soft pained expression, he kisses me gently, rises and turns to leave. I wait until I hear the clunk of the front door, before I bury my face in the pillow and cry again.

Chapter 40

The trill sound of the phone ringing awakens Sam. The room is in pitch-blackness which can only mean that it's still the middle of the night. As she swings her legs out of bed, a cursory glance at her bedside clock confirms that it's two-thirty. Her gut instinct says that phone calls at this hour are never good news. Racing to her lounge she grabs the receiver.

"Samantha Jones?" A male voice asks.

"Yes." Her heart is beating in her ears.

"It's Jake, Staff Nurse from Mercy Royal Hospital. Your mother has been brought in and has asked us to contact you."

"Oh My God, no! What happened? Is she OK?" She is panicked beyond belief.

"Yes, don't worry, your mother's fine. She's suffered a fall and we're doing some tests. She's in A&E."

"Thank you so much. I'll be there as soon as I can."

Replacing the receiver, Sam races around discarding her nightwear, throwing on the nearest-to-hand clothes and looking for her keys. Throughout the fifteen-minute drive, she considers the worst. Why would her mother fall? What if the cancer has spread further? What if this is the start of the end? She assumes that her mother was alone when she fell and if so, where was her father, the one time he's needed?

Arriving at the hospital, Sam grimly notes that parking spaces are in abundance for middle of the night emergency visits. The cold night air rips through her as she sprints to the A&E reception.

"I'm here to see Cheryl Jones, I'm her daughter," she tells the receptionist, who peers over her glasses to check the screen.

"Bay three, Dear. I'll buzz you through."

The curtains are pulled around the bay and Sam hesitates, listening for voices behind them. There are none. She peeps through the curtain to find her mother, almost the same colour as the white sheets she lies on, sleeping. Part of her head is covered with a wide cream bandage and her cheek sports a large bruise.

"Oh, Mum," she says softly.

Just then, a man appears beside her.

"Ah, are you a relative?" the young medic asks.

"Yes, I'm her daughter."

"Right. We're running some tests on your mother. We're not quite sure why she collapsed so we're keeping her in for observation. We'll be transferring her to a ward shortly - just waiting for a bed to be free."

"OK, thank you."

With not another word, he leaves. Sam silently curses that she didn't ask what kind of tests they were running and whether this is all linked to her mother's cancer. In fact, the questions start to crowd her mind as her mother opens her eyes.

"Hiya, Mum."

"Hello, Love," she says wearily.

"What happened?"

"I don't know. I was talking to your father..."

"Dad was with you?"

"Yes, he phoned the ambulance."

"Where is he now?"

"Oh you know him, he doesn't like hospitals. I came round at home and he saw me onto the ambulance."

"That was kind," Sam mutters under her breath, once again disappointed in her father and feeling justified in her suspicion that he is trying to side-line her. Why else would he not have phoned Sam himself? Didn't he want Samantha to know that her mother is in the hospital?

Cheryl gives her daughter a dark look but chooses to ignore the comment.

"Anyway, like I said, I was talking to him and the next thing I knew, I was flat on the floor. By the way my head feels, I must've hit it on the fireplace as I went down."

"Oh, Mum." Sam squeezes her hand, feeling nothing but flesh and bone.

"Has the doctor been round?" her mother weakly asks.

"Yes, they're keeping you in for observation. They're just waiting for a free bed and then they'll take you up to a ward."

"Good, that gives us a little time to talk."

"Talk? About what?" Sam asks warily.

"I was awoken the other night by a very loud banging front door."

Sam inwardly cringes. She wants to say many things to her mother but she's unprepared for a cards-on-the-table discussion right now.

"Would you like to tell me what it was about?" her mother persists, matter of factly.

"What did *he* say it was about?" asks Sam.

"Nah-ah – I want to know from you."

Sam sighs. "I suppose you could say that I'm having trouble acclimatising to him being back on the scene."

"Nicely put. You should be a lawyer, my girl." She pauses. "What is it about your father being around that upsets you so much?"

"I'm just not sure I trust him." Sam chooses her words carefully; she's acutely aware of the volatile nature of this conversation. One wrong word and they could be falling out at a time when they should be at their closest.

"I see. And what exactly don't you trust about him?" Her even voice barely covers the underlying tone of severity. Should Sam impart that she suspects her father is wooing her mother to claim financial reward? Can she take the risk of hurting her mother? Would it not be simpler to lie? "Come on, Sam, we've been close for too long for us not to be honest with each other. We've always told the truth, haven't we?"

Sam takes a deep breath.

"You're still married to him, right?" Her mother nods. "So he is legally entitled to your estate, isn't he?"

"Money, Samantha?! This is about money?!" Her hackles are up.

"No, Mum, no, it's not about money. It's about him taking you for a fool."

As soon as the words leave her mouth, she wants to press rewind and delete. "No, I don't mean that you're a fool, what I meant was…"

"I know exactly what you meant, Samantha, and I have to say I'm disappointed in you. You think I'm some blind fool being taken for a ride! Well thank you for the vote of confidence and for thinking so little of me!" Her cheeks are gaining colour from her anger. "And you know what, My Girl, I never would've taken you for someone who had their eye on the money!"

Her mother's disappointment crushes Sam like a lead weight.

"No, Mum, I haven't. I didn't mean it like that. Honestly, I'm just thinking of you, that's all."

"And what you'll get from me after I'm gone." Her mother's words spill out.

Sam decides it's time to stop talking. She doesn't want to upset her mother any further; in fact, she wants to erase the whole conversation. Her mother's angry eyes are brimming with tears.

"I'm sorry, Mum. It's all been a lot to take in, that's all."

There's a stiff silence, a stalemate in what is usually a loving mother and daughter relationship. Her mother's lips are set rigid and Sam feels like the world's worst daughter. Even in his absence, her father is the instigator of this altercation.

A ward orderly appears at the curtain.

"Mrs Jones?" she says, looking at Cheryl's plastic hospital bracelet. "Right, Lovey, you're coming with me to Grafton ward. Let's get you up there."

Cheryl smiles weakly.

"I'm coming with you, Mum." Sam says.

Averting her eyes, her mother nods her acquiescence.

Once on the ward, Sam opts for conversations that don't feature her father. They make pleasantries and skirt around topics. It's exhausting, and Sam eventually decides to make sure that her mother has all that she needs and bows out. They kiss goodbye and Sam leaves promising to return the following day with a few hospital essentials.

Sam heads along the corridor to the lift, breathing a large sigh of relief. What makes this whole situation worse is that her father comes out of it smelling of roses yet again – the angel to her devil. Riddled with guilt from upsetting her mother, she wonders whether she should be the bigger person and call her father to let him know how and where her mother is. She is scrolling through her phone contacts as the lift doors open. Inside stands an orderly with a frail looking bruised old lady in a wheelchair with her head in her hands. Sam steps in, still searching for her father's number. As the lift descends, the old lady lifts her head and their eyes meet. For the second time in twenty-four hours, Sam is shocked to her core.

The old lady is Marion.

Chapter 41

Upon recognising Sam, tears spring forth, running down Marion's bruised, cut face. Sam takes her hand and Marion winces.

"My God, Marion, what happened?"

Marion looks down, unable to speak.

"You're not telling, are you, Love?" The orderly says, putting his hand reassuringly on Marion's shoulder. He turns his attention to Sam. "You know her?"

"Yes, we dance together."

Sam kneels down next to the wheelchair.

"Marion, please, what happened?"

Marion raises her head, her eyes filled with pain and defeat. Sam gets a nasty feeling that she knows exactly what's happened and exactly why Marion isn't talking; it's common knowledge amongst the ballet crowd.

Sam turns to the orderly. "Where's she going?"

"To X-ray and then we're putting her on Parker ward. They want to get to the bottom of what happened." He lowers his voice somehow assuming that as Marion isn't speaking, she isn't hearing properly either. "The authorities will be called."

Marion lowers her head again.

"Can I stay with you?" Sam asks them both.

"Don't see why not, she's got no one else here," he replies.

Sam sits in the X-ray waiting area. Marion is physically damaged, but more telling is her inability or her unwillingness to speak about what has occurred. Whatever she has been through, she needs the support of her friends around her. With that, Sam walks to the hospital entrance and composes a group text to the Dixbury Dollies.

Hi guys. Sorry to give you bad news, but just bumped into Marion at the hospital. She's in a bad way – bruised and cut. She's in x-ray at the mo, but will be transferred to Parker ward afterwards. I'm with her, but if anyone fancies joining, please do. Love, Sam x

Hitting 'Send', she walks back to the waiting area. She idly browses the pile of last year's magazines, but can't focus. Could Jack be responsible for Marion's injuries? Did he finally lose it? Surely the reason that Marion isn't talking is that she's protecting him? Sam doesn't want to be judgemental and knows little about domestic abuse, but why would anyone stay with someone who is capable of doing that? Isn't a relationship supposed to be about mutual love and caring? Why share life with someone who causes unhappiness? Samantha shakes her head. She's not naïve enough to believe things are that straightforward. We're complicated beings who fall in love and can disastrously end up at the mercy of our chosen loved one. And if we're told on a daily basis that we're not worthy, we eventually believe it. The self-esteem exits but the person remains.

"You look far away," a voice interrupts her thoughts. She looks up to see Jason, the Physio standing before her.

"Oh yeah, I was. Hi! How are you?"

"I'm good, thanks. I was just picking up some notes on a patient."

"I thought you worked at your dad's practice?"

"Part-time there and part-time here. I like the private work, but my heart belongs to the NHS," he smiles. He must be over six feet tall and Sam strains her neck to look up at him. He is schoolboy gangly, with geeky black square glasses and floppy mid brown hair. He oozes an innocent charm and her heart warms to him once again. "So what you doing here?" he asks.

"A friend of mine is just having X-rays," she says, nodding her head backwards towards the room where Marion is. "She's in a bit of a state."

"Oh, I'm sorry, hope she's OK."

"Thank you, so do I. She's not looking good, and won't say what's happened to her. I'm trying not to put two and two together to make five."

Jason takes a seat next to Sam.

"What do you mean?"

Sam hesitates. She hardly knows Jason and doesn't want to create the impression of being a gossip.

"Sorry...you don't have to tell me," he quickly adds.

"No, it's OK, let's just say that her marriage isn't the best. I don't want to jump to conclusions though."

"Probably best," he says. "So anyway, how are your neck/shoulders/back?"

"Good, thanks."

"You gonna come back or did I cure you?" he laughs.

"Definitely cured!" she lies.

"So, you all fit and ready for that competition?"

Sam is flattered that he remembers.

"Yes, you should come along – 31st December at Dixbury Playhouse."

"OK, I think I will. I haven't been to Dixbury Does Talent for years!" he grins nervously. Sam finds his awkward youthful manner very appealing.

"Great, should be a good night!"

Just then, the door swings open and the orderly wheels out Marion.

"OK, that's my friend, I'd better go. Nice seeing you, Jason."

"You too. Hope to see you at the competition."

"Yeah, see ya!"

Sam catches up with Marion and the orderly, and they make their way up to Parker ward. Transferred into a bed, Marion looks smaller and infinitely more vulnerable. The white of one of her eyes is bloodshot red and the skin around it is turning a deep purple. Her hands have wounds that have been tended and covered. Of all her injuries, the shapes of finger marks indented into Marion's neck make Sam recoil. The orderly leaves and Sam draws the curtain around them and pulls up a chair.

"Marion, talk to me please. How are you?"

Marion's face oozes shame and sorrow. "Not great."

Jack has literally taken her voice, as it's barely audible.

"Oh Marion, you must tell them what happened. Did he do this to you?"

Sam can see the conflict in Marion's eyes. She is clearly on the cusp of wanting to tell her story, but at the same time is rapidly calculating consequences. If she has two voices battling to be heard, the voice of truth finally wins.

"He's not a bad man, you know," she croaks. "He just has a temper..." She puts her hand to her throat and tries to swallow. Her pain is evident. She is trembling and Sam places a steadying hand on her. "I've always accepted that it's just him, that the man I chose, my husband, has a foul temper..." She pauses to swallow again, the fear rising in her face. "But this time, Samantha, I thought he was going to kill me...he was out of control, blacked out, I think."

Sam has to lean in closely to hear Marion's wavering voice.

"I don't know if he even knows what he did."

"What did he do?"

"One minute he was fine, rational, drinking a cup of tea. The next, he threw the cup, and started hitting me..." Marion is steady and stoic, "...I tried to fight back but he overpowers me every time. But this time was different, he had his hands around my throat, his eyes were bulging. Over and over, he kept saying that I'd be sorry."

"Sorry for what?"

"For going to class, for wanting to compete in Dixbury Does Talent."

Sam's heart breaks for her sweet kindly friend who only wants to dance.

Marion doesn't shed a tear.

A nurse appears around the curtain.

"Marion," she kindly says. "The police and Social Services are here to see you."

With an expression of resolute determination Marion uses all her physical effort to force out her words with clarity.

"Please show them in."

Chapter 42

I'm intrigued to be meeting Steve but, in all honesty, I would rather be visiting Marion. After receiving Sam's initial text, I felt scared that Jack might be the culprit of Marion's injuries and then, judging by the following texts, it seems, sadly, I was right. The last message received said that Marion had talked to the police and Social Services. She has spoken out against her bully of a husband. I am overwhelmed with pride.

My internal monologue about deciding what to wear is off the scale. How do you want to look when meeting a long-term love who left you heartbroken but is back proclaiming his love again? I want that 'I'm OK without you and look what you're missing' look, mixed with a perfume that sparks memories of times together. I'm running late, so the decision has to be made pronto, and I wonder whether all decisions should be made quickly? Maybe I shouldn't ponder over facts, but just go with my gut instinct? It might resolve the relentless internal conflict I'm dealing with on a daily basis.

Applying make-up in the mirror, I stop and ask myself the question of all questions:

If it were a perfect world – what would happen?

My immediate response is that Steve would happily give me the house and we'd find peace and closure. Joshua would stay and we'd date, and I would dance to rave reviews at Dixbury Does Talent.

What are the chances of any of those happening?

Steve arrives on time and it's obvious that, in his effort to please, he's spent a long time getting ready. He looks scrubbed to within an inch of his life and he's even wearing the blue checked shirt that I used to like on him. As he leans in to kiss me on the cheek, I catch the familiar whiff of Tom Ford aftershave. He's evidently had the same idea as me as it's *the* scent that I identify with him.

"OK, where we off to?" I ask. Before he answers, I know his response.

"Da Vinci's." We both say together and laugh.

This is going to be a pulling-on-the-heartstrings trip down memory lane.

Arriving at the well-heeled Italian restaurant, the maître d' greets us warmly.

"Mr and Mrs Gathergood, so lovely to see you again. Welcome, welcome."

We haven't been together for so long that it jars to hear someone call us 'Mr and Mrs.' "I have the table you requested," he says, smiling at Steve.

We walk through the white table-clothed, dimly lit bistro to the far corner. It is the most privately positioned table in the entire place and it used to be 'our table'. Throughout our twelve years together, we spent many happy evenings here, dining on delicious Linguine Vongole, Tiramisu and washing it down with a nice bottle of Chianti. Sometimes, if we were feeling flush, we would round it all off with a couple of Limoncellos. Happy days indeed...

The waiter takes our drinks order and leaves us to peruse the menu.

"This is nice, isn't it?" Steve asks. The soft candlelight accentuates his handsome face, a face I know so well, one I was supposed to look at for the rest of my life.

"It is. It hasn't changed much, has it?" I say, looking around.

"No. I'd like to say the same about us."

"Yeah, well, that wouldn't be quite true, would it?" I say flatly.

"I don't know. I do know that I have been through some stuff but I'm out the other side."

"What do you mean?"

"Look..."

Just then, the notoriously quick serving waiter brings our drinks. We used to laugh at the speed that this man works; it's like he's permanently on fast-forward. He takes our order, smiles and leaves.

"Speedy Gonzalez is still here then!" Steve says. We laugh and then fall silent.

"You were saying?" I prompt.

"I thought that Justine was my future." Steve sighs. "I'm not sure now. I think you and me lost our way a bit, but Ames..." he says, placing his hand on mine. "I want us to try again. I miss you."

"Really Steve? What about the fact that she's carrying your baby?"

"Ah," he looks down. "It would appear that I'm not the only one Justine has dallied with."

"Ah, I see. And how did you find that out?"

"A knock on the door a couple of weeks ago and it's some guy called Mitch who feels the need to tell me the baby's his."

"Oh Steve, I'm so sorry."

He's the dog that left me – why am I sorry?

"When she came home, we had it out, and it seems that Justine doesn't quite know *who* the father is."

"So what happens now? Please tell me you're not going for DNA testing on Jeremy Kyle!"

"No, nothing as drastic as that," he laughs. "I packed my bags and left. I'm staying at Rob and Anita's 'til I find a flat."

I stare into my glass with an unsettling inkling.

"I know what you're thinking," he says. "And this isn't why I want you back now. I was having these feelings even before I found out about the baby. Justine and me, we just weren't right. It's you, Ames, it's always been you. I've been an idiot and I want to spend the rest of my life making it up to you."

He gives me his best puppy dog eyes; it's a look that used to turn me to putty in his hands. I'm taken aback by everything he's told me, but I'm not going to respond with a snap decision. Despite my earlier musings that quick decisions are the way to go, in reality, I'm not going to rush into anything. I do, however, have a burgeoning feeling of power. From being the helpless victim, I now feel that the scales are tipping. He is wanting me to choose him. I've never been a vengeful person, but there's a satisfying glow in my belly that this man, who abandoned me, is now the one on his knees. It is the karma that I have longed for.

Our food arrives and our conversation diverts to memories of good meals, bad meals and times when we might have drunk a little too much. We could spend many happy hours reminiscing over all the moments we've shared. But what about the future? We can't build a future based on remembering the past. Or should I see this as the transitional period that will transport us to the next stage of our lives together, 'Amy and Steve, Part Two?'

Looking at him, I feel a warm strong tug on my heart. He was my 'forever man' and I loved him with a passion. As a firm believer of choosing to love your partner, I could easily summon up the appropriate feelings to be in love with him again. The only question is whether we can rebuild the trust between us? Or moreover – as it wasn't me who broke it – can he restore my faith in him?

Finishing the last drops of wine and wiping my hands on the napkin, I readdress the issue.

"What we were talking about earlier, Steve..."

He looks up with nothing but hope on his face.

"I'm going to need some time. A lot has happened and it's not a decision I can make over a bowl of pasta."

"Two bowls then?"

"No, Steve!" I laugh. "You just have to give me some time. I do think what we had could be salvageable, but I think you need to woo me...and court me. I need to be able to trust you again, and that's going to take effort from you and time for me."

He looks so pleased that I wonder what he heard. Did I just say that we are getting back together again? I suppose in a way I did. I have just given him permission to date me.

"No promises, Steve," I add quickly. "We take it one day at a time, right?"

"Suits me...for now," he says with a determined glint in his eye. I know that look too well. He's a man who likes to get what he wants. He squeezes my hand affectionately. "I will be the best I can be, Ames. I'll prove to you that you can trust me again, that all that happened was a stupid blip. I swear I'll do everything I can to get us back on track. I love you, Ames."

His eyes are fiery and passionate, and I know his intent is true. My heart should be dancing with anticipation of my future happiness with the man I have loved for many years. So why am I left with a worrying feeling that the scales have just tipped again? And not in my favour.

Chapter 43

"That's wonderful, People, just beautiful," says Helena, clapping and smiling. "It's really coming together and I'm so proud of you all." Her eyes scan the room and land on me. "I know you're all putting in a lot of effort to make this work."

I smile.

"OK, right," she continues. "The plan for the rest of this session is to keep running through the dance. But each time, the focus will be different. So starting positions again, please, and this time we'll concentrate on arms. I want to see soft arms that are being held from your backs. No hunched shoulders, no tension in the neck, OK?"

We all happily take our positions, excited to be only three weeks away from the big night and eager to keep honing the dance to perfection.

In the absence of Marion, we have to leave a space in our formation. In Prayers and Pains, Sam filled us in on what happened at the hospital. We all listened intently. My fellow dancers' faces show care and compassion for our missing friend, once again reminding me that although we came together as disparate souls wanting to dance, we have bonded into a tightly-knit clan. We all have our foibles, we fall out from time to time, but we have a camaraderie that can't be broken.

We run through the dance repeatedly with the changes in focus. After the fourth time, we are making mistakes and with an hour still to go, Helena, in an unprecedented move, gives us a ten-minute break. Heading for towels and water, I catch up with Gloria.

"How's it going, Glo?"

"Apart from the emergency dental appointment yesterday, all is sunny," she smiles.

"Oh no, toothache?"

"'Kind of. I cooked myself a lasagne and it was more crunchy than al dente, and I cracked a back tooth. Luckily, there was no pain. My dentist is a dear. He fitted me in and sorted it out."

"Oh I'm glad that story has a happy ending."

Gloria looks at me quizzically. "Funny you should say that. The night that I broke it, I could feel it in my mouth, still attached but not whole. It got me thinking about life in general."

"Wow, Gloria, a tooth made you think about the meaning of life?" I tease good-naturedly.

"Ha ha, not exactly. As children, we lose our first teeth, don't we?"

I nod.

"Then we have our adult teeth and that's it for the rest of our lives. We don't grow more teeth. There I was, sitting there with my dying tooth, one that will never be replaced and it hit me, yet again, that life really is short. That lost tooth represented a part of me that is gone. And one day, I'll be gone."

"Not for a long time, I hope!" I interject. She smiles, shrugging her shoulders.

"So running my tongue around that cracked tooth, I made the choice to live my life. I've been making myself feel guilty for having feelings for Brian when I should be grieving for Stanley, but no more. Stanley loved me and that means he would want me to be happy, and what makes me happy now is being with Brian."

"I like your thinking, Gloria. You deserve happiness." I squeeze her arm. "Have you told Brian yet?"

"We had a little chat last night. I think he was rather pleased," she blushes.

"I'll bet he was."

"OK, back to the grindstone, folks." Helena claps her hands, putting an end to our happy interlude.

I hook Gloria's arm as we make our way back to the dance floor.

***

After more chatting and giggling on the journey home about Gloria's new determination to seize the day, I arrive at my house exhausted, sweaty and a little disappointed not to have seen Joshua at the end of class. I'm acutely aware that he leaves in the early hours of the morning to catch his flight and I wanted to wish him well in person. Instead I decide to text him.

Hiya. Was hoping to see you tonight at the hall. Wanted to wish you all the best for your trip. Really hope things work out for you. Thank you so much for supporting me in the last few weeks – I really appreciate you being there for me. Keep in touch – I will add you on FB – promise! Love, Amy xx

Just as I am about to hit 'Send', there is a knock on the door. My stomach flips at the thought that it might be Joshua and, opening the door, it does a double somersault, as it is the very man himself.

"Hiya! I was just texting you," I beam.

"Ah well, I saved you the cost of a text."

"Come in, come in, it's so nice to see you."

We go through to the lounge and he takes a seat on the sofa.

"Can I get you a drink? Coffee, tea, water, wine?"

"No, I'm fine thanks. I won't stay long, I'm actually on my way to my dad's. He's taking me to the airport. You have to be there three hours early, and seeing as my flight is at stupid o'clock, I've got to leave around now. Why were you texting me?"

"Just to say I hoped to see you at the hall tonight. I wanted to wish you luck and say goodbye."

"Right, thanks."

"I also said that I'd add you on Facebook."

"Wow, didn't realise our relationship had got that serious!" he jokes.

As ever, our laughter comes readily and we relax easily into each other's company.

"So how do you feel on the cusp of your great adventure?"

"Mixed, I guess. Excited, nervous, scared, a bit sad."

"A bit sad?"

To be leaving me?

"To be leaving friends and family."

"Ah, I see."

"How are you anyway? Made any life changing decisions yourself?" he asks.

"Well, I met up with Steve and he wants us to try again, so we kind of agreed to date."

I think I catch a flash of disappointment in his eyes but it passes too quickly to be sure.

"I'm really pleased for you, Amy. I hope it works out."

"So do I. He seems pretty determined to get back together."

"He must really want you if he can leave his pregnant woman."

"Oh, oh no, it turns out she wasn't totally faithful to him and there's a big question mark over the baby's father." I then quickly add, "But he says that he wanted me back before he found that out."

I realise that I'm sounding defensive and don't quite understand why.

"I'm sure he did, he'd be a fool not to."

There he goes again – making me blush with his compliments.

"Thank you, Joshua. And thank you for being my friend when I most needed one. You've helped me a lot through these past weeks."

We smile and he stands up.

"Well, I'd better get off. I just wanted to say goodbye. I hope things work out for you, I really do."

218

We walk to the front door. He turns and gives me a warm, gentle embrace.

"I'm gonna miss you," he says.

"Me too."

"You don't have to miss you as you'll be with you."

I laugh and playfully punch his shoulder.

"You fool!"

"Ow, that hurt!" he says, holding his shoulder in jest.

"Good."

Holding my gaze, he lifts my chin and kisses me lightly on the lips.

"Take care, Amy Ballerina."

"You too, Joshua Handyman."

He walks to his van and doesn't look back.

Chapter 44

Since Marion is still in hospital, the 'Dixbury Dollies' agree an unofficial rota of visiting. They don't want Marion to be alone. Samantha is the most frequent visitor as she can combine seeing Marion either before or after she sees her mother, who isn't actually faring so well. Tests to indicate why she collapsed are, so far, inconclusive, whereas Marion is making sure but steady progress.

Julay and Lucia are down for visiting Marion, so they meet at the hospital entrance and make their way up to Parker ward.

"Hiya, Mazza," Lucia says, smiling through a bunch of petrol station flowers.

"Hello there!" Marion responds brightly. Her face is still swollen and bruised, but her eye is no longer bloodshot, which means she looks more human and less zombie. "How lovely to see you! You ballet girls certainly look after me," she smiles.

"We're trying to," Julay says. "How you feeling?"

"Better all the time, thanks. Still aching all over, but I'm lucky not to have any broken bones. They should be letting me out soon."

Julay wonders where Marion will go, but intuitively feels it would be insensitive and an invasion of her privacy to ask. Lucia has no such qualms.

"Where you gonna go? You can't go back to Jack, can you? Is he still banged up?" she asks.

"They charged him yesterday with assault and he's out on bail," she says with a worried look. "Social Services are helping me find somewhere, like a women's refuge, you know..."

"Oh no they won't!" Julay says with such force that both Lucia and Marion turn to her in surprise. "You won't be going to any refuge! You'll be coming home with me! I've got a spare room and you're welcome to it for as long as you need it."

"That's very kind of you, Julay, but..." Marion starts.

"Yeah, nice one Ju," Lucia interrupts.

"...but I can't take you up on that, it's too much... I'd get in your way. But I'm very touched by your kindness, thank you."

"Nonsense, Woman!" Julay continues. "You have no home. I have a spare room. You will come to stay. End of."

"But really..." Marion protests.

"Really what, Marion? You don't have a roof over your head because of your pig of a husband. You shouldn't have to be in a refuge, you should be returning to your own home, but with the way things are, *he* is there and you are the one out on the street. It's unfair beyond belief." With cheeks turning red and fists starting to clench, she continues. "You'll have to wait and see what happens in court, and see if they get enough evidence to prosecute him. Or, worst case, they make you out to be a liar. Or turn it all around to make it look like you provoked him. And then...will the judge be lenient and give him a measly six month sentence? Will you always be wondering if he's waiting for you around the next corner? Will you always be living in fear, feeling vulnerable?"

Lucia and Marion are open-mouthed at Julay's outburst. Where did that come from?

Marion leans forward and takes Julay's hand.

"Who are we talking about, Dear, me or you?"

Julay's lip quivers. Visibly she tries to regain some self-control and taking a deep breath she says,

"Sorry, it was a long time ago, a friend of mine, Marilyn, her name was. Her husband was a horribly mean man, cruel beyond belief. I watched her go through hell. In the end, he went too far, split her jaw. Police arrested him; it went to court, only

222

for him to get a six-month sentence. Then he was back on the street."

"Where is she now?" Lucia asks.

"Like I said, it was a long time ago...fifteen years or so, and she died two years ago." Her eyes cloud over. "After he went to prison, she came to live with me where she lived for the rest of her life. He didn't touch her again but she lived with the fear of him everyday." Realising that telling Marion all of this wasn't the most sensitive thing to do, Julay quickly retracts. "But she was a different sort of woman to you, Marion, you won't cower from life."

"So you lived with her for all those years?" Lucia asks.

Julay blushes. "Yes I did."

There's a small silence.

"Thank you, Julay, I'd love to take you up on your kind offer, but only until I find my own place. I won't overstay my welcome, I promise."

"Done," Julay says and they shake hands, smiling.

"So when you back doing pirouettes, fouettés and those big jumps again?" Lucia teases, moving her arms in a balletic fashion.

"That might be a while. I'd love to be a part of the competition but it might have to be behind the scenes...the dresser maybe?"

"Well, we've still got three weeks, you might be fit for it by then," Julay says. "But anyway, we're planning a night out before then, on the twenty-second, a Christmas meal, you must come to that."

"Sounds good, lucky I've got my appetite back," Marion smiles.

"Is it partners for the meal or just us?" Lucia asks.

"Lucia, why do you ask? Do you actually have a partner to bring?" Julay bristles.

For once Lucia is coy.

"Maybe."

"Go on then, tell us about the latest unfortunate." Julay rolls her eyes.

"Look, I don't want anyone to judge me…"

"Dear, I don't think I'm in any position to judge anyone," Marion says.

"Fair point."

Marion snorts, being momentarily taken aback by Lucia's honesty.

"He's old, " Lucia says, burying her head in her hands.

"Old? How old are we talking?" Julay asks.

"Old, like you."

Julay sniffs. "Ancient then!"

"We look like grandfather and granddaughter…"

"Good grief, Lucia, how old *is* he?" Julay asks.

"Forty-two."

"OK, let's think about the maths here," Julay starts sarcastically.

"He's not old enough to be your grandfather, Dear." Marion soothes. "Do you like him?"

"You see, that's the thing, I really do. I joked about going out with fellas who are different and I've done it – I've got me an old boy and I really like him!"

"Then age doesn't come into it. You just enjoy yourself."

"If his disability buggy is fixed, I'll bring him along to the meal," Lucia cackles.

"If his disability buggy's fixed, I'd like to borrow it!" Marion laughs.

"Right, shall we find a doctor and find out exactly when you're getting out of here?" Julay asks.

"Yes, please," Marion smiles. Looking at her friends, she realises that, for the first time in ages, she is undoubtedly filled with hope.

Chapter 45

I'm making Chilli in the kitchen whilst Steve is in the lounge, lighting candles and choosing music.

"What do you fancy?" he calls through.

"Erm, something jolly...how about McFly?"

"Really? I'm not feeling the Mcfly boys." With that, he puts on U2.

Why bother asking if he doesn't want my opinion?

"Dinner will be about twenty minutes, OK?" I call out.

He walks into the kitchen and puts his arms around me. My gut instinct tells me that it doesn't feel right; it's just too soon.

"Steve, we're taking things slowly, OK?"

"So I'm not allowed to touch you?"

"Let's just have dinner and talk. Please?"

"OK. Your rules." He holds his hands up submissively.

I try steering the conversation in a less contentious direction. "How's work?" I know that the bookings of a painter/decorator have peaks and troughs.

"It's OK, plenty of jobs on at the mo, lots of houses need decorating, especially just before Christmas. How's the shop?"

"Good. Same for me. The run up to Christmas is busy as usual. I never quite understand why people want their hair coiffured for Christmas Day. Of all the days of the year, it's the one you're most likely to spend indoors with your family, no?"

"...looking at your painted walls."

"Ha! Exactly!"

"You see, I sort their houses and you sort their hair, and then they have a great Christmas. We always were the best team." He dips a spoon into the Chilli.

"Oi, get your snout out! I'm the cook here, and we're not a team in the kitchen...not with your culinary skills anyway." His lack of expertise in the kitchen was legendary. "I don't suppose you've improved, have you?"

"Nah, never will either." He looks shamed.

"I'll never forget that roast you did." I laugh at the memory.

"Some people like black roasted parsnips and carrots!"

"Some people maybe, but not me."

"Well, you've always been fussy."

"Excuse me, Mr 'Don't-Put-Cream-On-The-Pie-I-like-It-In-A-Separate-Dish' Gathergood."

"Hey, I can't help it if I like what I like."

We hold each other's smiles.

It's like we are finding our rhythm again. Our conversation, much like a ping pong match, bats back and forth jovially. When he left me, all those months ago, I was heartbroken and could barely function. The bond between us felt severed, and now, here together, we have a chance to reconnect. We can't spend time analysing and poring over old wounds, we need to move forward with this different version of us. I think about advertisements that rebrand products as 'new and improved.' I always feel it implies that the first version wasn't as good as it should have been. Is this what we are to become – the 'new and improved Amy and Steve'?

With dinner out of the way, I take the plates to the kitchen to clear up. Steve, once again, is the chooser of music. As I plunge my hands into the soapy water, I hear the strains of 'A Hard Days Night' coming from the lounge. Memories of Joshua flash before me as my heart jolts. I don't know if I can bear listening to The Beatles without him here. It was the soundtrack to our woefully short relationship. I hear Steve singing along and I desperately want him to stop. I am surprised to find my heart hurting. If Steve and I are to make a go of it, shouldn't I tell him about Joshua? If I did, what would I say? That we spent a night together fully clothed and kissed a few times? It's not actually what we did that prevents me from telling – it's the feelings I'm harbouring. But if I'm expecting honestly from Steve, then surely I need to be honest with him.

Wiping my hands on a tea towel, I walk into the lounge. Steve is reading the CD cover. I sit next to him and take it out of his hands.

"Steve, if we are going to build anything between us, then we need to be honest, don't we?"

"I have been!" he starts defensively.

"No, no, I'm not talking about you…"

His eyebrows rise. "You've got something you want to get off your chest?"

"Yes, just so we have a clean slate, I think you should know that I became friends with a guy in the last couple of months."

"Friends?"

"Yes, friends. He sort of supported me."

"Supported you."

"Steve, yes, you don't have to repeat everything I say." He looks hurt and I want to wipe that away. I want my words to convince him that I haven't betrayed him. "He is, erm, *was* the caretaker, well the handyman, at the hall where I dance. We struck up a friendship and went out once and spent some time together, that's all."

"I see. Did you sleep with him?"

I want to say 'no, we stayed awake all night 'cos he's Steven Tyler', but I refrain.

"No, I didn't." I look him squarely in the eyes so he can read my truth. "We did kiss, but that was all. He already had plans to move to New Zealand, which is where he is now, so it was never going to be a relationship. We were just friends."

"Ah, OK. So let me just get this straight…all the time you were crying about me being unfaithful, you weren't exactly squeaky clean yourself?"

"That's slightly different, Steve!" I splutter. "You had an affair whilst we were still together. I struck up a friendship and had a couple of kisses after you left me. It's not the same thing!"

He lowers his head. He knows I'm right but I can see that my admission has hurt him. I lean forward and touch his leg,

"I was crushed when you left me, Steve. I wasn't looking for anyone else and he was a kind friend to me. He left for New Zealand a few days ago and wished us all the best. He hopes we can work it out."

Despite my 'no touching' rule, I lean forward, put my arms around him and kiss him. The way he holds me, the feel of his lips, and the way our bodies pull together is comfortingly familiar. As he pulls away, his voice is gravelly.

"He's definitely not coming back?"

I shake my head and move nearer again, back into his arms.

Chapter 46

Samantha arrives at the Grafton ward with the usual newspaper and hard-boiled sweets for her mother. The wide pine veneer doors swing open as she walks towards the semi-circular reception. Being a regular visitor, and on friendly terms with the staff, she usually stops for a chat. Today is no different, but as she approaches, she catches Staff Nurse Jane asking a question of the receptionist.

"What's the name on file for Cheryl Jones' next of kin, please?"

The receptionist looks up to see Samantha, a few feet away from the desk, standing statue-like, frozen still. Jane immediately runs around the desk and whisks her off to a private room.

It's one of those box rooms that hospitals have for delivering bad news to families. They paint them in pale colours and hang bright flowered curtains. There are six wooden chairs with comfortable deep cushions and Jane seats Samantha in one and pulls up another to face her.

"Why are you needing my mother's next of kin?" she asks shakily, already knowing the answer.

"I'm so sorry, Sam, your mother died this morning," Jane imparts in a clear even tone.

"What?! How?" It's beyond Sam's comprehension. "I only saw her yesterday and she was fine. What happened?"

"You know her cancer was advanced?" Sam nods. "Well, sometimes, with all the extra pressure that the body takes from the cancer and the treatment, the heart just can't cope. She had a heart attack earlier today. We did all we could, but we couldn't resuscitate her. I'm very sorry."

Samantha wails the high pitch sound of an animal in pain, a raw piercing noise that alerts all in the immediate area that she is bereaved. Jane cradles her in her arms. With running nose and streaming tears, Sam tries to speak.

"But...I never got to tell her..." Big shuddering sobs make her words difficult to decipher.

"What's that?"

"I didn't tell her...I'm sorry..."

"Shh... shh... what do you have to be sorry for?"

"We had a fight. We didn't sort it out properly. Now I'll never be able..." Sam dissolves into giant racking tears again.

"Samantha, your mum knew you loved her," Jane says squeezing Sam's shoulders. "She talked about you all the time, you know. She was very proud of you."

Samantha nods, wiping her nose and eyes. She wants to believe Jane's comforting words but her all-consuming pain renders her incapable of thinking logically.

"Would you like a cup of tea?" Jane asks. "And is there anyone else we can call for you?"

"Yes, please, and yeah, could you call my father, please?"

***

An hour or so later, Sam's father arrives at the ward, looking ruffled and upset. They hug briefly. The staff leave them in the plain, box room with the door blinds pulled, telling them to 'take all the time they need'.

"I can't believe it, Love," her father says with shaking hands.

"Me neither. I only saw her yesterday and she was doing so well."

He looks down.

"I hadn't seen her. We'd been texting but I just can't do hospitals. Spent too long in one myself and can't face them."

"Yes, Mum told me."

"What happens now?"

"I don't know. They let me see her earlier. She looked so peaceful. Sorry, did you want to see her?"

He shudders at the thought. "Eurgh, no! That's the last thing I want to do."

"Of course."

Even being her sole parent, her father still doesn't endear himself to her. She can't help thinking that if he really loved her mother, he would have put aside his issues, manned up and visited her in hospital. She does, however, understand his reluctance to see her mother's dead body, but his contorted face, at the thought of it, is repugnant. After the dust settles, the plans of cutting ties from this man still stand. Sam looks across at him, biting his fingernails, and she contemplates what makes a father. It certainly isn't the person who is part of the physical act of making a baby, that's for sure. A father is constant, caring, loving and present, and that is most definitely not him.

"Are you heading back to Derby?" she asks.

"Thought I'd hang around, be here for the funeral, you know."

"Yes. Or if you wanted to go back, I could let you know where and when it is?"

He eyes her warily. "No, you're alright. I'll stay at your mum's until then. I can sort out her stuff if you like?"

The thought makes her stomach turn. She doesn't want him getting his hands on any of her mother's things. Sam isn't interested in the monetary value of items, but supposing he takes the small Buddha that sits on the windowsill that her mother adored? Or the ballerina painting that hangs in the hall that reminded her mother of Sam?

"Please, can we do that together? I feel like it's my duty."

"Sure, of course." He looks away uninterested.

There is silence. There's nothing for them to say and Samantha hasn't got the energy to force a conversation.

"OK, I think I'm going to head home," she says.

"OK, Love. I'll head out too. Give me a shout if you need anything."

Sam nods and turns to put on her coat. When she looks up again, she sees the back of him heading out of the door. Gosh, he didn't take long to run away.

'Mind you,' she says to herself. 'That's what he's always done best, isn't it?'

As she's leaving, she passes the reception desk.

"How you doing?" Jane calls out, beckoning her over.

"Pretty much as expected."

Jane reaches under the desk and lifts a cardboard box.

"These are your mum's belongings, OK?" She says passing it over. "And Sam, just to say, sometimes a grieving person wants to talk to those who were with their loved one at the end, so if anytime you want to talk, just give us a call or pop in. Alright?"

Samantha thanks her, bids goodbye to the staff, and clutching the box to her chest, walks out of the ward.

***

Once home, Sam puts the kettle on and sits on her sofa to look through the contents of the box. She pulls out the clothes her mother was wearing the night she was admitted, her glasses, magazines and slippers. Plunging her hand to the bottom of the box, she pulls out her mother's diary. Her breathing is uneven as she places it on the table. She sits and stares at it. Her mother's journal. She had kept one for as long as Sam could recall. Should she contemplate reading it? She wants to find out her mother's feelings in her last days but doesn't have the courage to open the pages.

Sam moves to the kitchen and returns with a mug of tea to gaze at it for longer. She wishes someone else were with her, someone else to speak her mother's words. She wonders if she should read it through her fingers the way she used to watch horror films?

232

Inhaling deeply and with trembling hands, she picks it up. Pressing it to her nose, she inhales deeply hoping to catch the scent of her mother. She doesn't, it only gives off a vague whiff of the hospital. She places it back down and it falls open to the last entry. Unable to resist Sam lifts the book.

Sunday 13th December.

It's midnight and I'm having trouble sleeping, mainly due to the woman in the bay along the corridor who is slightly hysterical. Poor soul, she's crying out, praying for Jesus. I'm just praying they give her some stronger meds!

I'm still thinking about that conversation Sammie and I had in A&E. I can feel an atmosphere between us. I need to sort it. She's my beautiful girl and has been my constant in these past years. She has been there for me, helping and caring. She's the best friend I've ever had and no one can ever take her place. I wish she knew that. John's attention is flattering, it's a long time since a man noticed me and I enjoy it. I feel young and desirable again, the old girl's got some zing in her yet!

I can't believe she'd think that I would completely lose my head and be careless enough to leave all my worldly goods (not that I have many!) to him. I've known him for many years and am well aware of his character and his love of money. Is he using me? Maybe. But maybe I'm using him to boost me up and give me some thrills before I shuffle off. Who could blame me? I may be a fool for love, but I'm not an ignorant fool, I'm just enjoying whatever life throws my way.

I must remind Sammie to never forget that life is for living.

P.S. Ooh the advantages of being awake at this hour is that the rather lovely Dr Hannekin is once again on night duty. Hope he passes this way! Smiley face (or whatever the young folk say.)

Half smiling, half crying, Samantha buries her face in the pages and whispers 'I love you, Mum.'

Chapter 47

Red checked tablecloths cover the long tables in Calutti Fruitti's. The Dixbury Dollies, as Sam insists on calling us, are seated at the window table. We have silver, red and gold cracker hats on and are a-buzz with conversation. The wine is flowing as we await the late arrivals of Lucia, Catherine and Josie.

"Before this celebration gets underway, I'd like to say a few words," says Helena, from her vantage point at the top of the table. "I've worked with many dancers in my time, and I can honestly say that none are as dedicated and hard working as you lot. It's been my pleasure to train you and I have great hopes for the competition. I'm sure you'll do me proud. I raise my glass to you all." Everyone toasts, clinking glasses up and down the table.

"And you've been so patient with us, and we think you're a brilliant teacher," Marion smiles, as a pink glow fills her cheeks.

"Thank you, Marion," Helena replies. "And it's so good to see you again, you've been missed."

Murmurs of agreement go around the table. Marion is still displaying battle scars, but living with Julay must be working out, as she's put on a little weight and looks all the better for it. Maybe physically she's still healing, but mentally she appears stronger than any of us have witnessed before. There's a quiet confident air of determination about her. Gone are the twitchy tics that were so much a part of her.

"What's happening with Jack?" I discreetly whisper across the table.

"His court case is next month. I have to be there, but I really don't want to," she grimaces.

"One of us will make sure you're not alone."

"Thank you, Dear. Julay said the same, she's already offered. The solicitor said that he might not get put away but she'll press for a restraining order. He doesn't know where I'm living anyway and to be honest, I don't think he'll come looking for me."

"Marion, you're my hero, you're doing fantastically!"

"Well, Julay has been incredibly kind to me. Watered and fed me, and made sure I'm OK. I'm blessed with good friends for what seems like the first time in my life." A small tear appears in the corner of her eye.

"You're worth it, Marion," I say, raising my glass to her.

Lucia appears on the arm of a man who can only be described as debonair and who she introduces to us as 'Geoff.' He has some silver hair that only serves to increase his distinguished look. He's well groomed and casually dressed. He pulls out the chair for Lucia to sit and she is fit to burst with pride. He whispers something in her ear that makes her giggle. We are all exchanging approving looks when Catherine and Josie join the party.

Gloria breaks away from her conversation with Brian and nudges me.

"What are you doing for Christmas?"

"Ah, I think I'm spending it with Steve."

"Well don't sound too happy about it!"

"No, it'll be fine, I'm sure it will."

"Keep convincing yourself and you'll believe it in the end," she smiles mischievously.

"He's truly sorry, you know. He wants more than anything for us to be back together permanently. He's trying really hard. We both are."

"I don't want to be the one to pee on your bonfire, or whatever that expression is..." We both giggle. "But if you and Steve being together is the right thing, then should it involve that much effort?"

Something registers that she's probably right.

"I don't know, we've got so much to get through. I need to be able to trust him again and we're just learning to love each other again. We stopped trying a while back."

Gloria stops herself from saying something.

"Go on, Gloria, say what you were going to say," I press.

"I don't mean to be harsh, My Dear, but maybe there's a reason you stopped trying?"

"Do you think so?" I ask gloomily. "You think we fell out of love before any of his shenanigans started, don't you?"

"Do you?"

I am stumped.

"I don't know, Gloria, I'm so confused."

"Darling girl, I don't mean to tell you what to do. You have to make up your own mind and I will, of course, support you in whatever you do." She touches my hand kindly.

"Thank you."

"Where is he tonight anyway?"

"Erm, he's at the pub, there's an important match on the telly."

She says nothing, but her thoughts are as clear as if she'd spoken them through a loud speaker.

The evening progresses in merriment with the retelling of ballet class bloopers. Geoff, who transpires to be the only partner present from outside the group, listens and laughs in all the right places. No doubt he's bored to death, but, with impeccable manners, doesn't show it. Lucia, however, remains true to form and ends up drunkenly trying to encourage us to 'do shots.' It seems an appropriate time for people to make their excuses.

Back at home, sitting on my sofa with a bedtime cup of tea, Gloria's words go around and around in my mind. No matter how she phrases it, she clearly doesn't think Steve is the right choice for me. I sink back in the chair recalling these past few months on my own – when I felt free to have fun with Joshua. A thought suddenly pops into my head and I jump up to find my laptop. Opening it, I log onto Facebook. I search for 'Joshua

Milne' and finding his page, my heart squeezes with joy to see his face smiling at me. My finger traces the screen over his picture and I can hear his voice, his laughter...and I can feel those kisses! I guess he's busy settling into his new life as there are no recent posts. I fire off a friend request and strangely feel closer to him. Should I be doing this? Does searching for him on Facebook constitute infidelity?

Steve is trying to reclaim his position as the only love of my life and I don't even know if Joshua truly reciprocated my feelings. Regardless of their intentions towards me, it strikes me that when I think of Steve I feel a sense of sad regret, and yet, when I think of Joshua my insides do a little dance.

Let it go, Amy, he's gone to live the life he planned.

And you're going back to the life you planned too.

I shut down the laptop, call for Basil, my most trustworthy bed companion, and head up the stairs to sleep.

Chapter 48

Christmas Day

Julay, Marion and Julay's younger sister, Bridget, sit down to the table covered in dishes containing all the trimmings of a mouth watering Christmas dinner.

"Oh Julay, this looks wonderful!" Marion enthuses.

"Always were the cook of the house, weren't you, Jules?" Bridget says, smiling. She is similar in looks to Julay only slightly shorter and plumper. She shares the same complexion, but her features are softer and her hair is naturally grey. She had arrived the day before and the three women had enjoyed a convivial evening of chatter and card games that had lasted past midnight. To Marion, this Christmas felt as Christmas should. She liked a drink but Jack always drank far too much. Every year, he would either be abusive, falling over, or passed out and every year Marion would end up alone.

"Thank you for this wonderful Christmas," Marion says with tears brimming. "I can honestly say I can't remember the last time I felt this relaxed." The women raise glasses filled with fizzy grapefruit, and toast to happy Christmases.

***

Sam, in the midst of mourning her mother, had not wanted to spend the day with her father. In fact, she couldn't think of anything worse. But he was lingering in Dixbury like a bad smell and finally, overcome with guilt, she invited him. Having committed herself, she could now only hope that the day would be exceptionally short. She gave him a start time of eleven in the morning and was praying that it would be Game Over by three.

"Hiya," she says, opening the door and forcing her best smile.

"Hi, Love," he says, stepping in. "I've brought you something."

He hands over a bottle of Lambrini that she knows for sure has come from her mother's meagre stock of wine. She was never the drinker.

"Thanks, want a glass?" she asks, knowing the answer full well.

"Got anything stronger?"

"Sure."

Sam's table displays all the components of Christmas dinner, minus the crackers. She draws the line at the forced fun of silly hats and bad jokes. Their conversation goes in fits and starts. Finding a safe topic, they chat for minutes but when that curtails, they are left staring into their food. When the first bottle of Rioja is finished, Sam makes the executive decision to open a second. The only way to get through this Christmas Day is to steadfastly drink through it. Tomorrow is another day.

***

Catherine opens the silver parcel, praying that it will be what she asked for. The advertisement that caught her eye in Dancing Times showed the most gorgeous pointe shoes she had ever seen. Most pointes are pink but those in the photo were bright, bold, pillar-box red. She wanted them more than anything. She had told her parents and they had frowned and mumbled something about money not growing on trees. Catherine had no idea how much they would be but something so beautiful was sure to have a weighty price tag.

As she peels off the last piece of wrapping paper she opens the box to reveal a tutu. It's the same colour as the shoes she desired – but it's a tutu. It's delightful and she loves it – but in a bottom corner of her heart she feels an unjustified disappointment. Maybe those red pointes were just too expensive.

"I love it!" she says to her parents who are staring at her expectantly.

"Oh, that's a relief," Josie says. "See Ed, I told you she'd love it!" her mother says to her father. "And I bet Helena will let you wear it in the competition!"

"Yes, I'm sure she will." Catherine forces a smile.

Having finished opening the presents, they gather at the table, ready to feast on a plentiful dinner. Her mother makes everything nice. Her creativity adds to every aspect of family life and this year is no exception as she has handmade bespoke crackers.

"Here, pull this one with me," her mother says to her.
As the cracker bangs apart, Catherine finds a red glittery card inside. She reads the words.

Christmas comes but once a year,
Bringing with it gifts and cheer.
But there's one gift you forgot,
It's behind the tree, you silly clot.

Catherine looks up at her mother and father who are sporting grins as wide as a mile. She races to the tree and forages at the back to retrieve the package. Filled with renewed hope, she rips at the paper with pieces flying off fluttering to the floor. She gasps involuntarily and her eyes light up at the sight of two dazzling red pointe shoes.

***

Lucia's larger than life, noisy family are all crammed into the lounge of her parents' small two-up two-down terraced

241

house. Lucia is one of seven children and five of her siblings are present with their families. The main rule of the house is that if you want to be heard you have to shout louder than the rest.

Lucia's elderly Italian grandfather, Mica, is sitting in the corner watching the joyful chaos of his son's family gathering.

"Luchi, come and sit with your Grampi for a second," he calls over to Lucia. Lucia adores Mica. Ever since she can remember, she's held a special bond with him. He is always dressed in a three-piece suit, replete with pocket watch, tie and braces. His thinning hair is combed to one side and he has small round wire framed spectacles perched on his roman nose. Lucia always finds comfort in his scent of cold tar soap and Brylcreem. When his wife, Noni, died, Mica was left to cope with the domestics of daily life and he didn't fare well, and so after a time, Lucia's parents suggested that he should live with them.

"Luchi, my darling, come tell me what's new in your life."

"Well, I've met a new man...he's rather lovely."

"Another new man? You're a popular girl" he pinches her cheek a little too hard.

"He's a bit older than me, but I really like him."

Mica looks over his glasses, "How old?"

"In his forties..."

"Argh, Luchi, don't worry about such things. I was twelve years older than Noni, God rest her soul, and it didn't make any difference to us. As long as he's good to you...he *is* good to you?"

"Oh yes, he treats me like a lady."

"I can see the colour in your cheeks, my beautiful girl. You enjoy yourself."

Just then, Lucia's phone buzzes and she quickly looks down at it.

"Is that him?" Mica's eyes twinkle.

"Yes it is, do you mind?"

He shakes his head. Lucia reads the message and smiles.

"Well?" her grandfather asks.

"He's wishing me a Happy Christmas," she beams. "He's with his children – he's divorced," she quickly qualifies. "But would like to cook me a meal this evening at his place."

242

"Go on, go," Mica urges. "But Luchi, you must be in bed by eleven. And if you're not, come home!" Mica roars with laughter at his own joke.

"Grampi, you're terrible!" she laughs and starts to text her reply.

***

"Sherry?" Brian asks Gloria as she bastes the turkey.

"That would be lovely," she smiles.

Gloria considers her decision to invite Brian for Christmas lunch a bold one. In recent years, she has spent the day sitting at Stanley's bedside, talking to him gently, reminding him of past Christmases, hoping that something might register. To be back in her own home, and with company, feels unfamiliar, but she acknowledges that she's readily warming to it.

Brian had happily agreed to spend the day with Gloria, informing his daughter and her family in Cambridge that he would join them on Boxing Day. He loves being around Gloria. In fact, he loves Gloria.

"Cheers," he says, chinking the small schooner to hers. "When shall we exchange gifts?"

"Well, the dinner is cooking nicely, so why not now?"

Sitting on the sofa, they open gifts from family and friends and save the ones for each other until last.

"Go on then, you can open mine," Gloria says.

Brian unwraps the present to find The Nutcracker CD with two tickets to watch the English National Ballet in March stuck to its cover.

"Thank you, My Dear, I, well *we* shall enjoy these very much." He smiles warmly at her and pecks her on the cheek. He leans over to the tree and fetches a small gift that is balancing on the branches. Gloria can tell from the shape that it's a ring box and her stomach goes into knots. He hands it to her. "Go on, open it," he urges.

She feels sick with nerves. What if this is what she thinks it is? She likes him very much, she might even be falling in love with him, but this is too much too soon. She can't contemplate an engagement, but how can she reject his gift on Christmas Day?

She reticently unwraps the gift to find a ring box. She looks up at him nervously and slowly opens the lid. To her complete joy and relief, she sees the infinity symbol of a silver friendship ring.

"Oh thank you, Brian, it's absolutely beautiful!"

"I'm your friend, Gloria. If a time comes where you want more, then so be it, but until that day, I remain forever your friend." He places the ring on her finger, admires it and kisses her hand.

***

We sit at the dining room table and Steve and I pull a cracker. The loud noise makes Basil yelp and we agree not to pull another. Steve then turns his attention to carving the turkey, which earlier he, with no culinary prowess, told me to add spices to.

'Ames, honestly cardamom is the way to go,' he'd said. 'They were raving about it on the telly - let's be adventurous!' And, in the spirit of new beginnings, I'd fulfilled his request. With the first mouthful, I am positive that this is not the way to go. I am irrationally cross.

"Steve, this is revolting! The turkey's ruined!" I whine, sounding like a six-year-old.

"Aw c'mon, Ames, it's not that bad, and anyway, I was only trying to help."

"Help I could've done without!" I bite back.

A cold silence ensues as we eat the trimmings without the bird. We're finished and washing up by two-o-clock.

"Hey, why don't we head to the pub for a last one?"

"Really Steve? That's what you want to do?"

"Yes, Ames, that is what I want to do and in the past it was what you wanted to do too!" he retorts, a touch tetchily.

"I'm not even going to answer that. You go – just go!"

He doesn't. He remembers that he is trying to woo me back; that I am his forever person.

"Oh look, I'm sorry. I won't go. Let's put our feet up and watch some rubbish telly, eh? Sorry. And I'm sorry about the turkey too."

With his best 'begging for forgiveness' expression, he crosses the room and puts his arms around me.

"Steve," I say, taking his arms from me. "I should be the one that's sorry. I'm not being fair. I just can't do this."

"Can't do what?"

"Us."

Chapter 49

Well that was a Christmas Day like never before, I reflect, sitting wrapped in my soft favourite blanket. It really didn't matter that the turkey was inedible, or that the cracker upset Basil; what did matter was my reaction. I already knew, in my heart, that we were trying to breathe life into a dead relationship. I didn't plan for it to end on Christmas Day. He was quite right that my timing stank, but I now feel a sense of relief that the deed is done.

Steve, understandably, was confused. He wondered if there was more he could have done; if I could see my way clear to giving him one last chance. When I told him that I just wasn't happy and that instinctively I felt us reuniting was wrong, he became defensive. He asked me if it had anything to do with 'that fella who legged it off to New Zealand.' (I didn't like his implication of a man 'legging it' away from me, but I let it pass.)

'No,' I'd said, and I was telling the truth. The decision to end our marriage for good really has nothing to do with Joshua. He's gone – didn't even accept my Facebook friend request, but what he has done is plant within me the dream of meeting someone else, someone who makes me feel alive, someone who makes me dance inside and out.

Dixbury Does Talent is my immediate focus and, after that, I shall continue the ballet classes. They're good for me. The 'new year, new me' doctrine doesn't hold water for me, but this year, it's rather apt, as I shall most definitely be evolving.

Before Christmas, a lovely young couple viewed Rose Cottage. They liked it very much and I liked them. Unfortunately, we chose to reject their offer, as it was far too low. As I wish to sever all ties with Steve, I'm going to suggest that we reconsider their offer; it's not like we've had other interest. If we can all agree, I'm then going to look for a small one bedroom flat over the cheaper side of Dixbury and create for myself a new safe haven. I'm going to paint the walls white and shed all the stuff I've squirrelled over the years and go chicly minimalist. I'll visit the newly opened Ikea and buy flat-packed furniture and fashion a simple, stylish apartment to suit a modern singleton. I'm not going to start wearing purple or burn my bra, but I am going to embrace life, build my own dreams, and literally dance to my own tune.

***

Despite the Bank Holiday, Gina agreed to come into the shop on Boxing Day to help with some chores, and I arrive to find her already getting the coffee on.

"Hiya G, great to see you," I say, kissing her on the cheek. "Good Christmas?"

"Yeah, y'know, the usual. Drank too much, stuffed me face, conked out on the settee wiv me cracker 'at still on." I laugh, loving her lack of pretension. "'Ow 'bout you?"

"Ah, let's say I've had better. I spent the day with Steve, as planned, but somewhere around lunchtime it all went a bit wrong. I realised that I'm kidding myself – I can't go back to him." I pause for thought. "I guess it's about broken trust, but it's also that I just don't feel the same towards him anymore, y'know?"

Gina nods sagely.

"I want to be with someone who makes my heart zing!"

"Like that other fella, eh?"

"Yeah. Don't get me wrong, it's not about him, but he gave me a glimpse of the feelings I should be having for Steve, and I don't. Me and Steve are dead in the water. I really didn't plan to end it, but I did."

"Blimey, Babe, on Christmas Day? Brutal!"

"I know, I know," I wince. "Don't make me feel worse than I already do."

"Come 'ere," she says, wrapping her arms around me.

"G! What's happened?" I ask, sniffing her like a dog. "Where's Vera Wang?"

"Me Barry bought me a new one. It's Beyoncé's! Classy innit?"

"Very lovely indeed," I say. "Hey G, before we start, will you do me a favour?"

"Let me guess. You want the 'New Me, I'm Single, So Cut All Me 'Air Off' 'aircut?'

"Got it in one!"

"'Course I will."

"Elfin crop please, and show no mercy."

"Get yourself to the basin, Babes. Let's do this!"

***

Because of Christmas we missed a couple of rehearsals so we meet on the Sunday afternoon to get some extra practice.

"Before we begin," Helena starts. "Can we just say how sorry we all are to hear your sad news, Samantha."

"Thank you," she chokes. "It's a difficult time and I wasn't sure whether to come or not...but dancing has always been my salvation, so I thought I'd try."

"Well, thank you, we're so pleased you could make it, and you know we're all here for you, don't you?"

We all caringly smile and nod at her, and Lucia, who is positioned next to Sam, squeezes her hand.

"Right, People, we have four days until show time!" Helena declares. Some giggle nervously. "It's time to polish the edges but not to start panicking. You all know your parts well, and I have every confidence in you."

"I've missed so much, Helena, I don't know if I can catch up," Marion says.

"Yes, I've been thinking about you. Let's go through the piece and see where the gaps are and we'll work on them. What do you all think of squeezing in another practice before Thursday? How about Tuesday evening? It would be ideal for a dress rehearsal. I know the hall is free as the Dixbury Singers don't meet through the holidays."

Everyone agrees.

"I have something to say," Lucia says, raising her hand in the air. "My new fella, Geoff, runs a limousine company and has offered us the use of a limo to get us to and from the competition."

"Oooh, that sounds rather luxurious and wonderful!" Gloria enthuses.

"I've never been in a limo!" adds Marion.

"That's very kind of him," says Helena. "I think, on behalf of us all, we would like to accept," she says, scanning the room to check for agreement.

"Right, so can you give me your addresses at the end tonight and I'll work out the route to pick up everyone. The driver'll drop us at the hall and return later to pick us all up."

"Sounds marvellous. Please thank him," I say, thrilled at the occasion this is becoming.

"OK, that's settled then," Helena says. "Now let's do a quick Prayers and Pains. Prayers?"

"To leave tonight feeling confident for the competition," I say.

"To pick up all that I've missed," Marion adds.

"To keep my knee back in that pirouette," Julay chips in.

"To enjoy the dancing!" Gloria smiles.

"To be the best partner to my ballerinas," Brian says.

"Not to wobble!" Josie laughs.

"To dance with my heart and my feet," Samantha says.

"To impress you all with these..." Catherine pulls out her red pointe shoes, and her wide proud beaming smile says it all. We all coo and fuss over the unique pointes.

"They're beautiful! I can see you've started breaking them in, so please put them on and get them performance-ready," Helena encourages. "Right. Pains anyone?"

"Still not one hundred per cent, but I'm actually looking forward to moving and stretching out," Marion says.

"Take it easy, Marion. You're going to be my main focus tonight, I want you feeling confident and without pain, OK?"

Marion nods.

"Could I ask a question please?" Brian asks.

"Certainly," Helena says, turning to him.

"What are we called? Don't we need a name to enter the competition?"

"Oh, thank you for reminding me," Helena says, putting her hand to her forehead. "I had to get the form in quickly and didn't have time to consult, so I entered us under the working name of "Dixbury Ballet." But I did say I would confirm our agreed name. So what do you all think?"

"How about what you call us, Sam?" I tease, pushing her in front of the bus.

"Amy!" she laughingly scowls at me.

"Come on then, what is it?" Helena asks.

"The Dixbury Dollies," Samantha says, blushing furiously.

Everyone laughs.

"What a fine name, although I'm not sure I'd make a very good 'Dolly'" Brian chuckles.

"Sorry, Brian," says Sam.

"I don't suppose it matters too much, the company *is* mainly women."

"No, no, it's a silly name."

"How about The Dixbury Dancers?" Lucia pipes up. "That way if we ever change our style of dance, we can!"

"That's a good idea, especially as I was thinking of introducing a tap class in the new year," says Helena.

"Well then, Ladies and Gent, looks like we are The Dixbury Dancers!" Gloria says. "Let's dance!"

Chapter 50

Sam pads to her front door and picks up the pile of letters from the mat. Flicking through, she mentally ticks them off, 'bill, bill, late Christmas card, bill, bill...mmm...what's this?' It's an official looking white A4 envelope. She sees the stamp of 'Hardy, Joyce and Hendricks' on the back. Once again, she finds herself sitting on the sofa staring at an unopened document. It has to be the will. This is going to need industrial strength tea. She heads to the kitchen.

Returning with builders' tea, she takes a deep breath, picks up the envelope and opens it. She scans the legal speak, and gets to the part where her mother's decision of who gets what is written down. To truly believe the words, she reads them twice. She has inherited all of her mother's estate. She quickly checks to see what has been left to her father and is bemused to find that her wonderfully astute mother has left him their wedding photo and a bottle of whiskey that she'd won in a raffle.

Sam then has an uneasy feeling. Supposing her father has seen the will and is angry at his meagre share? He is still in her mother's house. Will he take what he feels he rightly deserves? Imagine he takes something of sentimental value that Sam wants? She quickly dresses and races over to the house.

Using her mother's key, she lets herself in.

"John?" she calls. There's silence. She walks through to the lounge and shivers at the cold. The heating can't have been on for a couple of days at least. She makes her way through the

251

house, looking for clues as to where her father might be. She draws up the courage to go into her mother's bedroom. Everything looks in order and there's no sign of her father's belongings. Returning back downstairs, she catches sight of some papers on the sideboard. As she nears, she recognises that the ripped up document is her mother's will.

Samantha sighs with relief, knowing that the ties, that didn't really bind them in the first place, are now irrevocably cut.

Chapter 51

I stand by my front door, waiting for the limo. We had our final dress rehearsal the night before last and it went splendidly. The main dancers' costumes are impressively eye catching, and the rest of us wear coordinated separates that present us as one, yet manage to maintain elements of individuality. We ran through the dance a handful of times and then stopped. Helena didn't want to over-rehearse us. She told us a story of schooling a class of children to perform in a show when she'd rehearsed them to death. (Not literally.) Come the big day, these children performed as robots instead of dancers and Helena had learnt her lesson. We ceased dancing, changed our clothes and headed home, with her words ringing in our ears:

"Before you sleep at night, go through the steps in your head, but do not dance them again until you're on that stage."

I had tried to 'go through the steps' in bed but found that I fell asleep before I reached the end of the dance. I convinced myself that it must mean I know the steps well enough.

I hear a horn tooting outside. I look out of the window to see a shiny white stretch limousine. It belongs in Las Vegas and looks out of place sitting on an English country lane.

I ruffle Basil's head. "Wish me luck, Bas."

I grab my bag and costume, and head up the path towards the sound of giggling emanating from the car. To an outsider, it would look like we are embarking on a hen party rather than a ballet performance.

"Hiya!" I say, climbing in. This is my first time in a limo too, and I am open-mouthed at the gaudy decadence inside. Around the sides, there's a bank of navy blue leather seats with turquoise fluffy cushions. The floor is covered in a shag pile carpet, a flat screen television divides us from the driver and to top it off, there's a stocked drinks bar.

"OK, next pick-up is Julay and Marion," says Lucia, ticking off her list. "And then, Miss," Lucia addresses Helena. "May we sample the complimentary bottle of champers? Dutch courage and all that?"

"Just one glass each, then; I don't see why not," she smiles, doubting that The Royal Ballet have a similar custom.

The chatter and laughter continues to Julay's house where, much like me, they are waiting at the door. With a limo full of increasingly nervous ballet dancers, we realise that we are far too early. Even allowing time for sizing up the competition and warming up, we are still a couple of hours premature. Lucia presses the intercom to the driver.

"Hey, Henry, any chance we could go for a spin?"

"No problem, Madam, where would you like to go?" he answers in his deep Welsh brogue.

"Shall we go out to Bowden and around the lake?" she says, looking at us for agreement. We all nod.

"Certainly," he says, switching off the intercom.

Heading away from Dixbury, we relax into our seats and Lucia opens the champagne. We shriek as the cork ricochets off the ceiling, narrowly missing Marion's nose.

"Gosh, I don't need any more injuries, thank you!" she laughs.

We glide through the open countryside.

"OK, Dixbury Dancers, it's time for the motivational pep talk," Helena says. "You all know the dance back to front, although I don't want you to do it that way!" she laughs at her own joke. "Ooh, I think the bubbles have gone to my head!" she says, thinking better of drinking and placing her glass in a holder. "So what you have to do tonight is *enjoy* it. We won't have the opportunity for a stage run. so just be prepared for the lights.

They might blind you, and you certainly won't be able to see the audience..."

"Always a good thing," interjects Samantha, and we laugh.

"...but try thinking of them as smiling, encouraging supporters who want you to do well."

"Even though most of them will be rooting for another act!" Julay says.

"But you trick your minds into thinking that they're solely championing you. So much about dancing is in the mind. Believe that you are the best dancers in the world. Dance with ease and confidence and if you remember nothing else, remember to breathe! Breathe life into the dance. Breathe and you will appear in control with grace. If you make a mistake, breathe and carry on. I swear no-one will notice."

"They will if I pee my pants!" Lucia raucously laughs.

"There will be no mishaps like that," Helena chuckles. "Well at least I hope not," she adds, under her breath.

My gaze drifts outside to the greyness of the landscape. I look up at the rain filled clouds and then turn back to look at my companions. If outside is bleak winter, inside is cheery summer. Catherine, our young star and her mother, Josie, who are now firmly part of the group, are snuggled up watching the world go past the window. Lucia is looking at photos on her phone and, judging by the big smile on her face, I presume they're of Geoff. Helena is discussing with Gloria the merits of past ballet dancers compared to those of today. Samantha and Brian are laughing about a recent television programme. Julay and Marion are discussing whether there is enough milk in the fridge for their bedtime hot chocolate. Warm feelings and giddy excitement fill this pimped up elongated car. We drive for miles, past farmhouses and tractors, slowing occasionally to let a stray pheasant cross the road, until we reach glorious Lake Bowden. In the summer, the banks are lined with people fishing but today it's eerily deserted. Henry continues driving us around the wide lake.

"OK, let's play a game," says Lucia excitedly. "Let's play questions!"

We all look at her dubiously.

"Questions? What does that entail? If that's not a stupid question," Marion asks.

"OK, we take it in turns to pose a question to the group and then we all answer. It's fun!"

"Doesn't sound it," Julay remarks dryly.

"Come on, we've got at least another hour in here," persuades Lucia.

Most nod in agreement. "Right then, I'll give you the first question. If you had to, would you rather eat worms, offal or vomit?"

"This is considered fun?'" Gloria chides good humouredly.

"Worms," I say.

"Really? Lucia questions my answer, which I doubt is part of the game.

"Well, unless they're alive of course!"

"Fair play to you, worms it is!"

"I've eaten vomit." Josie speaks up. In surprise, we all turn to her. "Well, I didn't mean to. What happened was I'd baked a cake with lots of yellow icing and fresh cream for Ed's birthday. We ate it at the table. Later as I was clearing away I saw, what I thought was, some of it on the kitchen floor. I leant down and scooped it with my finger and automatically popped it in my mouth. What I didn't know was that this one..." she says, nudging Catherine. "Had felt ill and had rushed through the kitchen to the toilet to be sick but hadn't quite made it."

A chorus of groans and giggles fill the car.

"See? I told you this'd be fun!" Lucia smiles. "Right, who wants to ask the next question?" It falls silent as no one can think of anything. "OK, I'll go again...would you rather stand up to your waist in sludge, ice cold water or poo..."

Just then, a loud bang resonates and the limo judders. Gradually, we lose momentum and are left stationary, in the middle of nowhere, wondering what the heck just happened.

Chapter 52

The door opens to reveal Henry displaying a worried expression.

"We seem to have a problem," he says, stating the obvious.

"What happened?" Lucia asks.

"I don't know. There was a loud noise and the engine cut out. I'm not mechanically minded, me, so I don't really know. It just won't start. I think whatever it was might have triggered the immobiliser." He imparts his lack of knowledge with gravitas.

"So can we phone the rescue services?" Helena asks.

"That's a good idea," agrees Henry.

He returns a moment later holding a mobile phone.

"I don't seem to have any reception."

"Which network are you on?" asks Sam.

"Vodafone."

We all check our phones and find that we have three different networks between us but the only one with reception is mine and it's only one bar. I try making the call but seemingly one bar isn't enough. Feeling mildly panicked, Helena asks Henry where we are. He informs us that we are about 'ten miles or maybe more' from Dixbury. Helena looks at her watch calculating what to do next.

"Right, we have to be at the competition for six thirty at the latest and it's nearly five o' clock. We have no mobile phone signal and none of us knows one end of a limo from another, right?" Helena's eyes are wide with hope. "Nobody here *is* a mechanic, are they?" People shake their heads.

"I work around them every day but their skills haven't rubbed off on me yet," Sam replies despondently.

"OK then, People, I suggest we start walking and hopefully, we'll pick up phone signal, and then we can call for a couple of taxis to come and get us. What do you think?"

"I think it's the best plan we've got," says Gloria.

I think to myself that it's the *only* plan we've got.

Henry stays with the limo, and we promise that when we get signal we will call Road Rescue for him. We walk for ten minutes but with bags and costumes weighing us down, we don't get very far. Ever the gentleman, Brian insists on carrying more than his fair share, but even with his help, we still have far too much luggage and not enough strength. Helena keeps looking at her watch and tries to quicken the pace by walking faster. It doesn't work as some of the troupe just can't keep up.

"We are going to make it, aren't we?" I ask, falling in step with Helena.

"We should do. Just depends on whether we can up the pace, or at least maintain it," she says, clearly not believing her own words.

"We need to think of this as our warm up." Lucia tries to lift spirits. "Let's sing and march!"

"No!" everyone choruses.

And that's when it happens. A solitary blob of water plops onto my nose. I look up to see the angry clouds threatening to burst. Within a few moments, the blackened sky erupts and the rain falls in torrents so hard that it hits the ground and splashes back up our legs. As our means of transport was a limo we don't have an umbrella or a rain mac between us. Worse still is that the deluge of water slows us down even more. We trudge along, heads down, for what seems like hours.

"Look! A bus stop!" says Marion.

"Don't think there are many buses around here," offers Brian.

"No, but we could shelter until the rain stops?"

Helena surveys her bedraggled dancers. We're soaked through, our hair is stuck to our heads and rain is dripping off the tips of our noses. Any costumes not covered in polythene have been stuffed inside our coats, which give us the appearance of being bulkily fat.

"OK, Guys, let's stand in the shelter for a bit, and hope for it to pass," sighs Helena.

"We can check our phones, maybe we have service here," Gloria says optimistically.

We haven't.

Nobody says a word but we're all painfully aware of the time. We have twenty minutes to get to the venue, yet we're standing in a leaky bus shelter in the countryside, not knowing quite where we are, with no phones and in the worst storm we've seen in years. It wouldn't even be possible to thumb a lift. How many cars could accommodate ten of us?

As the skies continue to tip tons of water over the bleak scenery, we stand in the bus shelter shivering, feeling our feet and our spirits sinking. The storm rages on, treating us to a sensory display of lightening forks and ear crashing thunder. If it weren't for the fact that we're supposed to be somewhere else, I could quite easily enjoy the spectacle.

The rain doesn't stop as much as ease when we agree to leave our leaky shelter to venture out again. Fifteen minutes later, we hear a phone ringing. We all delve into our pockets and bags. It's Lucia's.

"Hiya Geoff!" she says. "Yeah, we're a little way away. The limo broke down and we've had no phone signal....yep, well you could come and get us, but there are ten of us....OK....we're near the crossroads of Toremodden and Shankley," she says, reading the white country signpost ahead. "See you in a bit, mwah mwah."

By the time she's finished her call, Gloria is busy calling Road Rescue and Helena is calling the theatre.

"Geoff is coming to get us and his mate, Andy is bringing his car too so at a pinch, we should all get in."

"That's great! " I exclaim. "Looks like we might make it after all!"

"Let's hope so!" Marion adds.

"GREAT! TIME TO WARM UP!" Lucia shouts above the noise of the downpour, and enthusiastically starts star-jumping in the rain.

Chapter 53

Geoff and Andy arrive and, sopping wet, we all pile into the cars. I am in the back of Geoff's BMW, and I squelch onto the seat, dripping rainwater over the plush interior. Glancing at my watch, I am now wondering whether we'll not only arrive on time, but also whether we'll be able to dry off and be performance-ready. As Geoff speeds through the lanes, it's starting to feel like we are falling at the last hurdle.

Andy's car is ahead and pulls in Dixbury Playhouse's car park. I see the passenger door open and Helena hurling herself from the car like she is the victim of an ejector seat. We thank our kindly drivers and make our way through the stage door. We stand in the corridor, awaiting Helena's return.

"Well, that was an adventure we weren't expecting, eh?" I say.

"Certainly was." Gloria smiles, patting herself down. Her normally sleek hair is matted and tangled, but as it's Gloria, there's still beauty in her disarray. Looking around at my compadres, I feel the need to giggle. Rarely have I seen such a weather-beaten bunch of folk. Dressed in sodden heavy clothing, hairstyles wildly askew and muddy shoes, they look a sorry bunch, and I love every one of them.

"What's tickled you?" Sam asks.

"You lot," I say stifling a giggle. "And long may it continue. I'm not one for speeches but this journey with you guys - and I don't mean today's - has been a blast. I love dancing with you, and I'm so pleased to count you as friends. And you all look like you've just stepped out of a washing machine and are drip drying."

"We are!" Josie laughs. And then, standing in a puddle of our own making, we all laugh slightly deliriously at the ridiculous state we're in. The jollity dies quickly as we see Helena approaching with a stony expression.

"I don't know how to say this, " she sighs. "They won't let us enter. The competition's already started. Even though we had the form in on time, the stipulations are that we had to be here at six thirty for the briefing and the spoken run-through. I'm so sorry. They said we can use the facilities to dry off but after that, I suppose we might as well go and sit in the audience and watch."

As downcast as the weather, our spirits sink.

Just then, a tall spindly man with a small moustache appears in the corridor.

"Ms Saunders?"

Helena turns to face him.

"Mr Hennessey?"

"I have just consulted with the adjudicators again and they have agreed that, although it *is* too late to take part in the competition, they have asked if The Dixbury Dancers would like to perform at the end of the competition to close the show?"

Helena turns back to find nine smiling faces.

"What do you say, Dixbury Dancers?"

"We say YES!" Lucia says, punching the air.

"This is better than being in the competition. We can't lose!" Sam adds.

"Gives us time to dry off too." Julay says holding out her drenched skirt.

"Mr Hennessey, thank you very much, we accept." Helena smiles and heartily shakes his hand.

We head to the changing rooms, buzzing once again with the prospect of performing. We manage to peel ourselves out of our wet garb and set the hand driers blowing hot to warm ourselves.

"We need a cuppa," Sam says.

"You're not wrong, Samantha." Julay adds. "We could put our costumes on with warm-ups on top, get our hair done, and then go and find some tea and coffee?"

"And then sneak into the audience," I say.

"Sounds like a plan," Josie agrees.

Leaving our clothes draped around the changing room, we make our way to the coffee bar, purchase large hot drinks and then slip into the back of the theatre. Being held on New Year's Eve, it always surprises me that it's a popular event. I always assume that people want to be drinking, dancing and kissing on this night of the year, but looking around the auditorium, it seems I'm wrong. With the exception of the back three rows, it's packed.

The dark stage shines a single spotlight on 'Ian The Marvel' who is trotting out some fairly standard magic tricks.

"For the love of Jesus, Mary and Joseph, we're better than him," Lucia whispers to me.

I snicker. "The beauty of us not competing is that we can say that about every act, and no one can prove us wrong."

"High five," she says, raising her palm to me. I look to my other side and find Samantha craning her neck.

"What's the matter, Sam, searching for how the magic works?" I tease.

"He's here!" Her eyes are wide and sparkling.

"Who's here?"

"Jason...Mr Physio."

"Ooh, lemme see...where is he?"

"There...one, two, three, fourth row back." I am now craning my neck.

"Which one?"

"The one who looks taller than the rest, with the glasses."

"Ah, I see him."

"Isn't he lush?" Sam gushes.

I wouldn't say lush...

"He looks very nice, Sam."

'Ian The Marvel,' a name I consider to be ironic by the time he's finished his act, is followed by a singing pensioner, and then it's a ventriloquist who takes us up to the break.

"Right, Dancers, we've got a fifteen minute break and then it's the second half which I reckon will last for about twenty minutes," Helena says. "Say we meet in the changing rooms as soon as the break's over?" We all agree and then disband. Half the group head off for another warm beverage while Lucia makes a beeline for Geoff, and Samantha for Jason. I join Gloria and Brian to critique the acts we've seen so far.

"Do you wish we were still competing?" I ask them.

"Not really," Gloria replies.

"What about you, Brian?"

Brian takes Gloria's hand and smiling at me says, "I think we're the winners already, don't you?"

Chapter 54

Whilst Helena is finding the right person to help set up our music, we are waiting in the changing room to warm up. Julay steps up and volunteers to lead us in our usual exercises. As most of the acts in the contest don't require a place to change clothes, we have the room to ourselves. We slowly and methodically warm up all parts of our bodies. Helena arrives back in the room just as we are finishing by jogging on the spot.

"Thank you, Julay," she says. "Are we ready, People? I'm sorry that we didn't get the opportunity to compete, but there's always next year and just think how practised and polished we'll be by then."

"I'm up for next year," Sam says, still glowing from her chat with Jason.

"Me too," beams Marion.

We all concur.

"Wonderful, same time next year then." Helena claps her hands. "OK, we stay backstage from now on, and after they've announced the winner, we will be welcomed to the stage. Please enjoy the experience of dancing for an audience, especially as we're not being judged."

***

"...and the winner is Mavis Trudeau and Bentley."

The performing dog beats Ian The Marvel – who'd've thought...

"Big round of applause for our winners!"

The compere goes to shake hands with Mavis but she offers Bentley's paw, much to the audience's amusement. "How about this dog, eh, ladies and gentlemen?" he says, with an affected laugh. Mavis takes her bows and from where we're standing in the wings, it does look like Bentley is also bobbing his head. A deserved winner, I'd say.

"Well, Folks, that concludes our competition. I'd like to thank..."

As the compere starts to list the many people and organisations that have made the evening possible, we huddle tight in a small circle.

"OK, this is it, your moment to shine," Helena whispers. "Remember, keep your arms soft, raise your eye lines, point your toes...and breathe." We release our arms from each other in time to hear our introduction.

"...to close the show, please give a warm welcome to The Dixbury Dancers." There is such loud applause, whistling and whooping that I wonder whether Helena has paid people to turn up and support us.

My palms are clammy, my heart beats out of my chest, and I seriously consider feigning illness to avoid performing. But fight wins over flight, and I gingerly step onto the stage.

We take our starting positions with Catherine, Brian and Julay centre stage, and the rest of us framing them in a pose. The music begins and I can no longer hear my heart. I watch my fellow dancers to keep time and slowly start to enjoy the much-rehearsed steps to Tchaikovsky's finest.

All the recent sorrow that I've been channelling into my dancing is replaced with joy. Now, as I dance across the stage, I feel a sense of completeness and accomplishment, an inner confidence that I didn't possess before. I know now that whatever life may throw at me, I will be OK. I lose myself to the dance and experience a freedom coming from within.

Marion has a wobble, Julay forgets a step, Lucia misses the little leap and Samantha chickens out of the double pirouette but none of it matters. We are there together, creating an ending to an evening, putting ourselves up there to be criticised or praised. We are committed and brave. Brian was right earlier. We are already winners.

We finish the dance to thunderous applause. The houselights are raised a little as we make a line at the front of the stage to take our bows. The clapping and cheering go on for so long that I wish that we had The Royal Ballet's thick heavy velvet curtains to endlessly reappear around. From the wings, Helena gestures that we should step forward one at a time. Starting from the far end, my talented dancing friends take individual bows to well deserved rapturous applause. I'm the last in line and as I lean forward in a deep bow, a single red rose falls at my feet. I pick it up and, in true ballerina style, delicately smell it, whilst my eyes dart around the room looking for who might have thrown it. It's then that I see him. Standing in the side aisle, with his unruly hair, wide smile, and clapping wildly – Joshua.

Are my eyes deceiving me? Is that really him? What is he doing here? I'm completely aware that my mouth is ajar and, as the applause starts to die, I remain fixed on him as we turn towards the wings to file off.

"Oh My God, Oh My God!" I say, as we reach the changing rooms. "It's him!"

"Who?" Sam asks.

"Joshua! He's here! In the audience! He threw this at me!" I say, holding up the rose.

"Well I never!" says Gloria, smiling from ear to ear.

"Oh My God, Gloria – it's JOSHUA!!"

"Yes, I heard you the first time," she laughs, shielding her ears from my high-pitched squawking. "You know what this means don't you, My Dear?"

"No, what?!"

"He came back for you."

The After

It's been a month since the night we didn't win the competition but stole the show. I sit here looking out over the garden, with my Sunday morning tea and toast, thinking of all that's happened since.

Helena was so proud of us, her protégés, that she immediately started thinking of other possible shows and competitions we could enter, hence we are continuing with the two classes a week. She says we're improving all time.

In the ensuing weeks, Gloria and Brian have been spending more time together, and have even planned an Easter mini-break to the Cotswolds. I couldn't be more pleased for them, and have great hopes that her friendship ring will be joined by another ring soon.

After the court's decision that Jack should go to prison, Marion still decided to accept Julay's offer of sharing her house, and they remain happily co-habiting. An odd couple maybe, but they seem to exist perfectly as the yin to the other's yang.

Young Catherine spied some electric blue pointe shoes in the window of Chappelle Dancewear, and has mounted a campaign to persuade her parents to buy them for her birthday in March. Something tells me that Josie and Ed will buckle under the pressure.

My lovely friend, Samantha, is relieved that her father has dropped off the radar once more. She has decided to sell her mother's house, and plans to use the money to retrain as a sports physiotherapist. Jason has offered to help.

Lucia remains smitten with Geoff and is even considering taking herself off the 'Too Many Monkeys' dating website.

And me? After the performance, I changed back into my still ever-so-slightly damp clothes and rushed to the foyer to find Joshua standing there, hands shoved deeply in his pockets, looking a little nervous. As I'd approached, he'd shrugged his shoulders.

"Couldn't do it, Amy."

"Do what?"

"Be without you."

I smiled and he kissed me. Simple as that.

"What about Steve?" he'd said, pulling away.

I shook my head. "I couldn't do that either."

We stood there grinning.

"What happened to the barnet?" he asked, ruffling my cropped hair.

"What happened to yours?"

"I was trying to fit in with the sheep."

I laughed.

"So, New Zealand didn't work out, eh?" I asked.

"No pork pie, not enough Beatles and no you."

"In that order? Pork pie beats me?"

"Only the one with the egg in it."

We laugh, holding each other's gaze.

"Oh..." I'd said, poking him in the ribs. "...why didn't you accept my Facebook friend request, eh?"

"Cos I don't want to be friends, I've got plenty of friends. With you, Amy Ballerina, it's love or nothing."

I swear I melted.

"Love it is, then," I said.

"Love it is."

As I sit here now watching him tidying the garden with Basil running round his feet, I smile, because that was the very moment we started *our* dance.

THE END

Acknowledgements

I'd like to thank all the people who have influenced, inspired and helped me along this journey. There are many and if I miss any particular names please don't take offence – I'm truly grateful to you all.

So in no particular order, huge thanks to -

Matthew Talbot – for letting me pick your brain.

Joanie Gray – for nonchalantly giving me a plot twist.

Nozomi Abe – for being my sounding board and support.

Jo Greenhalgh and Karen Jenkins for saying all the right things after reading the first few chapters.

Lucie Pratt, Diane Weston, Helen Talbot, Cindy Risby, Elsa Sinclair and Siobhan Zysemil for your encouragement and positivity.

MH Ferguson – for your encouragement and for believing in me. I owe you for your invaluable advice and editing skills. Thanks also for introducing me to Murray McDonald, who freely gave me the wisdom of his experience.

All the marvellous dancers in the classes I attend who provided the initial inspiration.

Phil Collins, my sister from another mister, for your friendship, always being there and for believing I could do this.

My gorgeous sisters, Viv Wilson and Laura Schlotel for all your love and support.

My mother, Joyce Munton, for a lifetime of love and for always championing my ventures.

And finally to my most treasured loved ones, Malcolm, Ruby, and Beattie who encourage, support and love me despite the fact that I 'disappear' regularly to dance or write.